Praise for *Before the Devil Fell*

"Hauntingly atmospheric and relentlessly suspenseful, this dark and compelling mystery reveals a shocking bedrock of buried secrets—and shows what can happen when traditional New England witchcraft meets the light of modern day. *Before the Devil Fell* will keep you guessing on every unpredictable—and unsettling—page."

—**HANK PHILLIPPI RYAN**, author of *The Murder List*

"The paranormal elements are subtle, gradually creeping in around the edges with unsettling effect. Both mystery and weird fiction fans will be pleased."

—*PUBLISHERS WEEKLY*

"An appealing, atmospheric yarn."

—*BOOKLIST*

"A fresh take on New England witchcraft thriller."

—*THE DAY*

"Neil Olson is an unassumingly subtle writer, and *Before the Devil Fell* is not the kind of thriller that goes boo, but the kind that makes you think—about human nature, daemonic nature, and a lot that lies between."

—**MADISON SMARTT BELL**, author of *Behind the Moon*

BEFORE THE DEVIL FELL

Also by Neil Olson

The Icon
The Black Painting

BEFORE THE DEVIL FELL

A NOVEL

NEIL OLSON

HANOVER
SQUARE
PRESS

HANOVER
SQUARE
PRESS™

Recycling programs
for this product may
not exist in your area.

ISBN-13: 978-1-335-07084-5

Before the Devil Fell

First published in 2019. This edition published in 2021.

Copyright © 2019 by Neil Olson

This edition published by arrangement with Harlequin Books S.A.

Hanover Square Press
22 Adelaide St. West, 40th Floor
Toronto, Ontario M5H 4E3, Canada
HanoverSqPress.com
BookClubbish.com

Printed in Lithuania

MIX
Paper from
responsible sources
FSC® C021394

For my father, Neil Bradford Olson,
who loved ghost stories.

BEFORE THE DEVIL FELL

"Until an hour before the Devil fell, God thought him beautiful in Heaven."

—Arthur Miller, *The Crucible*

The house is alive as he wakes. A bright flash echoes in his retina and burned metal stings his nose. A presence lurks nearby. Perhaps a specter from the dreamworld, hauled to the surface. He does not hear the screaming until it stops. Panicked voices rise from somewhere, but he cannot focus on them. Only on his dread of the unseen thing. He is in danger; he must get out of the house.

Cold mud sucks at his feet. Beyond the light of the kitchen windows, there is nothing, just enveloping darkness. He won't remember later how he got outside. His mother or her friends would have seized him had he passed through the circle, so he must have used the back stairs. The field was a forest of cornstalks days before, but they are all cut down. Stubs now, high enough to trip him, and mud gets on his hands, on his pajama knees. His ankle hurts, and his mother's voice cuts through the night. Calling his name. That voice should draw him back, but drives him on instead. He has not shaken the presence. He does not dare look behind him.

A light is in the field, near the tall pines that mark the neighbor's property. A dim lantern at ground level. He runs toward it until he sees a figure standing beside the light. Blond hair. The girl who lives beyond the trees. His feet slow, he walks quickly now instead of running. He barely knows this girl, and finds her strange. She shows him things that he cannot remember later. Frightening things. So he does not understand the compulsion that guides him. The light, the girl, the lines carved in the dirt at her feet form a place of safety. If he can get inside it, the presence will not harm him. He wants to run, but her stillness instructs him. He must not show fear, and he must not stop. Step after step, with death at his back, he walks swiftly and silently toward the girl.

CHAPTER

ONE

"So, what's up with the girl?"

"It was a dream, Beth."

The bland university function room was packed with academics. Even in a corner, Will and Beth nearly had to shout at each other. Will took a long pull on his beer and scanned the crowd. The students were all upper class or graduate level, several of them from his seminar. Huddled together and looking nervous, the poor nerds.

"I don't think they'll run out," Beth said.

"What?"

"Of beer. You can slow down."

In some mythic past, these student-faculty mixers were boozy affairs, sure to produce at least one tale of a professor embarrassing himself heroically. In this new age, they had become tepid events. Serious types drinking seltzer and lime and gesticulating with bread sticks. At the refreshment table, Will had to specially request the beer, a watery "lite."

"We should have snuck in a flask."

"So you could breathe whiskey over Dean Wagner?" laughed Beth. Will's teaching assistant was tall and dark eyed, with a low laugh and a sharp wit. And tonight, a probing manner. "The dream. It's based on something," she pressed. "You told me once. There was a storm and the house got hit by lightning and—"

"Someone died. Yes."

"But the girl is only in the dream?"

"No," Will replied. He had forgotten until now that he had told her of his troubled youth. Trying to make the stories funny, though they were anything but to him. They had spoken of it one time, over drinks, but she was not the type to forget. Why did he mention the dream tonight? Because he felt a need to share with someone, and knew Beth would keep it to herself. And because after a long reprieve, he was under siege again. First once a week, then twice, now nearly every night. "She was there, in the field. I'm not sure of the details. I was only five."

"She was your neighbor."

"Yes."

"Were her parents hippies too?"

"She lived with her grandfather. Dartmouth professor. The house was filled with books, wall to wall. Anyway, why are you focused on the girl?"

"That's who you're running to, in the dream. Seems like she's the key."

"To what?"

"Understanding it."

"What's to understand?" said Will, annoyed. The beer bottle was empty, and he had promised himself to stop at two. "Dreams are just mental garbage."

"Okay." Beth sipped her soda. "So why were you telling me?"

"I don't know," he mumbled. "It was on my mind."

"It must have been. Because that wasn't even the girl I was asking about."

At first he thought she meant Asa, the pierced and pink-haired ghoul from his Myth and Folklore seminar, who was slithering across the room in a serpentine fashion. Headed their way.

"You mean Helen?"

"Is there someone else?"

Not for years, thought Will sadly. And not for a long time to come.

"I haven't spoken to her in weeks."

"Wow." Beth seemed genuinely surprised. "So this is for real, this..."

Breakup? Such a weak word, something that happened to high school sweethearts. He and Helen were in their thirties, had been together four years, lived together for two. He had visited her family far more times than he had seen his own mother in that span. Anxiety rose up, and Will squeezed his eyes shut. The darkness, the burned smell, his mother screaming into the night as he ran. From what?

"They weren't hippies," he said, forcing down the panic. "My parents."

"I'm sorry, I didn't mean to—"

"No, no, I realize I paint them that way. Not my dad, but my mother's crowd. The flared denims and long hair and mystical chanting. But I mean, it was nineteen seventy-five. Could you still be a hippie then?"

"Sure," Beth maintained. "It's a state of mind. They're out there now, with gray ponytails and tie-dyes yanked over their guts. Starting internet companies."

"The Revolution," said Will.

"What did she call it? That séance thing your mom did?"

"Spirit circle," Will replied uneasily, trying to share Beth's enthusiasm.

"Spirit circle," she echoed with delight. "Who were they trying to contact?"

"Darned if I know," he said, wishing desperately for a real drink. "God? Aliens? The Great Spirit?"

"Professor Fairy Tale," shouted a voice so close that Will jumped. Asa was beside him. Green peasant skirt low on her hips, a skull ring dangling from her long nose. Her hair was more purple than pink tonight, and her bulging eyes drilled into him. "You're hiding from us."

"I'm doing no such thing," Will lied.

Asa was flanked by her reliable wingman, Viktor, and plaid-shirted... Pete? Will's wandering mind created nicknames for students, and this kid was always just Plaid.

"Professor Fairy Tale?" Beth repeated, both defensive and amused. "That's not very nice."

"Who are you?" Asa demanded, getting into Beth's space, which is what she did.

"Beth Gonzales. And you are?"

"Asa Waite." They shook hands like boxers at the weigh-in. "You're the TA for Prof's American Lit survey, yeah?"

"That's right," Beth said. *And you're that wacko Will told me about*, she did not say.

"Professor Fairy Tale is what he called himself the first

day of class," Viktor explained, a bright smile nicely set off by his black beard.

"Which was so great," Asa said, her lips red from whatever she was drinking. Or perhaps from feeding on an underclassman before coming here. "Like, this is who I am and what we do, and you can like it or get out."

"It wasn't a challenge," Will corrected, disturbed by her misreading. "Just a little self-deprecation."

"You're all enjoying the seminar?" Beth asked, in her den mother voice. She seemed so much older than these kids, though she was only twenty-four.

"Very much," Viktor said. "Fascinating stuff."

"I never thought I'd find an actual class like this," Asa declared. "I'm going to do a paper on incubi."

"Wait," Beth said, "that's the thing that comes in the night and…"

"Screws you in your sleep," Plaid filled in.

"Lays upon you," Asa enunciated, aiming death rays at Plaid, "and saps your life energy. But there's more to it than that. Incubus is male, succubus is female."

"And which are you?" Beth asked. They all stared at her. "Which are you *writing about*? Isn't that what I said?"

"Both kinds," Asa replied, leaning in confidentially. "It's partly research, but mostly based on my own experience."

"Right," Beth said brightly, turning to Plaid. "What about you?"

"I guess I wasn't expecting it to be so *serious*," he said, with a nervous smirk.

"He thought we'd be reading *Harry Potter*," snarked Viktor.

"I did not think that. Maybe Tolkien?"

They all laughed.

"We'll get there," said Will. "Celtic mythology is dense, but it lays the groundwork for a lot of later stuff. Hey, be grateful. I used to put Carl Jung right in the first week's reading."

"Psychology," Asa huffed dismissively.

"There's more to Jung than that," said Will. "But ultimately, what else are we talking about?"

"Come on, Prof," the young woman said. "It's a new millennium. No one has to be ashamed of what they believe. The spiritually tuned-in will lead the way."

"To where?" Plaid asked.

"My aunt was goth before that was cool," said Asa. "Got abused in school, cut herself, that kind of thing. She leads a Wiccan circle now, and she's never been so happy. Fulfilled. It's everywhere. I'm not saying that's *my* thing, but—"

"It's bullshit," Plaid said. "Wicca, come on."

"Okay," Will intervened, "let's not be contemptuous, Pla—uh, Pete."

"You don't believe that stuff, Mr. Conner, do you?"

Now they all stared at him. Even Beth.

"What interests me, the reason I created the seminar, is to better understand the myth-making impulse. Why do we all do it? Why do all cultures have versions of the same stories? What do we seek in the otherworldly that our reason can't supply?"

"But it's not real," Pete insisted. "That seeking happens in the mind. Right?"

"Yes," said Will. "Or is shared between minds. Which doesn't make it less interesting."

Asa stared into her cup. Purse-lipped and profoundly disappointed, Will could tell.

"I'm going to find food," she said, starting to move away,

but stopping short. "There's a book I saw. At Argosy. It was behind glass, they wouldn't let me look at it closely. I'm ninety percent sure it's a grimoire. I'm going to get that sucker and bring it class. And blow all your tiny minds."

"You do that," Will said. "That would be very cool, in fact. Just don't steal it."

She smiled and sauntered off. Viktor and Pete followed, waving quick goodbyes.

"Well," Beth exhaled. "She's everything you said."

"She keeps me on my toes."

"You realize she's nuts?"

"Let's not be judgmental," he counseled. "She'd fit right in where I come from."

"Grimoire?"

"Book of magic," Will clarified.

"They have those at Argosy?"

"I doubt it, but they exist. I mean, books purporting to give magical instruction." Will hesitated. "Our neighbor the professor was supposed to own one."

"Dream girl's grandfather? No way. Did you read it?"

"No. Come on—don't try to make something out of it."

"I'm not making anything," she protested. "You just had one freaky childhood."

"Yeah, and look how sane and boring I turned out."

"You're trying to understand them," Beth said, eyeing him curiously. "Your mother. All the loonies you grew up with and ran away from. You're studying this stuff to figure them out."

"That's insultingly reductive, Ms. Gonzales. I expect more from you."

"Well, I'll try to broaden my mind. Maybe I'll leave my window open tonight and see what crawls in to visit."

* * *

In the taxi home, Beth's words pursued him. He was aware, in a general way, that the untamed atmosphere of his youth, the eagerness of adults to retell old tales and believe in unseen things, fed his creativity. He would not have spent the hours studying and teaching folklore without that early shaping. That was one thing. It was quite another to say he was trying to decode his mother. Whatever genuine knowledge of the arcane existed in those old families in that little town north of Boston had died out generations ago. Abigail and her crew were pot-smoking, wine-slugging losers, shouting songs from *Hair* and wishing they had been at Woodstock. There was nothing Will needed to understand, except the one thing nobody would tell him. Which had led to his latest argument with his mother.

Abigail called three weeks before, just as the semester was starting. She was having dreams about the night Johnny died and wanted to talk to Will. In person. It was infuriating. For years he had asked for details about the incident, and she always refused. Now, suddenly, it couldn't wait? He told her he could not possibly get there in September, which was true. It was also true that somewhere in the last decade a scar had formed over that fearful recollection. Without deciding, Will had simply stopped wanting to know. And, simultaneously, had stopped having bad dreams. Since her phone call, the dreams were back. And the unwanted questions.

He bailed out of the taxi a few blocks from home, to walk off his agitation. On a side street near Second Avenue, he passed a bar. Trinity Pub in yellow letters over the door. Will went inside. It was dark, cramped and loud. But the patrons were adults, not college kids, and there was an open spot at the bar. The Yankees were playing Baltimore on the television above. 2003 was supposed to be the Red Sox's year, but Will was skeptical. It was always supposed to be their year.

He drank a whisky in two gulps and a Guinness more slowly. The tightness in his chest relaxed. Will didn't look at anyone and no one bothered him. The Yanks were mauling the Orioles' pitcher, and leading five-two when he slapped down some cash and swung his jacket off the stool.

Back outside, the breeze had picked up and Will could smell the East River. He was near his apartment now. Light from a corner deli glowed on the far avenue. Plane trees shot out of the broken sidewalk, leaning over the road. There were few lights on this block and he stumbled. The anxiety had worn off, and he was a bit drunk. A short Latino kid in a T-shirt and apron hosed out plastic tubs by the deli's basement entry. He squeezed off the hose and stepped back to let Will pass. The sidewalk was soapy, and Will had to watch his footing. And then something was wrong. The shape of the young man, seen from the corner of his eye, became distorted. *Don't look*, Will told himself. *Do not look, just walk by.* But he couldn't help it. He had to look.

Beside him, in the shadow of the brick wall, was a grisly mask. Black lips peeled back from yellow teeth. Bloodshot eyes stared out of the wrecked visage with hypnotizing intensity. Bad energy radiated from it—malevolence, or a desolation so intense it colored the space around the thing. Yes, the thing, because what else was it? Not a man. The mouth dropped open and it staggered forward, forcing two hoarse syllables from its ruined throat.

Murder.

Will reeled. Toward the street, stepping on the plastic tubs and going down hard. Knee, elbow, and then his forehead all banged against the wet concrete. Thoughts retreated, his mind unwilling to process what it had seen, or anything else.

A low, guttural chanting of voices. Some laughing, some deadly serious. A panicked rushing, up and up, and then a blinding flash of light.

The mottled bark of the plane tree filled his vision. Its trunk soared heavenward to the pearl sky of nighttime Manhattan. No stars. A shadow loomed and Will flinched, covering his face.

"Mister. Mister."

The Latino kid was withdrawing the hand he had offered. Will looked closely at the face. A hint of mustache above full lips. Fear in the eyes. It was all the poor guy needed, some well-dressed gringo falling over his buckets, hurting himself. And just like that, so much for the dream of America.

"I'm good," Will said, but it came out a whisper. The kid reached out his hand again and Will took it. He needed the tree as well, but finally got to his feet. His vision swam. The elbow hurt, and his forehead stung. He would feel worse later.

"Okay now?" the kid asked hopefully.

Will studied him a while longer. Trying to figure out how he could have mistaken the face, but there was no mistake. One face had nothing to do with the other.

"Yeah," Will said more clearly. "I'm fine. Thanks."

He was distracted from the fear of his dark apartment by the flashing red light on the answering machine. Two rapid blinks. Two messages. His mind went immediately to Helen, but before he could hit Play the phone rang again.

"Hello?"

"Will? Is that you?"

"Yeah."

"It's Muriel." His mother's friend. He was surprised not to recognize her voice, but then she did not seem to know his. Maybe nobody was themselves this evening. "I'm sorry, did I wake you?"

"No," he answered, a throbbing setting in behind his eyes. "No, it's okay."

"I tried you before."

"I was at some faculty thing. What is it?"

"It's about your mom," Muriel said stiffly. "Will, it's not good news."

It never was.

CHAPTER

TWO

Muriel was at the house when it happened. She and Abigail had some kind of argument, with Abby raving about a dream of Will in peril. That was familiar—she'd had those before. Yet something new had been added, agitating her dangerously.

"I tried to calm her," Muriel said. "Think I did more harm than good. She went marching out the back door. You know those damn concrete steps."

Cracked, uneven. Throughout childhood, Will had been warned against running down those stairs. You'll fall and break your head, Abby would scream. Joke's on you now, Ma.

"A shallow coma." He repeated Muriel's phrase. "What is that?"

"Better than a deep one, I guess. You need to come up, Will. Soon as you can."

He took a train from Penn Station early the next morning. The New York he left was summer green, but in New England it was already fall. Yellow patches flashed by the train window. The Saugus marshes were a forest of beige cattails and sea grass. Sugar maples flared orange, and it was not even October. His mother's timing was brilliant, as always. The semester had just begun, and the school would struggle to find a fill-in. Will could not even tell them when he would return.

Muriel was headed out of town, but stuck around long enough to meet him at the train. She was leaning against her battered green Subaru in blue jeans and a jacket, brown hair askew. Her hazel eyes looked him over closely.

"What happened to your face?" she asked.

"Fell."

"Some fall."

"Do I look that bad?"

"No," she said, squeezing him quickly. "You look good."

"So do you," Will replied.

"Liar."

In fact, she seemed worn. At forty-eight, she was five years younger than Will's mother, but looked older. Exercise and a native toughness were clearly no match for the cigarettes and whiskey. Or was it some bad strain of DNA that had killed so many in her family so young? For all that, her mischievous smile stirred something in him. A reaction inextricably tied to his first romantic yearnings. As a teenager, Will had a thing for Muriel, and evidently still did.

"Hospital," she asked, "or home first?"

"Hospital."

"I figured. Get in."

The Subaru bucked and stalled. Will remembered Muriel as a good driver, so it must be the car getting old. Several travel bags were on the backseat.

"Where are you headed?" he asked.

"New Hampshire. See my Mom. I was supposed to leave first thing this morning, but I wanted to be here for you."

"Sorry to mess up your plans."

"I called Joe." She never said *your father*, always *Joe*. "Last night, after we spoke."

She said it tentatively, like she might have overstepped by doing so. Which, of course, she had, but Will was grateful.

"Thanks."

"He'll wait to hear from you before he does anything." She glanced over at him as they sailed along a twisty road of oak and pine and dilapidated clapboard houses. "Were you drunk? When you fell?"

"A bit," he said.

"Not my business, but isn't thirty-three a little old to be getting plowed and falling down stairs, or whatever?"

"It was a wet sidewalk. It was dark. There were some buckets."

"Okay."

"It's not like I get drunk and fall down every night, Mure." He sounded too defensive, even to himself. *Who are you*, he wanted to say, *my mother*?

"Never mind," she said, accelerating up the ramp onto the highway, then merging into traffic without seeming to look. A skill that impressed Will, who had never owned a car. They drove in silence for a while. There was color on

28

the trees, mostly yellows. A black turkey vulture wheeled overhead.

The hospital was a big brick pile off the first rotary in Gloucester. It looked like the kind of place you went to die, Will thought. But what did he know? Anyway, there had been no time to take her anywhere else.

Muriel wouldn't come in. "I don't want to be the first one she sees when she wakes up. She was cursing at me when she fell."

"I'm sure she won't even remember."

He touched her arm. She squeezed his hand and gave him a pensive smile. Then leaned toward him, practically into his lap. When she banged the glove compartment with the side of her hand, he jumped in his seat.

"Sorry," she said, digging through a stack of papers for a loose scrap.

"It's okay." What had he thought, that she was going to kiss him?

"Here's my cell," Muriel said, handing him the paper after scribbling on it. "Call me with a full report. Her car is here. I had someone drive it over, so you can get home in that. I really need to get on the road. My mom will be nervous."

"You were good to stick around," he said, distressed that she was not staying. Loner that he was, he still didn't like facing this on his own.

They hugged again, awkwardly, and Will got out of the car. There was a cool breeze off the Annisquam. He had barely slept in two nights and the bracing chill woke him. He took a moment to collect himself, then headed for the sliding glass doors.

Intensive care was on the first floor. The duty nurse was

lean and hard faced, but her manner was kind. The doctor would not be back until next morning, and questions of treatment or prognosis must be directed to him. She could tell him that the brain was swollen, but they were able to minimize fluid buildup with medication and had not needed to drill. Heart rate and breathing were stable. She was on a respirator, but that was just a precaution.

"That sounds encouraging," said Will.

"We've seen a lot worse around here," the woman replied.

"But she's still in a coma."

"That's correct," she said. "There's been some muscle movement. Spasms in the hands and face, but she hasn't woken yet."

"You expect her to."

"That's a question for the doctor," said the nurse, with a bland neutrality that could only come from years of practice.

"She's been out a whole day," Will said. "Isn't that a long time?"

"More than six hours is serious," she conceded. "But it's too soon to draw conclusions."

Then she left him alone with his mother. Abigail. They had shaved the hair around the wound and what remained, flattened by bandages, was dull and lank. Not the lustrous black curls he had known his whole life. There was an IV line in her arm, and a clear mask over her mouth and nose. Her skin was paler than its usual pale, and there was bruising under the eyes. But the most striking thing was the slackness of her face. The flat mouth, the hollowed cheeks. Will tried to remember a time when he had not seen that face animated. She had dark moods, like anyone. Yet even then, there seemed a dormant energy, collecting up to burst back into life. He rarely saw her sleep, but when she did—a nap on the sofa, maybe—there was always movement. Her long arms thrashing around. Eyes shifting under the lids, the mouth pursed and twitching. And now this deathly stillness.

Will dragged a heavy vinyl chair to her bedside, the legs squealing against the tiled floor. He took his mother's left hand in his own, surprised at its coldness. Then surprised at himself. She always had cold hands; it was a joke among her friends. When had he forgotten? When had he last touched this hand? Christmas, nine months ago. Which had been his first visit in a couple of years. They had fought almost the whole time. Abby asking why she hadn't met Helen yet, why he didn't visit more often, why he didn't call his father in Seattle—the same father she had warned him against trusting. Will scolded her over the sad state of her house and finances, her drinking and smoking: you'll have a stroke before you're sixty, and I'll have to take care of you. He was angry with her, deeply and constantly. For his traumatic childhood. For her weirdo pals, her eccentric behavior. She embarrassed him.

He knew that his anger was justified. Knew too that it would not go away easily. It was just hard to make it important at this moment. He placed his hot forehead on her cold hand and closed his eyes. *Can you feel that, Ma? Can you feel me here?* He waited for the expected welling up of grief in his chest. Waited eagerly, in fact. What sweet relief from this numbness, from this emotional sedation that would be. Sadness was all he could manage. And exhaustion. The cold hand answered nothing back.

Later, he sat by the nurses' station, trying to finish forms

Muriel had started the day before. There were things for him to sign. He could barely take in their meaning, but was pretty sure he was agreeing to make medical decisions on his mother's behalf, and to pay for whatever her lousy insurance did not. Abigail taught art at the Alternative School and was a substitute teacher in the public system, and Will was used to covering some of her expenses. He scribbled his signature and the date three times and dropped the forms with the night nurse.

"Coffee?" he asked her.

"There's a machine. Down this corridor, then left and all the way in back."

"Thanks."

The alcove in question held multiple machines. Candy bars, sandwiches, coffee. In front of the last stood a young woman in faded jeans and a powder-green shirt like the nurses wore. It took a moment for Will to realize she was looking not at her coffee choices but at him. It took another moment for him to realize he knew her.

"Hey, Will."

She was smaller than he remembered. The bright hair had gone straw-colored. The soft face had acquired some definition, but the serene expression in the blue eyes exactly matched his memory. That smile had once unnerved him, presaging as it so often did some scary knowledge, or wondrous vision. But that was long ago. Long before they had become casual friends, then lost touch completely.

"Samantha."

"When did you ever call me that?" she said.

Not a line in her face, and yet she was two years older than Will, if he remembered right. Two years, or two hundred.

"I'm sorry. Sam."

"That's better. You want coffee?"

"That's what I'm here for," he said, the tiredness too obvious in his voice.

"How is she doing?" Samantha asked, turning her profile to him now and dropping coins into the old machine.

"You know about my mother?"

"I know most of what goes on here. Went to see her earlier. Just sat by the bed and talked a little, you know?"

She handed him the steaming paper cup of coffee. Dark, no sugar, the way he took it. He didn't ask how she knew, or offer her money. The Samantha he remembered had little patience for niceties. She did not get coffee for herself, which made him wonder why she had been standing there in the first place.

"Thanks," Will said. "And thanks for checking on her. I appreciate it. There isn't any change."

"Her car is in the south lot, near the entrance. Muriel Brown asked me to drive it over."

"She said someone had—I didn't realize she meant you. I guess I have a lot to thank you for."

"Thing is—" she tipped her head, and slid one foot forward and back "—it means I need a ride home tonight."

"Right. Of course. Well, I was…"

"Going to stay until visiting hours were over," Samantha finished for him. "That's fine. I've got people to see, and I can always find things to do."

"Great. That's great, thanks."

"Stop saying that."

"Okay," Will agreed sheepishly. He tried to remember when he had last seen her, what he had heard about her in the last… Fifteen years? She had gotten married some time back, he knew that much. "Where are you living these days?"

"Didn't your mom tell you?" She seemed more amused than surprised, and probably guessed within a moment that his mother had told him very little of late. "I'm back in my grandfather's house. I'm your neighbor again, William."

CHAPTER

THREE

It was hard for Will to remember a time before Samantha was a presence in his life. Before the lightning strike and the night in the field, he had been aware of the spooky girl next door. Trotting up the long slate walk beside her grandfather, she seemed harmless enough. But racing like a wild animal through the woods behind their houses, or flitting about the low candlelight in her house, she was a daunting and beguiling presence. Two years older, that would have been enough, but there was more to it. She would stare without blinking, and always said what was on her mind, even if it hurt or frightened you. She had no friends that Will ever saw, and did not seem to need them. But on certain nights, when Will was already in bed, he would creep to the window and look out. And see her by the lilac bushes, blond hair white in the moonlight. Gazing up at him.

"It pulls you, right?" Sam said.

He glanced away from the dark road to the woman in the passenger seat. Trying to connect her with that blond specter from his youth. The same steady gaze. The quiet, uninflected tone. But where memory made that voice hypnotic and foreboding, the woman beside him seemed merely withdrawn. He had to remind himself that they had become friends later. That he had known her, though less and less well, right through high school. That her unnerving presence in his childhood had been forgotten years ago. Only resurrected now by dreams.

"The car," she clarified. "There's a tugging to the right."

"Yeah?" he replied, coming out of his trance. He loosened his grip on the wheel and could indeed sense a slight drift. "I feel that."

"What did you think I meant?" she laughed.

"I had no idea, to tell you the truth."

He laughed too, late and feebly. *It pulls you.* Such a Sam thing to say, and so uncharacteristic that it should refer to something as mundane as steering.

"You weren't even listening," she said without rancor.

"No, I was…"

"Thinking about your mom. Why wouldn't you be? That's a tough thing to have happen."

With anyone else Will knew, this would be an opening to discuss her own troubles. God knew Samantha had them. Her father died when she was very young and her mother ran off to Florida with some guy. Leaving her to be raised by her bookish, absentminded grandfather. Strange as her upbringing was, Sam never complained about it. And would not now.

"Her vital signs are good," he said.

"She's strong. I could feel her strength while we were talking."

He let the *we* go without comment.

"But she's been unconscious too long."

"She's going to be all right," replied Sam. "The body knows what it needs."

He was both comforted and irritated by the words. Was she a doctor now?

"Do you work at the hospital?"

"No, up at Cedar Hill," she said. The nursing home. Or whatever the correct name was for such places. "But a lot of our patients end up there."

"Yeah, I guess they would."

"So I visit them. It's not part of the job, just something I do. Watch the road."

"What?" he asked. "I'm watching."

"You're drifting a little." She was looking in the rear-view mirror.

"I'm not," he protested. And how could she even tell, with all these curves? He tried to see what she was looking at. Another car slowly gaining on them. Big deal, he wasn't going to speed up on this road.

"Don't speed up," she said.

"Do you want to drive?"

"Nope, you're doing fine."

"What do you do at Cedar Hill?"

"Physical therapy."

"Really? That's cool. I didn't know you were doing that."

"Strictly speaking," she said after a pause, "I assist the

therapists. You need a degree to be official. I only have a certificate from this course."

"Have you thought of getting the degree?"

"I was in school for a while. In Boston." Her voice took on a halting, distant quality that was unfamiliar to Will. "My husband didn't like it."

"He didn't...so you stopped going?" Will failed to keep the dismay from his voice. He needed to be careful. Other men and women had relationships like that—it wasn't for him to judge. But Sam was the last woman in the world he would expect to be held down by her husband.

"I wasn't very good at the work," she went on.

"I remember you doing well in school."

"When my grandfather was helping."

"You're as smart as anybody I know," he insisted.

"Thanks," she said quietly. "But I think I'm not good at focusing my mind that way. You know?"

"Conforming it to textbook knowledge?" he asked. "Or do you really mean you're not good at sucking up to egotistical professors?"

Sam didn't respond, so he glanced at her. She was smiling big at him.

"Yes," she said. "That's just what I mean."

"I bet you argued with them all the time."

"I did," she agreed with merriment. "Don't miss the turn."

He almost had. He really didn't know these roads in the dark anymore. The car behind turned with them, right on their tail now.

"Shit," groaned Sam.

Before he could ask what was wrong he heard a single sharp wail and saw blue lights flash in his mirrors. Will jolted upright in his seat, swerving a little and then correcting.

"What is this?" he protested, pulling slowly onto the grassy shoulder.

"My ex-husband," said Samantha flatly.

The police car stopped twenty yards behind, lights still flashing.

"Your ex-husband?"

"He's been following us since the hospital. I wasn't sure it was him until now."

The cop didn't dawdle like they usually did. Checking the plates for warrants, exerting authority via delay. Instead he launched himself from the cruiser, leaving the door open, and strutted quickly toward them. Compact, muscular, with dark hair and skin that looked deathly pale in the pulsing blue light. Will rolled down the window.

"License and registration," the cop snapped.

Will's age, or around there. Familiar. One of the Duffys. Not Brendan, who went to school with Will, but a brother. Round face, dark eyes. A small mustache and an angry clench to the chin. Will pulled out his wallet and dug for the seldom-used license. Sam opened the glove compartment and an avalanche of paper landed in her lap.

"You know your left taillight is out?" the cop continued. His tone made it sound like a moral failure.

"I didn't. It's my mother's car."

"Will, you remember Jimmy," Sam said calmly, sorting through the mass of envelopes, maps, postcards. "Jimmy, this is Will Conner, who—"

"I know who he is," Jimmy snarled, bending down so his face was even with Will's, but looking past him to Samantha. Rage in his black eyes. Will could feel the fury coming off him like heat waves. "What are you doing with him?"

"You know," Sam said, "I don't even know what a registration looks like." Jimmy kept staring, and she finally turned her gaze to him. Her mouth a hard line, her voice the same. "I don't have to explain anything I do to you."

"License," Will said, handing it out the window, his muscles flexing oddly. "I was just giving her a ride home. She drove my—"

"This is expired."

"Is it?"

"What did I just say? Look." Jimmy shoved it back at him and Will examined the awful picture. Shaggy brown hair, needing a shave, eyes half-closed. He looked homeless and stoned. Then he found the black letters: EXP 6/30/2003. Three months ago.

"I didn't realize. I never use it."

"Step out of the car."

Will felt a sudden adrenaline surge. He did nothing for a moment, then reached quickly for the door handle.

"Jimmy Duffy," Samantha shouted, freezing him. "This man has just come from the hospital where his mother is in a coma. What are you trying to prove?"

The cop stood upright, mouth moving without producing sound. He turned his back to them and wandered several yards away, into the middle of the road. Will ground his back teeth and squeezed the useless license until the plastic edges dug into his hand. He glanced at the sharp turn ahead, imagining a vehicle whipping around it too fast. Flattening the stocky little man like so much roadkill. Jimmy strolled back over to the window.

"I heard about your mother," he said, voice more subdued. "I'm sorry."

"Thanks," Will replied.

"It sucks. I hope she'll be okay."

"Well. We'll see."

"I could cite you for about four violations," Jimmy said more sternly. "But I'm going to let it go this time. Get that license renewed. And fix your mother's taillight."

"I'll do that."

Jimmy stared a few more moments at Sam.

"You headed home?" he asked. When Will nodded he said, "I'll follow you. Make sure you get there safely."

He strode back to the police cruiser and flung himself in, killing the flashing blues. Will waited half a minute, then turned the ignition too hard and the car ground to life. He pulled slowly back onto the road and drove toward home at twenty miles an hour. He sincerely hoped it pissed off Jimmy.

"You all right?" Sam asked after a while, her voice light and easy again.

"Fine."

"I'm sorry. He hasn't done anything like this in a long time."

"I didn't remember you married Jimmy Duffy."

"Five and a half years," she said. "Almost two now since the divorce. He was real sweet at first."

"That didn't last, I guess," he said, checking the rearview for his escort. Jimmy was hanging well back, almost lost in the turns.

"Bad stuff happened," Sam replied. "We got impatient with each other. Got mean."

"I never heard you shout like that," said Will, almost smiling.

"Well, I had to do something. One of you was about to get hurt."

"You think?" He was genuinely surprised by her words. "He was ticked off, but I don't believe he was going to hurt me."

"He wasn't the one I was worried about," Sam said.

"What do you mean?"

"You were very angry."

"No," he scoffed, "I was a little shaken, that's all."

"You were furious, Will. You still are. It's in your voice," she maintained. "In the way you're sitting. I can smell it. Are you really not aware?"

This was more like the old Sam. Laying him open to inspection. He was aware of tension in his body. Anxiety, stress, fear. He had not registered anger, but knew those ingredients could alchemize anger in an instant. There had been some unidentified but bad intent within him when he reached for that door handle. And she had read it.

"You've always had a terrible temper," she added matter-of-factly.

"My friends in New York would laugh at that idea," Will replied. "Anyone I work with. They would find that so funny." Yet he did not deny it.

"I'm sorry," she said.

"I wasn't offended."

"I mean I'm sorry you don't have friends who know you better."

At least I have friends, he wanted to reply. Poor Sam. What did she have? An angry ex-husband. A missing mother, a dead father. Was there any family left at all?

"I should know this," he said hesitantly. "Is your grandfather still around?"

"He's alive, if that's what you mean. Not in the best of shape."

"He's not living at the house with you."

"No," she said sadly. "Grandpa is…retired from the world."

Will didn't press her. The old guy must be in his eighties, and it sounded like he was up at Cedar Hill or one of its equivalents.

"So you're alone."

"I don't know. I never feel alone in that house."

They crested the low rise, which had seemed like a hill in his childhood. Though Will could make out little in the darkness, he knew that beyond these oaks was the tall, gray, many-dormered house of Thomas Hall. Samantha's grandfather. Built by *his* grandfather more than a century ago. Which barely classified it as old in this colonial town of sea captains' mansions and ancient taverns, set at odd angles to the road. Through a stand of pine and across a field that once held corn was the aluminum-sided rattrap owned by his mother. Will pulled over where the slate path to the Hall house began, leaving the engine idling. Jimmy did the same about fifty yards back.

"Thanks for the ride," said Sam.

"Please. Thanks for everything you've done today."

"You want to come in?" she asked. "See the old place?" Will scanned the rearview, not sure how to answer. "Don't mind Jimmy," she added.

"I'm not worried about him," he answered. "But it's late, and I haven't even been to the house yet."

"Okay." She touched his leg, then opened the door. The

dome light failed to come on. That would be violation number five, thought Will.

Samantha shifted in the seat and looked at him in her steady way. Even in the dim light, those eyes were unnerving.

"Remember that I'm right next door," she said. "I don't know how many friends you have other places. But you have one here who knows you. Understand?"

"Sure," he agreed.

"I'm your friend, whatever happens. Good night, Will."

Then she was out of the car and heading up the walk. The porch light was on to greet her, though Will remembered the house being dark when they drove up. Maybe it was on a timer. She skipped up the steps and went inside without looking back, but Will kept idling awhile. *Whatever happens.* And just what do you imagine happening, you strange girl? Jimmy must have gotten bored sitting there. The patrol car started forward again, rolled past Will at a crawl, then accelerated into the night.

CHAPTER

FOUR

He woke in darkness. His eyes tried to conform the ceiling and walls to his New York apartment, finally accepting them as his childhood bedroom. There had been a sound and he awaited its repeat. Only silence. He could not even say what the sound had been. A voice? But he was alone in the house.

Will had not remembered the place having a smell, but it hit him coming in that night. Jasmine and vanilla. Burned cooking oil, cigarettes, must. Some of it belonged to the house. Much of it was the smell of his mother, though there had been no trace at the hospital. She had left her scent at home. Home. Was it still that without her here? Without friends and strangers trailing in and out? There must have been times when Will was alone in the house, but he could not recall a single one.

Wandering through rooms, he had been struck by their compactness. He knew the place was small, but he felt like a giant in a dollhouse. Somewhere there was a memory house big enough to contain all the scenes and images in his mind. The flushed faces of adults, stumbling about the bright kitchen. Slanting autumn light picking out dust motes above the dining room table. Arthur the cat racing down the stairs while Abigail laughed. Snow sticking to his bedroom window. Watching *The Fog* or *Alien* on the sofa with his mom. Kissing Christine Jordan by the front door. Too many moments to process, like an old box of photos upended suddenly in his head. Still alive somewhere, still happening. He would never return to that house.

The green digits on the clock said it was 2:00 a.m. Not long since he'd gone to bed. Will heaved himself up, meaning to head for the bathroom, but some old instinct guided him to the window. His skin prickled against the cold seeping through. A quarter moon hung high in the starry heavens. You didn't see skies like this in New York. It was one of the things he missed. The tops of the lilac bushes bent, shook and stood up again as a breeze passed across them. A figure stood among the bushes.

Will leaned until his head knocked the glass. Was it a figure? A darkness like negative space, roughly in the shape of a person. Sam? Isn't that where she used to stand when she watched him? No blond hair, though, and so still. Could anything living be that still? He stared hard, determined to catch the smallest movement.

Images invaded his mind. A narrow sidewalk, a looming presence. That hideous face. A single word.

Murder.

He stepped back quickly. As if the face had been right there before him. But the glass held nothing but night, and the faintest reflection of his own face. Eyes wide, their wetness catching ambient light. The line of his nose, his forehead. He went back to the window, knowing before he looked that the figure was gone. Not gone, but had never been there, any more than the face in the shadows behind the deli had been. Will went around the house checking doors and windows, then answered the call of his aching bladder.

In the morning he could not be certain anything had happened. The house was more familiar in daylight. Less threatening. Except for those steep, narrow stairs, which he hated. He made instant coffee—all he could find—and drank it on the front steps. It was late—he should be at the hospital. But he needed caffeine, and a few minutes to himself. He closed his eyes and let the sun bathe his face. Wind rustled the rhododendrons. He glanced at the stump of the lightning-struck pine. His mother had resisted cutting it down, even after the incident. Then his gaze shifted to the thick clump of lilac, swaying innocently. No one hiding there. He could not see Samantha's driveway, but assumed she was at work. Across the street, where once there had been fields, there were houses. Big ones. They had been going in one or two at a time over the last decade, and he was only truly noticing them now. The farm still existed, though shrunken. Selling produce from early summer to late fall. He would go over there at some point.

On the arc of road beyond the lawn, a car slowed to a stop, then backed up cautiously to the house. Maroon Volvo. Older model, with rust on the chassis. A woman with short gray hair rolled down the window and called to him.

"Is that Will?"

"It is." He knew the woman, but couldn't come up with her name. One of those fixtures of the community who made it a point to know everyone's business.

"How's your mom?"

"Stable." He stood and wandered down the lawn toward the car. "I'm going to see her in a few minutes."

"Please give her my best." A lined face and lively blue eyes. Sixtyish. Yet Will had the uneasy feeling that she had been sixtyish for the last thirty years. Margaret something-or-other. "We're all very worried."

"I'll tell her."

He felt no need to go into the details of her condition. Assuming the old crow didn't know them already, which would be a naive assumption.

"So many awful accidents these last years," the woman said. "You heard about Marty Branford?"

"Yeah, I think I might have been here when that happened."

"Were you?" she asked, oddly intrigued.

"Sure, it was last Christmas, right?"

Marty was a paranoid crank, worried about everything. It almost figured a guy like that would die of a gas leak in his home.

"Of course. Are you here alone?"

"Yes," he confirmed. "Just me."

"I thought Muriel was taking care of you or something."

"She's seeing her mother," Will replied, the woman's name suddenly coming to him. "I'm thirty-three years old, Mrs. Price."

"I know, I know," she replied, flashing yellow teeth. "And a college professor. We're all very proud of you."

"Assistant Professor. But thank you."

"Call me Margaret. I mean, how long have we known each other?"

Too long, he was tempted to say, but her smile seemed so genuine that he felt mean. Was it so bad having people keep tabs on you, worry about you? Even if they were mostly about satisfying their busybody natures.

"Is your father coming?"

The question threw him, as did any discussion of his father.

"No. I mean, he's aware. He would come if I needed him."

"It is a long way from Seattle," she said, not very convincingly.

"Yes."

"You know that strange Hall girl has moved back in next door."

"Samantha? Yes, I did."

"Of course, you're probably friends." Her tone was less apology for the previous remark than indulgence in his bad taste.

"She's been very helpful."

"Muriel Brown and Samantha Hall," she sighed, shaking her head. "God help you."

"I'm really fine, Mrs. Price. Margaret. How is, uh, how's everything with you?"

"Me?" She seemed perplexed by the question. "No worries about me, dear. I worry about other people—that's how that goes." Her smile was warm again, but with a hint of mischief as she put the car into gear. "I am always exactly the same."

* * *

For God's sake, Ma, why did you move back to this creepy town? They're all crazy.

Will glanced at the open door, unsure whether he had spoken aloud. Did it matter? Couldn't all these witches read his mind? He'd pulled up the chair beside the bed again, his mother's cold hand in his own.

We couldn't stay with Dad, I get that. But why come back here? Because it's where you grew up? There was a whole world out there, any number of places we could have started over. You could have finished your degree. Moved to New York like you always wanted to do, taken a shot at being an artist. We could be friends now.

He leaned over and put her hand to his forehead, as he had done yesterday.

I guess that's a lot to ask. For you to have had the courage to do that alone. No money. That would have been hard as hell, and scary. Even scarier than coming back here, where at least they knew you. Distant relations, but they took you in. Old Mr. Hall. Renting you the house, then selling it to you for almost nothing. Well, who would have bought it after a man was killed by lightning on the second floor landing?

Will lifted his forehead from her skin. Looked at her face—the pinched, pained expression. Definitely thoughts going on in there, and not happy ones. The doctor said she should wake today, it was time. If she didn't, it could indicate something seriously wrong. Well, it was late afternoon and she was still under. Will knew he had to bring her out, but these angry thoughts were not the way. He tried to focus his mind on happier memories and put his forehead back against her hand.

His mother in the kitchen. She was a decent cook, though her penchant for hummus and brown rice put Will off health food for years. But she was a wizard at baking. Chocolate chip cookies, Toll House she called them. Bread, pies, apple cake with cream cheese frosting on his birthday. The sweet and spicy flavor filled his mouth, made his stomach churn, even though he had not tasted it in years. He could see her standing over him as he ate. It made her happy to make him happy, but mostly she had no idea how to go about it.

Baking? Is that the best you can do? Will squeezed his eyes shut harder, tried to block out the angry, cynical voice.

And do you remember what happened next, after the cake? You were supposed to go to the Topsfield Fair. Except she was too drunk to drive, right?

That was one time.

No, three or four. Out there in the driveway, hammering on the horn, insisting you climb into that death trap just to prove she could do it. And Muriel on the sofa, waiting out your tears.

Willie, look at me. You can't get in that car with her.
I know.
I'll take you over there tomorrow. You're a good kid. You're strong—you'll be all right. God bless Muriel.

He sat up suddenly, dropping the cold hand. His own hand was shaking and sweat glazed his forehead where it had touched her flesh. Why was this so difficult? Why was it so hard for him to forgive a wounded, lonely woman? Who had been barely more than a child herself when he was born. Who had lost the love and support of her husband at that very moment. Who had been given none of the tools necessary for being a good mother, but had done her best anyway. What was this devil inside him that could not forgive?

Movement in the corner of his eye. Did she flex her hand? He grabbed it.

"Ma, it's me. Can you hear?" That same pained expression, but it seemed more focused now, more intentional. "Squeeze my hand. Can you feel? Squeeze."

Nothing. Had he imagined the motion because he was so desperate to see it? Or was it another spasm? The nurse told him yesterday she had been doing that. It meant nothing. It was the same with her expression, a random tightening of muscles, no more. And if he read intention there, why assume it was toward waking? Why not just the opposite? Maybe she was hurt worse than they knew. Maybe she'd had enough. Will slumped and put his face against the bed. He had been on emotional guard for too many hours, and he did not care who saw his distress. He was tired. Sleep seemed not to replenish him, except with nightmare fragments to pick through during waking hours. When this was done, he would sleep for real, and for a long time. His nose itched. The sheets were rough and smelled vaguely of bleach.

Something touched his head and his body tensed. Had someone come into the room? There again, the lightest touch. Fingers stroking his hair. A blunt nail jabbing his ear. He turned his head very slowly, as if afraid of startling her. His mother's long white arm was moving of its own volition. Patting his head. Her eyes were open but unfocused.

"Sokay," she breathed.

"Ma?" he whispered. Then more loudly, "Ma, can you hear me?"

"Sokay, honey. Jus…jus gib me minute."

He did not move. He wanted nothing to upset the moment. If it was just a dream, he was in no hurry to wake. Then a body intruded between them. A nurse, gently pushing him back.

"Mr. Conner? If you could move aside, please?"

Will wanted to resist but fell back in the chair, his vision swimming. A second nurse darted into the room for a moment, then was sent by the first to get the doctor. He heard his mother's voice weakly answering questions.

"She's awake," he said to no one, his voice trembling. He turned to the doorway and saw a familiar figure. "Sam. She's awake."

Samantha stayed where she was, smiling at him.

CHAPTER

FIVE

He took the scenic route home. Following the winding coast road past clapboard houses of white, yellow, red. Every second house an antique shop. How did they all stay in business? Clam shacks, seafood restaurants with waiting lines out to the street, the marina with a dozen blue tarpaulins pulled tightly over pleasure yachts. The white steeple of the Unitarian Church. The occasional view out over the marshes to a strip of blue evening ocean, and the dark hump of Hog Island. This was the part of town everyone came to see. The part he actively avoided for the touristy feel, and for certain unpleasant memories. It was beautiful, actually. He should drive this way more often.

At a roadside farm stand he pulled over, not ready to be

home. They had put away their produce for the day, and there was a sign that announced No More Corn. But there was a big pile of early pumpkins. Many striped with green. It made Will unaccountably happy to see them. He dug Muriel's number out of his wallet and tapped it into his phone.

"She's awake. She knew who I was and seemed to understand what had happened."

"That's great, Will. Could she remember anything?"

"Wasn't clear," he replied. "She didn't seem agitated. I sent your regards, told her how worried you were."

"What did she say?"

"Nothing. But she smiled."

"Well," Muriel said. "Okay, I'll take a smile. How are you holding up?"

"Fine."

"You eating?"

"Oh yeah." In fact, he'd had nothing but hospital sandwiches for two days. And bad coffee. He could use some real food. "How's *your* mom?"

"Truthfully, not so good," Muriel said. "I need to stick around."

They talked a little longer and disconnected. Now came the hard part. But it would not get easier, and somehow sitting here staring at pumpkins and the little duck pond in the green dell below made him calm. He dialed his father's number from memory. Hoping for interference or an answering machine. Instead he got the old man.

"Don't beat around the bush," Joe Conner said.

Will did not, reciting the facts as efficiently as possible. Keeping his voice neutral. Sounding more like a doctor than the doctor had. His father said nothing while he spoke, and for a while afterward. Will pictured him. Short and muscled, in the Jimmy Duffy mold. Standing in the gleaming kitchen of his big house, squeezing the receiver hard enough to crack it. Always one step away from blowing up. The guy went through phones.

"Good," Joe finally said. "That sounds good. No sign of brain damage? I mean, more than usual."

It wasn't funny, but it was the kind of thing his father said. Even his mother was always claiming her brain was addled from "all those drugs I took" whenever she couldn't remember something.

"She can move her feet and hands," Will replied. "Answer simple questions. She knew who everybody was. More than that will have to wait for tomorrow."

"They'll keep her a few more days?"

"Yeah."

Then a pause and a deep breath.

"You need me to come out?"

"No," Will replied immediately. "I got it covered."

"You sure?"

"Absolutely."

"Okay then," Joe said. "Just as well, 'cause it's busy as heck here, and Patty would kill me if I had to run off and deal with this."

That was Will's cue to ask how Patty was, but he really didn't give a damn. Any more than she did about Joe's first family.

"I wish you had brothers or sisters to help you," the old man mumbled, sounding like someone else. Will didn't know how to answer.

"That seems unlikely at this late date. But I'll talk to Ma about it."

"I don't mean that Joey and Tricia aren't your family," his father said quickly.

"I didn't take it like—"

"They talk about you a lot."

"Dad, they met me once."

"But they remember. They get the books you send. And the, ah, the CDs and stuff. They always ask how you are, when you're going to visit again."

The words were rushed and eager, and Will felt a sudden tenderness for his father he could not have imagined even moments before. They were not close. They spoke twice a year. The kids would be teenagers now, wrapped up in their all-consuming teenage lives. Not thinking about some half brother they didn't know.

"You should come out for Christmas," Joe said.

"Yeah? And what about Ma?"

"Right. I guess that wouldn't work."

You know damn well it wouldn't. That's why you offered.

"Look, I have to go. I'll call when there's more news."

"Call in a few days, news or not. And Will, you be… You know, you're always…"

"Okay, Dad."

He was driving somewhere with Christine Jordan. Which was awkward, because she was dead. She kept smiling at him and tossing back her brown hair. He smiled too, but there was a thick sadness within him. He adored Christine, and was amazed to discover that she liked him too. It was good having her near again, and he did not want the ride to end. But it was also wrong. The dead could not come back. At some point he would have to tell her, and he dreaded it. The knowledge took all pleasure from the moment. He felt old. His hands on the steering wheel looked worn and knobby. Was he old now? He couldn't remember? She was young and lovely and smiling at him. Just seventeen. She would never be any older.

A knocking came and went. He thought at first it was the engine, but couldn't sustain the illusion. The car was gone, Christine was gone and he was staring at another strange ceiling. The green sofa was to his right, the bluish-black painting of the raven above it. His mother's work. She had been into ravens for a while. To his left the window was full of night. Will was on his back on the beige carpet of the living room. He had lain down here after coming home. For a minute, to rest. His spine and the darkness told him it had been more like hours. The knocking had stopped, but someone was in the house.

Sam entered the room. Someone else might be alarmed to find him on the floor, but her expression was only mildly curious.

"Do you need help?"

"Standing? I might."

"Tell me when you're ready," she said, crouching beside him. She wore jeans and a yellow cotton sweater, and her eyes looked him up and down, settling on his face.

"I thought I locked the door," said Will.

"You did."

"Muriel give you a key?"

"I figured you might need me," she answered, "that's all."

She helped him to sitting position, then stood and headed for the kitchen.

"You still hate going up those stairs, huh? Is there any food in this house?"

"I don't know," Will mused, surprised by her strength. How easily she had lifted him. Maybe shifting and hauling old people around at the nursing home did that. "I'm sorry. Are you hungry?"

"No," She gave him a faintly annoyed look over her shoulder. "You are."

They determined quickly that his mother's refrigerator could furnish nothing edible, and Sam invited him over to her place. Will accepted. Not bothering with a jacket, which he soon regretted. It was a chilly night, autumn taking hold. He moved warily, looking around at dark clumps of bushes, the swaying oaks. She didn't wait for him, but walked ahead, like a scout. Her pale sweater was a beacon in the darkness. There was strength in the deliberate way she moved. He liked watching her. Liked the way her ass swayed in those jeans. Will laughed quietly at himself. He was too tired to feel embarrassed, but it was odd to think about Sam that way. She was not like other women, or like any other creature he knew. Yet she was a woman. Surely, underneath the fear and fascination, he had once harbored a childish crush for the mysterious girl next door. Her porch light guided them through the pines. He had a memory of hiding here as they played flashlight tag with four or five other kids. Sam behind him, breathing on his neck. Waiting to be caught by the light beam, or to race off and find a new hiding place. She waited on him now, holding back a spiky bough so it would not slap him in the face.

"That was fun, huh?" she said in the darkness. "Those nights."

"You mean playing tag out here?"

"That was the only time I did stuff with the neighborhood kids. And only because you made them include me."

He did not remember, but she might be right. Memories were flooding in again. Danny Larcom stuck in the apple tree. Brendan Duffy with the flashlight, shouting obscenities to make them laugh and give away their hiding places. Arthur the cat rushing after him, wanting in on the game. Samantha's budding chest pressed against his back, her arms around him, her lips at his ear. Telling him things. Apologizing for something. And then someone else was in the pine grove with them. Someone they could sense but not see, and a terror seized them both. The memories became more real than what was around him, and Will stopped, unable to move. Sam took his hand.

"You're in a bad way, William. Come on."

The house was as he remembered it. Narrow hallways and large, wood-paneled rooms with high ceilings. Old bookcases stuffed with ancient, dusty volumes were jammed anywhere they would fit. The corridors, living room, study, even the airy dining room. Only the kitchen was free of them.

"I think this is still edible," Sam said, dragging a frozen grayish-purple slab from the freezer and dropping it in a bowl of warm water.

"Did one of your ancestors kill that?"

"Margaret Price brought it with a bunch of other groceries. I can't remember when."

"Does she think you can't shop for yourself?" Will asked.

"She doesn't think anyone can do anything for themselves." Sam bent down to rip open a big paper bag of potatoes. "I'm surprised she hasn't been after you."

"She has," he confessed. "Drove by this morning. She

seemed appalled that no one had been assigned to care for me. Wait."

She had been about to stab the potatoes with long silver nails. He took them from her warm hands and brought them to the sink to wash.

"Do you have a brush?"

"The dirt's good for you," she answered, fishing a little brush shaped like a bear out of a drawer and handing it to him.

"The *skin* is good for you," Will said, scrubbing gently under cool water. The task was soothing. His hands looked strong, useful. Not old and knobby. "I don't know about the dirt."

"Did she warn you to stay away from me?" Samantha asked. "Margaret?"

He waited too long to answer. There was no point in lying to Sam anyway.

"Not exactly."

"She thinks I'm dangerous."

"*Strange* was the word she used." Will placed the potatoes on the counter.

"*Dangerous* is what she meant," Sam answered calmly, stabbing the potatoes a little more fiercely than necessary. "A lot of them think that."

"Priccs don't like Halls," he said, the words out of his mouth before Will had registered thinking them. Sam gave him a surprised look, or as close as her face got to surprise.

"Haven't forgotten all that seven families gossip, huh?"

The Seven Families. How long since he had heard the phrase?

"I don't know where that came from," he said. "Something somebody told me. Maybe my mother."

"Or Margaret Price," she said. "They were the leading families once. Up in Maine, maybe all the way back to England."

Her grandfather. Of course, it was old Tom Hall who told them this stuff. Will could hear his deep, rumbling voice, broken up by long pulls on his pipe. The click of teeth on the enamel mouthpiece, and the sweet smell of the smoke. The family chronicles were imparted with a smile or wink, as if it was not meant to be taken seriously. The lessons on Greek and Roman history and philosophy—the professor's courses at Dartmouth—were the important ones, but the family stories remained buried in Will's brain. Wars, voyages, feuds. Evil pacts with witches, brave or cowardly men and women.

"Natural they would butt heads back then," Sam continued. "But it's not true anymore, about them hating each other."

"Tell Margaret."

"Maybe she still feels that way. About me, anyhow. Although she did bring me food I didn't ask for. But your mother is a Hall, and Margaret seems to like you fine."

"She condescends to me the same way she does everyone," said Will.

"Imagine that. You being a professor and all."

Will thought he heard an edge to her words. He was probably imagining it, but he didn't like the silence that followed.

"I wish I could remember those stories," he said.

"Ask me," Sam replied, disgust creeping in that he was not imagining. "I remember every damn thing I've ever heard."

"Wow," he deadpanned. "What a useful skill."

"You kidding? It's a curse. You want a beer, William?"

They emptied most of a six-pack of Harpoon IPA, talking. About his Mom, about their lives since high school. There were silent stretches too. Will had gotten used to silence, living alone, and Samantha had always been good with it, so it felt companionable, not awkward. When the potatoes were done, she decided the meat was ready to fry. The kitchen got so smoky Will had to open the windows, but the steak was surprisingly good.

"You're hungry enough that anything would taste good," Sam said. "Anyway, thank Margaret, not me."

"It has to be a good cut, that's true, but you also need to cook it right. You've clearly mastered the art."

"Jimmy liked steak. I don't eat it much myself."

Will reached for his beer, then put it down again, shaking his head.

"I still can't picture you and Jimmy Duffy together."

"Well, don't strain yourself. There's nothing to picture anymore."

"I'm sorry, that sounded—"

"I was waitressing at The Clam Digger." She cut him off. Determined to get this story out without being interrupted. "He came in all the time. With the other cops, that was their place. He was nice to me, didn't treat me like a weirdo. We were both lonely. Had nothing else in common, really, but it worked out for a while. Then I had a baby that died. And things kind of fell apart after that."

"Oh, Sam. I didn't know."

"It didn't live more than a couple of days. I knew it wasn't going to. I wouldn't let him name it. He was so angry about that. Then I had a miscarriage the next year.

That was it—I was done. And we were alone again. In the same house, you know? But alone. So I left."

"And he hasn't accepted it."

"Not in two years," she said, staring at the table. "Maybe not ever."

"He must really love you," Will replied, knowing he shouldn't say it. But the truth of it had struck him forcefully through her words. She looked at him a long time.

"He wants a son more than anything," Samantha said. "And I can't give him one. So maybe you're right. Maybe he does." She stood again. "You want to split that last beer?"

"Sure. Unless you have something stronger."

She kept walking past the refrigerator and out of the room. He saw her shadow move into the dark study, and pictured her grandfather in the squeaking leather chair. Speaking tightly through the clenched pipe. *Judging only by the tales left to us from Plato*—click, suck, smoky exhale—*we'd be forced to conclude that Socrates was an insufferable ass who got exactly what he had coming.*

Sam came back into the room with a mostly full bottle of Maker's Mark in her hand.

"I remembered Grandpa always kept a bottle in his desk," she said, rummaging for glasses in the cabinets over the counter.

"And you haven't raided it before now?" Will asked. "How old is that?"

"A few years. Does bourbon go bad?"

"Not in my experience."

They did not speak again until the first pair of shot glasses were empty.

"That is good," said Sam. "I didn't remember liking it. So Will, how are you?"

"Better now," he replied. "Thanks for dinner. And the booze."

"How is New York?"

"Loud. Hot. I didn't get away this summer. Fall should be better, if I ever get back. I like my students, and teaching is a good distraction."

"You could teach someplace else," she suggested, refilling their glasses.

"My mom's always saying that. Wants me to come back here."

"Lots of colleges around these parts."

"I couldn't live here again, Sam."

"I know," she said gently. *Did she?* "This place haunts you."

Will leaned forward to take the glass, avoiding her eyes. He couldn't deny the sentiment, but wished she had chosen a different word.

"I have a tricky relationship with home. A lot of people do."

"Is it better in the city? Do you feel free of it there?"

"Free of what?" he asked.

"The burden," she replied. "The haunted feeling."

"That was your word."

"How is it you're not married?"

"Come on," he laughed nervously. "You can't make something of that. Lots of people aren't married."

"Not good-looking guys in their thirties," she replied, her gaze not leaving him. "With good jobs. Okay, you could be a womanizer."

"Or gay."

"Right. But you're neither of those things."

"No," he agreed. "So what's my problem, Doctor Hall?"

"You're haunted. You have been since you were five, and it's screwing up your life."

He was getting annoyed now. She was a perceptive, intuitive woman, but she had not known him in more than a decade. It was arrogant of her to think she could diagnose his troubles. He tossed the rest of the bourbon back and closed his eyes against the burn. When he could speak again he looked at her.

"Thanks for this, Sam. Dinner, being around. Everything. I really appreciate it."

"I didn't mean to offend you."

"No, I just need sleep. Can't seem to get enough."

"You can talk to me now," she pressed on, quietly but firmly. "Or somebody else later, but you'll have to talk about this."

"Stop."

"It would be better if it was me. I can help you."

He stood up and was suddenly dizzy. *Drunk again. Well done, William.* He looked around for his jacket, remembered he hadn't brought one. He could just walk out, but that would be childish. She had been kind to him. Will went over and squeezed her shoulder.

"Good night."

She didn't reply, didn't even move as he left the kitchen. And yet somehow she was behind him when he reached the front door.

"It doesn't matter that time has passed," Samantha said to his back. "Stuff has happened to us, okay. Some bad stuff. It doesn't change anything between us."

"It changes everything. We're different people."

"We're connected."

"How?" he demanded, wheeling on her. She was closer

than he thought. Less than a foot away, and his shoulder nudged her back. "How are we connected?"

"I called you and you came. That night, in the field. I summoned you."

Her face was calm as ever, but her voice was high and tight. He could smell fear even through her whiskey breath. It was costing her something to force these words out. Which didn't make them any less nuts.

"The house had been hit," he said. "There was yelling and screaming. I was panicked. I was running for my life."

"Yes, right to me."

"I was just running. I had no idea where or why."

"But you knew when you saw me," she persisted. "You knew to come to me."

"I saw the lantern."

"You knew I would protect you, even though you had no reason to believe that then."

"Sam." His anger was gone, and he was exhausted. He could have fallen down on the threadbare carpet and slept right there. The blue disks of her eyes were huge and close, swallowing him.

"I was inside my circle," she said firmly. "I performed all the steps perfectly. And you came to me, just like I imagined. The thing is…" Her voice faltered and she broke eye contact. She must have taken a step back, but it seemed more like she simply shrank. "The only thing is, you didn't come alone. Something came with you, out of that house."

If she spoke any words beyond those, Will did not hear them. He went out the door without closing it behind him. Rushed down the wooden steps and raced through the darkness for home.

CHAPTER

SIX

She was sitting up when he arrived.

"Hey, Ma."

"Come here," she said weakly, patting the edge of the bed. "Come over here."

He sat down on the hard mattress and she put her arms around him. She could not have lost much muscle in three days, but her arms felt thin. She smelled faintly of body odor, and strongly of soap and disinfectant. When she did not release him after several moments, Will put his arms around her. Then leaned into her as she rested her head on his shoulder.

"My boy," she murmured.

"That's me."

"Is this what I have to do?" she asked, though he could hear the smile in her voice. "Fall and break my head?"

"Arm or leg would have been fine," Will replied. "I would have come for that."

"Yeah, I always overdo it."

There was a vague slur to some words, but mostly she sounded tired. A coma was not as restful as it seemed, apparently. She finally released him and sank back onto the stacked pillows.

"You look terrible," she said.

"Me?" he laughed. "You should talk."

"I have a reason."

"Well, I've been a little stressed the last few days. Slept better last night," he lied. His poor sleep had nothing to do with her. He was, however, hoping to avoid another encounter with Samantha.

"Tell me what I missed," Abby said.

"The last three days? Not a hell of a lot."

"Tell me anyway."

He filled her in on what the doctor had said. Then gave brief and sanitized accounts of the phone call with his father, his doings with Muriel, Samantha, Jimmy Duffy, Margaret Price. All of their fond regards.

"Sam came by today," she said, an uncertain look on her face. "She was sweet."

"She's been by every day," Will reported.

"Poor girl. Still acts like she's twelve years old."

"That's just her manner," he said, unable to stop himself. He had no real desire to defend Sam. Was it merely the need to contradict his mother reasserting itself so quickly? "She's been through a lot."

She gazed at him steadily.

"You been seeing much of her?"

"Some," he admitted. "She's been helping me out."

"She was so crazy about you," Abby said fondly. "You were her pet. And her best friend, and the little brother she never had."

"And she was the scary sister I never wanted," Will replied, desperate to get off the topic. "What did the doctor say this morning?"

"They'll test my reflexes and stuff this afternoon. Again." She closed her eyes, the very prospect of more tests making her weary. "See if I need therapy before I go home."

"Have you walked?"

"To the bathroom and back. I need to get a little steadier before they let me out."

"So, another few days?"

She gave him that level gaze again. This calm, sane-seeming version of his mother was almost unnerving.

"I'm keeping you from your work, honey."

"Don't worry about that."

"I'm sorry."

"Please don't think about that," he insisted, with the vehemence of a guilty conscience. "This is where I need to be."

"You shouldn't have to deal with this alone. We can... Hey, how is Muriel? Has she been by, I don't remember?"

"She's with her mother," Will replied, taking her hand.

"Her mother, oh...the Alzheimer's is worse?"

"I guess. Also, she's a little nervous about seeing you."

Her expression was as puzzled as he had expected it would be.

"You and she were arguing when you fell," Will explained.

"Right," Abby said, some hazy recollection fighting its way through. "She was there. Oh God, poor Mure." Like everyone in these parts, she said it with a flat *u*, like *burr*. The local accent always clanged in Will's ears after he'd been away for a while.

"She's kind of twisted up about it."

"I've been having dreams," she whispered. "These awful dreams."

"You mean while you were under?"

"Then too. But before, the last few weeks. From when you were a kid. I've been dreaming of the night Johnny died."

John Payson was a blue-eyed, blond-haired, ne'er-do-well son of one of the old families. Everyone loved Johnny, all the grown-ups. Will was five when he died and could not remember him clearly. What he recalled was a big, hairy, loud man he had not liked very much. Johnny had been Abby's off-and-on boyfriend, and a member of the spirit circle. And he had been fried to death by lightning at the top of the stairs. Twenty feet from Will's bedroom door.

"Maybe you shouldn't think of that stuff right now," he suggested.

"You don't get to choose what you dream, honey," she answered. "But you're right. Because they're so real, I keep thinking of them when I'm awake. I keep remembering stuff I don't want to."

Sadness welled up in her eyes and she closed them. This could not be good for her, but how did he make her stop? He took both of her hands in his own. Still cool, but he could feel the life in them now.

"Is Joe here," she asked. "Is he coming?"

"No," Will replied.

"Figures."

"I told him not to. I kind of insisted, actually."

"Don't hate him, Willie."

"I don't," he assured her.

"He didn't do anything wrong. Me, now. I've done everything wrong."

"Stop it. No more of this."

"I want to talk," Abigail said.

"Not today. Let it go for a while."

She opened her eyes and looked at him again.

"Please tell Muriel it's okay. I'm not mad. Tell her to come see me."

"I'll do that," he promised.

Last day of September. The anniversary of Christine Jordan's death, but he had chosen not to think about that. The morning had been chilly, but the afternoon was clear and blue and warm. Late-day sun turned the backyard grass a glowing emerald. Will walked barefoot in that cool grass, sipping a beer. As content and relaxed as he had been in many days, weeks maybe. He had shopped for groceries at Shaw's and seen no one he knew. Then to the farm to buy early apples and cider. There had been no evil dreams for two nights. The beer was the first he'd had since that night at Sam's, and he drank it for pleasure, not medication. Tomorrow was October 1. The witching month, and his mother was coming home.

He gazed at the strip of white impatiens, dividing the lawn from a small rose garden. Three of the rose plants were dead, but four others were still blooming, a yellow and three reds. He would buy her new ones to replace the casualties. Or did you wait for spring to plant roses? Somewhere under those healthy plants were the ashes of Arthur the cat, friend of his youth. A small stone with an *A* on it used to mark the spot, but it had disappeared over the years. Will looked down the street to Muriel's house, but her driveway was still empty. He had thought she might be back by now. Across the field and through the pines he could see lights on at the Hall place, but he was continuing to keep his distance from Sam.

The sun disappeared behind the oaks, a chill came into the air and Will went inside. It was cooling off in the house also, and he traversed the shadowy rooms of the first floor lowering windows. Returning to the kitchen, he flicked on the overhead—only one bulb working—and considered dinner. The refrigerator and shelves were full, to meet any possible food whim of his mother's, but he wasn't that hungry. Maybe soup. He stood by the sink, finishing his beer. Sniffing the grassy scent through the window and watching the impatiens acquire that bluish glow they got at dusk. Brightening as everything around darkened. The phenomenon lasted only a few minutes until the white flowers faded as well. A shiver passed through him. Will set down the beer and reached across the sink to close the window.

Bathed in milky light, the room behind was reflected in the wavy glass of the window. Dim and distorted. The four glass-fronted cabinets. The array of steel and ceramic pots and pans on the far wall. The rusting kettle on top of the ancient gas stove. The white refrigerator. The figure in the dining room doorway. Slender, with brown hair to her shoulders, and a white T-shirt stained red in front.

Will?

The voice was hoarse. Strained but recognizable. Her

nose had been crushed by the dashboard and her neck had snapped. Who had told him that?

Will?

Scared, pleading. She did not know where she was or what had happened. She wanted him to explain, to comfort her. He had no comfort. He shivered again and closed his eyes. There was a slow, unsteady shuffling of feet across the linoleum, approaching him. Her legs had been broken in multiple places. How did he know that? Who would have been cruel enough to tell him details like these? And yet stories circulated after traumatic deaths. In small towns. Rumors, gossip, truth and invention hopelessly mixed.

Will?

The nerve endings in his neck and back began to ache, awaiting her touch. She must be right there behind him. Arm outstretched. Small, cold hand, bloody fingers about to brush his skin. He listened for her breath, but his own blood roaring in his ears drowned out everything. Her coffin had been closed. He had not been able to see her a last time. Not that it would have been her, just an abandoned husk. Why should he not look now? How could it be worse than what his imagination had created and recreated over sixteen years? She needed him. Didn't he hear the pleading in her voice? Where was his courage?

Will opened his eyes and turned around.

She took a long time to answer the door. When she did, she said nothing, just looked at him. Looked long and carefully at his face. He could only guess what she saw there. Will could summon no words, but it didn't matter. She did not need to be told.

74

"Come in," Samantha said at last, stepping out of the way.

Will didn't move. Just swayed in place, three or four feet from the open door. Some instinct had propelled him to this spot, but now his momentum failed.

"I need to understand what's happening to me," he said at last.

"I know," she replied, reversing her motion and stepping onto the porch. She took both of his hands in hers and drew him to her. "Come inside now."

CHAPTER

SEVEN

"I'm not the best person to explain this," she said, placing a steaming mug in front of him. "I have to imagine what it's like for you. For me, it's just how things are. But I guess I'm all you've got."

Will wrapped his trembling hands around the hot mug. The brew was a murky yellow and smelled flowery. He was determined not to interrupt, not to be evasive or skeptical. Not to think at all, if he could help it. Especially not to think about the scared, broken thing that had or had not been in his kitchen.

"There's stuff around us all the time," Sam said, sitting across from him with her own mug of the concoction. "Stuff people don't see. Maybe they used to when they were young. You did. Friends that aren't there, the way other people are. Probably we don't even see them like they really are. Just a picture our mind makes."

She was already losing him, but he didn't speak. She seemed to understand.

"Do you remember Toby?"

The name was instantly familiar, yet he had to fight the impulse to disavow. The instinct of ignorance. As if someone else controlled his mind, and had for decades. Relax. Wait for it. The little wooded gully behind the house. The leaves May green. Sam uttering some singsong chant or incantation while they watched her in fascination. They. Two of them. Will, and Toby. Round, chortling and red faced. A little boy, but not a little boy. He didn't live anywhere but there in the woods.

"Toby wasn't real," he said. Already he had broken his resolution.

"Or Alice?"

A plain-looking girl with pale skin and gray eyes. Gloomy and solemn. They let her hang around because they felt sorry for her. She was older, at first. Then she was their age, then younger, then gone. He had not thought of her in twenty-five years.

"She was yours," Will said, struggling with this. "I invented Toby and you invented Alice. Children have friends like that."

"They do," she agreed.

"They weren't real."

"Well, maybe they weren't what they seemed. Drink that."

He took a sip. It was bitter, and familiar.

"My grandfather has this genealogical research," Samantha said. "Books he's collected. Family trees. I look at it sometimes. There was an Alice Hall who would have been my great-aunt. She died in this house when she was seven. Spanish flu. I even found a photograph. Want to see?"

"You think they were ghosts?"

"You know, that's one of those words. There are these ideas you bring, these…"

"Cultural references," he supplied.

"Right," she said. "Thanks, Professor. Anyway, it's not useful."

"But that's what you mean."

"I know people can leave a piece of themselves behind. Especially if they die young, or die badly. It's not them, but it's real."

"You still see them?" he couldn't help but ask.

"I've seen Alice. Not for a long while. I see my grand-mother."

"When?" he asked.

"All the time. I saw her today, in the herb garden. She's there a lot."

Could he go down this road with her? Surely there was a line between opening your mind and losing it.

"Was it Christine you saw?" she asked.

The brew surged in his throat, hot and acid. He managed not to spit up. He had to stop being surprised by her. To accept that she knew things about him, however that might be.

"Why did you say that?"

"Because this is the day she died."

"Of course," Will sighed. Feeling foolish. "I didn't expect anyone else to remember."

"She was important to you," Sam said. "You loved her."

"No. We were seventeen, it was…"

"What's important to you is important to me."

"Would you stop with that." His words had no force. He could not tell her what to feel. That he had become an adult in the last fifteen years, had experienced a full and complicated life completely out of her sight did not seem to matter at all. He had forgotten her, forgotten them all. But she had not forgotten him. And anyway, it now seemed that he had not really forgotten anything.

"Is that how it works?" he asked. "Anniversaries of their deaths?"

"Some say. Some say certain times, or even in certain places, the line between what's seen and unseen gets thin. There's whole religions that believe that."

"Not you?"

"Maybe it's true," she conceded. Leaning back and putting her sneakered feet on the kitchen table. "How would I know, when I see things all the time? Mostly I think it's about the people who do the seeing. It runs in families. Runs in ours."

"Not mine," he protested.

"Sure it does, you're half Hall. Go back far enough, and most of this town is related. And it could be those people who have the sight are drawn to places where the sight is clearer."

"Like this town?"

"That's not for warming your hands. Drink, it'll calm you."

He took another sip. That familiar bittersweet taste.

"What's in here?"

"Mayweed. Willow bark, a little honey. Few other things."

"My mother used to make this." Will remembered at

last. "Something like this. When I was upset. Mayweed and honey. Hers was sweeter."

"Of course she made it," Sam said, getting up and going to the cabinet. "I'm sure she made all kinds of remedies you don't recall. She's a Hall woman."

"Meaning she's a witch?" he asked sharply.

Sam gave him a long look, the overhead light making a bright halo of her hair. Then shook her head slowly.

"That's another one of those words I don't use." She came back to the table and put the sticky honey jar and a spoon in front of him. "Here you go."

"They don't burn them anymore," he taunted. "They have ceremonies out in public. You can go down the road to Salem and join a coven."

"I don't need to go to Salem to do that," she said quietly, sitting again.

"No?" he asked, his false bravado curdling instantly.

"They're here," she confirmed, her voice firm and a little scolding. "In all of these towns hereabout. And most of them *do not* do their business in public." She closed and opened her eyes. "I don't consider myself one of them."

"What word do you use?" he asked.

"Hall women are healers. Going back generations. Back to Maine, anyway. Probably back to England. They're in tune with whatever place they live. The trees and plants. The herb lore, the energy. They might do some songs or chants, but I think of that more like prayer. You know? Ritual. They heal, they help people."

Will could feel himself falling into her words, the spell of her words. The idea of this community of women, healing and enfolding him. *It's a lie*, the voice in his head said. And he shook himself, as if from a dream.

"That's a nice story, Sam. But my mother was a drug-addled hippie. She was no *healer*."

"Every generation reinvents what it means. You think our ancestors weren't eating and smoking herbs and bark and flowers? Just to see what they did? You think magic mushrooms were just invented?"

"Come on," he said. "Your ancestral healers testing medicinal properties is not exactly the same thing my mom and her buddies were up to."

"They had the impulse, but they lacked teaching."

"What teaching?"

"There's supposed to be a knowledge-keeper every generation. Or more than one, maybe, who passes this stuff on to the next generation."

"That stopped at some point?"

"I don't know if it stopped," she said, not looking at him now. "But maybe it stopped being done the right way."

She knew more than she was saying. Which was odd for straightforward Sam.

"No one taught you," Will said. "But you know how the system is supposed to work."

"Yeah."

"How? Who told you that much?"

"My grandfather, for one."

"Tom Hall?" Will said, taken aback. "Told you this stuff?" But then it made sense, if you looked at those old family tales in a different way.

"Of course," she replied. "He studied local history. Knew all about the seven families. He always smiled when he talked about it, but he knew. Old Mrs. Price too."

"Margaret?"

"Not her," she scoffed. "Her mother. She was always nice to me—I don't know why."

"Maybe she saw something in you," he suggested. Wondering now if Margaret Price's seeming agelessness was not simply his confusing generations.

"I think that might be it. It wasn't that she liked me so much, but she would look me over real close. Ask me questions. As if she sensed something."

"Your witchy strength."

"Whatever," she replied. "I guess she did teach me things."

"Spells and incantations?"

"No, nobody taught me those. But I learned a few on my own."

"Yeah? How?"

She looked uncomfortable again. They were getting near what she wanted to talk about, but oddly it was him having to pull it out of her. That was fine. The tea was calming him, and they had already come this far. He might as well hear it all.

"A few days ago," he started. "You said that you called me and I came. That night of the storm. When John Payson died. What did you mean?"

"Johnny…" She took a deep breath and continued. "Johnny was spending a lot of time hanging around our house then. You remember that?"

"No. I don't remember those days very clearly."

"He was a Payson, but he had Stafford ancestors. And Halls. Actually, he claimed a connection to all seven families. The missing link, he called himself."

Will finished his tea. He had never added more honey.

"I didn't think his generation cared about all that," he

said. "Seven families, the history. I thought it was peace, love, drugs and rock and roll."

"Johnny was a little older. Twenty-eight or nine. He'd been out West, all over the country."

"Draft-dodging," Will said, having heard that much before. It was during that same cross-country exile that Johnny stayed briefly with Will's parents in California, before his dad shipped out to Vietnam.

"Right," Sam said. "He studied with some Zen master in Los Angeles. Stayed on Indian reservations, hanging with the medicine men and chewing peyote. When he finally came back, he had hair halfway down to his butt, silver bracelets. All these ideas about space and time and consciousness."

"You can't possibly remember that," Will said. "You were six or seven."

"I remember a lot. More than other people. But I'm sure I was told things too."

He noted that even after her scolding, she wasn't drinking her own tea. He pushed the honey jar at her, which elicited a brief smile.

"Nah. If you can drink bitter, so can I."

"Johnny came marching home," he prompted her.

"I'm guessing about this. Nobody wanted to talk about Johnny after that night. But I think he came to see our families, the healers or witches or whatever you want to call them... He came to see it as one more thing, you know? Zen, dream catching, the earth goddess, spirit cults. Just one more piece of the mystical whole."

"Is that how you see it?" he asked, genuinely curious.

"And unlike those other traditions," she pushed on, "this

was the one he was born into. And there's my grandfather. Always taking in strays, helping people out."

"Like he did my mother."

"And he's got these shelves and shelves of books about everything."

Will got it. Johnny was full of ideas. Full of himself and in love with the world, but returning with nothing. No money, his family dead or moved on, except for his brother Doug. He needed someone to help and guide him. And here's this old guy with a library designed to let the young man explore his theme. Investigate his past for the raw material to make something of his life. Tom probably ate it up.

"My grandfather liked him," Sam said, answering his thoughts unbidden, "Liked having anyone around who was curious about books and ideas. He was still grieving for Grandma Jane, and I guess he needed someone else to focus his attention on. He and Johnny bonded."

"Seems like Johnny charmed everyone."

"He had the knack," she agreed. "He could dazzle the younger people with his half-assed philosophy, and he could flatter the older ones, like Grandpa or Doc Chester. He would listen to Doc gas on about African tribal rituals all afternoon."

"It must have been tough for your grandfather. You know, to have Johnny die like that."

He remembered Tom being around that night, for the aftermath. Trying to calm his mother. Talking to the police. Yet wearing the same haunted look as all the others.

"It was. They were fighting a lot right before it happened."

She was gazing just over his left shoulder. As if someone there was providing the story. He shivered involuntarily and resisted the urge to look.

"There was a book," said Sam. "One particular book Johnny got obsessed with. Old. Hundreds of years, I think, with old-fashioned writing. Passed down through the family."

"The grimoire," Will said, rather than asked. "The book of spells."

"I guess Grandpa didn't mind at first, but after a while they started to argue."

"Do you know why?"

"Something in the book." She closed her eyes, then looked at the tabletop. Anywhere but at him. "He had marked one page with a strand of hair."

"Hair?"

"Yeah, so it wouldn't be obvious. But Grandpa noticed it. He noticed things."

"And so did you," Will added. He placed his hands on the table and leaned forward, to get her attention. "What was on that page?"

"A summoning spell." She looked at him shyly.

"Summoning what?"

"It was in a whole section of spells like that. Spells you shouldn't use. Enchantment. Shape-shifting. Summoning."

"Summoning what, Sam?"

"The kind of spells you needed other people for," she said, like he was missing the point. "Many voices together, that creates power. I think he was trying them out in your mother's coven."

"My mother's..." He could say no more, his throat suddenly tight.

"What have we been talking about?" Sam said, exasperated. "Coven, conventicle, spirit circle. Call it what you like."

"It's not, it's not about what I like," he stuttered. "It matters."

"Only because you're a teacher. They're just words, William."

"It matters what *they* thought they were doing." He had to keep wetting his lips to speak. All that sweet calm had burned away, just like that. "I teach myth and folklore. I know what covens are. I know what kind of beings they seek to summon."

"Those are stories," she said.

"So it's not the same?"

"Look, there are things we know, things that are here." She chose the words carefully, her attention fixed on him again. "Like Toby or Alice. Call them ghosts, shades, whatever. But there are other things too. Not from here." Will had the strong impression *here* did not mean Cape Ann. "Things most of us never see, and never should. But sometimes they cross over. Some are powerful. When we encounter them, it's overwhelming. Our mind can't take it in. We don't even remember what we've seen, only that feeling of being overwhelmed. And we give them names. Gods. Angels."

"Demons," Will said. Her only response was that even stare.

He sat back in the chair. They were awfully far down the rabbit hole. Did he gather the strength to continue, or rush back to the surface? Would he laugh at all of this tomorrow? He might, but he could not laugh right now.

"And that's what happened that night," he said finally.

"Johnny brought the spell and they tried to summon one of these beings. My mother's *coven*."

"I think so," she said.

"But something went wrong."

"Yes."

"What?"

"I don't know," she whispered. Her eyes were damp. Will could not remember ever seeing her cry. Was that right? Everyone cried. She gave him a humiliated glance, then stood up and left the room. His legs were numb from too long sitting in the hard chair. Even standing slowly, he became dizzy, and by the time he reached the hall she had vanished. Yet he knew where to find her.

The study was dim. Just a low light from the desk lamp. Except for the windows and four old framed photographs, every patch of wall was covered in bookcases. Dark wood, dark spines, absorbing light and giving little back. Samantha leaned against the desk, her arms folded and back to the door.

"Is it here?" he asked, his words swallowed by wood, leather and paper.

"I've looked for it," she answered. Not needing him to explain that he meant the book. "The last few days. I haven't been able to find it."

"You read the summoning spell." He saw a rain-soaked girl in the lantern light. The symbols drawn in the mud at her feet. "And you performed it that night."

"I don't think I understood." She turned halfway toward him, her face shining in the lamplight. "I mean, what it was for. I knew what I wanted, and I learned all the steps."

"What did you want?"

"What every child wants," Samantha replied. "A friend.

It was so easy for other people, but I never got the trick of it. Still haven't. I didn't notice at first, I thought I had friends. Then I realized that nobody else could see them. They weren't the same as real friends. So I learned the spell and summoned one. I summoned you. And bound you to me in friendship." She glanced at him. "Funny, huh?"

It seemed pointless to say again that he had been running in panic. He had, in fact, run into the field. Right to her. And she had scared him in those days. Though not as much as whatever was pursuing him.

"Something came with me, you said."

"I saw the lightning strike the pine tree," Sam answered. "I didn't realize it had jumped to the house. Then I heard the screaming. And I thought…" Her lips shook, then her whole body. He went to her and put his arms around her. She was rigid at first, unused to being held. Then she relaxed into him. "I thought I did it," she whispered. "My spell. I thought for a long time that I killed Johnny."

"No," he murmured, rocking her gently now. "It was a storm. Just a freak thing."

"Later," she said, swallowing hard and talking into his dampening shoulder, "I figured out that they were doing it in the house while I was doing it in the field. They messed up. Or I did, I don't know. But Johnny died. And something arrived. Maybe what they were trying to call, or maybe something else."

"You saw something," he said, still rocking her, closing his eyes against whatever came next.

"In the field," she breathed. "Behind you. Right behind you. Only a shadow. I felt it more than saw it, but I saw it too. I've never been so scared in my life."

"What happened?" he asked.

"You stepped inside my circle, and you were safe. It wouldn't come closer."

"You spoke words," he remembered. Commanding words, but he could not recall what they were. She took a long time to answer.

"A protection spell. It shouldn't have had any effect on a...being like that."

"Nothing hurt us."

"No," she agreed, pulling back slightly and looking straight into his eyes. "But it didn't go away either. Did it?"

He felt his body get heavy as his head grew light. Felt he might fall. And then it was her holding him instead of the other way, though they had not moved.

"I can't go back to that house tonight," he said, dread nearly choking him.

"No, stay here. Stay with me."

She had lost her serenity. She was vulnerable in a way he had never seen. A weak and frightened human, like him. He thought of her in the field that night, warding off some imaginary monster. Whatever the true cause of their mutual fright, it had been a brave thing for a young girl to do. He felt a keen tenderness for her in this moment. The little girl and the woman both.

"I am your friend," Will said.

"I know."

"I'm sorry I forgot."

"You never forgot," said Samantha.

CHAPTER

EIGHT

He closed the car door too hard, and a dozen grackles exploded from the maple overhead. Winging up and over the roof of the house. The day was as gray and chill as yesterday had been warm and lovely, but that was autumn in New England. Will opened the trunk as the others got out of the car. Muriel lifted his mother from the passenger seat and Sam came back to help him unfold the wheelchair.

"I am not using that," Abby protested.

"You are," he said, wheeling it over to her.

"I don't need it."

"Use the chair," said Muriel.

"That was just to make the nurses happy," Abigail insisted, attempting to push Muriel aside. "You have to get wheeled out if you want to leave that damn place."

Then Samantha was in front of her. Small, immovable.

"Sit," Sam commanded, touching the older woman's sternum with one finger. Abigail collapsed into the chair, her expression momentarily blank. "And here we go," Sam continued, swinging behind the chair and pushing before Abby could stand up again. They were all deferring to her as the medical expert.

Will went ahead to open the door while Muriel got Abby's things from the car. The house seemed to expand again with four people in it. Will could feel the walls pushing back, feel the place breathing. In relief, perhaps, at the return of its mistress. Abigail practically sprang out of the chair once they were inside, and Sam had to steady her. His mother looked around, bewildered.

"What did you do?"

"Vacuumed," Will answered. "Opened the drapes, so it didn't feel like a mausoleum."

"Where's the couch cover?"

"In the dryer now. It was filthy."

"Jeez," said Abby, running her hand over her buzz cut. With the hair around her wound already shaved, she had asked the nurses to finish the job so it could grow back evenly. None of them could get used to it. "You were good to do all that, honey."

She seemed more uneasy than grateful.

"Will needs to keep busy," said Muriel protectively. The way she did when he was in trouble, when he had done something wrong.

"I'll put the dirt back exactly where it was if there's a problem," he said.

"No, Willie, don't—"

"He's just being funny, Abby."

"Why don't we all have a little sit-down?" Sam suggested.

They did. Samantha made another concoction in the teapot. This one more dark and astringent, with a licorice aftertaste. Will put it aside after a few sips, but noted that his mother drank it without hesitation or surprise. Then it occurred to him that Sam had not brought any ingredients, unless they were hidden in her pockets. She had made the brew from whatever she had found in the jars on his mother's counter. Muriel had a beer, despite it being eleven in the morning.

"This is just like your grandma made it," Abby said finally, smiling at Sam.

"She's the one who taught me."

They all knew her grandmother had died when Samantha was two, so there was no need to say anything. Muriel rolled her eyes and took a particularly large gulp. Five minutes later, Abigail was falling asleep.

"You need to lie down," said Sam, lifting Abby gently from the sofa. "Why don't you two get some air."

Still in compliance mode, they took their jackets and made a circuit of the house.

"You okay with them alone like that?" Muriel asked casually.

"Which one are you worried about?"

"Just asking."

"I'm fine with it. What does everyone have against Sam?"

"I got nothing against her," Muriel said, running her

hands through the deep green rhododendron leaves. "These look great. Mine are brown and dying."

"You have to trim them pretty aggressively," Will said.

"You want to come over and do it?"

"I used to."

"I remember. And I always underpaid you."

"Oh, Muriel," he replied, tone light and teasing, to mask his sincerity. "I could never repay you all that I owe."

But she saw through the act.

"It's sweet you feel that way, but it's not true. Looking out for you was a pleasure, not a burden. I got no kids of my own—you're as close as I'm going to get."

He didn't know what to say, so he took her hand and squeezed. Rough, calloused. She worked for the phone company, but was always doing stuff outdoors. Working on fishing boats in her twenties. Painting houses. Messing with car engines back when you could, before computers ran them. The only girl in a family of men. Her one female cousin, Louise, died of a heart attack at fifty-three. Her oldest brother died of cancer in his forties. The next one drowned alongside Muriel's boyfriend when their fishing boat sank, twenty-three years ago. There had been assorted men since, all of them drinkers and risk takers. Like her father and brothers. She never married.

Back at the front of the house, Will's gaze fell on the new properties across the street.

"Does anyone actually live in those places?"

"Sure," she said. "Most of them. They go for big bucks, way more than I could afford."

"Somebody's making money."

"Same jokers who've been leaning on your mom and me to sell."

"Wait." He turned to her in surprise. "Who's leaning on you?"

Her face tensed, and Will could see she was annoyed with herself.

"*Leaning* is the wrong word. More like a hard sell. I assumed Abby told you."

"We haven't been talking much," he confessed. What else had Abigail been dealing with that his petulance had prevented him from knowing? "Who's leaning?"

"You know Lucy Larcom?"

"Sure, Danny's mother. I forgot she sold houses."

"Buys them too. Pushy broad," Muriel pronounced. "Anyway, she's just fronting for this real estate group that's been building all over Cape Ann. They want to bulldoze all these old places and put up a bunch of McMansions."

"Christ. Would you think of selling?"

"No. Your mom and I sort of made a pact." She elbowed him gently. "That is, until they knock the price up another hundred grand."

Would his mother sell the house? Would that be a bad thing? It was small and cheap. She could use the cash, and she might be happier elsewhere. Will could not deny the pang he felt at the idea. For better or worse, this place was home.

"The thing about Sam," said Muriel, circling back to the place her mind had never left, "is that she means well. But I don't have to tell you she's a little off. She's got that certainty about things. The way truly crazy people do."

"Nah, Sam's all right."

"I don't want her making you crazy. She used to do that when you were kids."

"I'm not a kid."

"No, but you're vulnerable right now," Muriel replied. "And she's been filling your head with something. Am I wrong?"

She waited him out as they reached the front of the house a second time and started around again. As if encircling it with a protective spell. He wouldn't speak, at first. Then he couldn't stop. He did not mention everything. No word of his mother's so-called coven. But he did speak of his dark dreams, and of many things Samantha had said. The ghost friends of their childhood, the demon in the rain, the fact of his being "haunted." Before he was done, they had circled the house again, then wandered down the road. Past Muriel's house, nearly to the lane that led to the farm. She, in turn, was quiet for many moments after he finished.

"You're going to tell me none of it's real," Will declared, without accusation. What else could one say to such fantastical stuff? He was both afraid of her calling it nonsense, and afraid she would not.

"No," Muriel said. "No, it's real enough."

"You think?"

"It's real, but it's not in the world. It's inside you."

"I don't know what you're trying to say."

"They're…what's the word? Projections. The girl, Alice. Whatever spooky thing you think you're seeing outside the window. You project them into the world, in a way that's very convincing. They're real, but they're not out there." She waved her arm toward the damp trees, the dying lawns, the road. Then tapped her chest. "They're in here."

"And you know this because…"

"Because I grew up in this town where everyone is haunted by something."

"Including you?" he pressed.

"Sure. So I've read a lot. About why people see these things, and feel these things."

"You've read about that?"

"Yes, I read," she insisted.

"I know you do," he agreed. Her house was littered with books on self-realization. He had teased her about them before. She was defensive about her lack of a college degree, and did not take the teasing well. "This is Eastern philosophy, or what?"

"Not so much," she replied. "Psychology, mostly. But more than that, it's looking at what people do, listening to what they say. A lot of people think they see things. A lot of people call on powers outside of themselves."

"Christ, Mure. You want to be more specific?"

"Okay, how about the batshit crazy old biddies in this town?" she said, turning and heading back the way they came. He followed.

"What about them?"

"Charms and potions and ancestor worship," she spat. "Nothing has any value unless it's from an old book. Or it was something great-grandmother used to say. It's sickening."

"That's a little harsh," he said, sticking his hands in his pockets nervously.

"You think it's harmless? It's not. It encourages helplessness. Looking for signs, listening to ghosts. Instead of figuring it out yourself. It bleeds down through the generations. It messes people up, young people."

Was she thinking about his generation or her own? Both, no doubt. She certainly intended him to draw a lesson from her words. They were what he needed, weren't they? Isn't this why he had spoken to her? Good old Muriel, with her head screwed on right. She would tell him what was what. Her theory made more sense than the fairy tales Sam was feeding him. So why did the words strike him as bitter and defensive? A woman from the most cursed and down-wardly mobile of the seven families. An insider who was made to feel like an outsider, and had embraced the role. Muriel was like him. Solid, dependable, with a cauldron of molten rage at her center. Sam was an outsider too, always had been, but it did not matter to her. She was sufficient unto herself. And her ideas, crazy as they were, sounded more like truth.

Muriel turned to speak. Then grabbed his arm and yanked him toward her fiercely. A strong kinetic force brushed by his opposite side, and only then did Will hear the engine. The car had swerved to avoid him, but maybe not far enough if not for Muriel. The vehicle slowed briefly, then accelerated. Dark red. Possibly a Volvo. A common enough car around here, no reason to make assumptions.

"Jesus, watch where you're walking," Muriel scolded him.

"What, I was just—"

"You were halfway into the road. Are you hearing what I'm telling you?"

"Yes," he said, as convincingly as possible.

"No," she replied, coming slowly to a halt. "You're not."

They were standing in front of her house again. Gray with lavender shutters and a wraparound porch that made it look larger than it was. He had always liked the house, more than his own. But the rhododendrons were indeed in bad shape, and there was mold on the clapboards above the porch. What had happened to house-proud Muriel? Was her mother's drawn-out decline distracting her, or was it just age and disappointment?

"I hear everything you're saying," Will replied, still getting his wits back. His shoulder stung from the hard tug. "And it makes a lot of sense."

"But you're not really taking it in," she said, going up the steps to her door. He followed.

"You're not coming back to the house?"

"I'll come by later," she replied. "When it's less crowded."

Meaning when Sam was gone.

"Well. Thanks for being there this morning."

"Happy to help," Muriel said, perfunctorily. "But you really didn't need me."

"We did," he assured her. "I did."

She stroked his face and he leaned in to kiss her cheek, just catching her lips. She didn't move, and he was about to lean in again when a memory came. Christmas of his junior year of college. The three of them tipsy after too much wine with dinner. Some bad movie on television and Abby asleep in front of it. Muriel and Will in the kitchen, laughing about nothing. Then kissing deeply, up against the refrigerator. Something he had wanted to do for years, which she must have known. A sad smile was on her face as he pulled away.

That was nice, kiddo. But that's not how it is between us.

Not then and not now. He stepped back.

"Tell Abby I'll come by later," she said, pushing the door and stepping inside. "And if you need me for anything, you let me know. Got it?"

CHAPTER

NINE

He was being stalked. Will couldn't know for sure if it was Jimmy Duffy in the police car that kept showing up in his rearview mirror. The vehicle kept its distance, and if Will slowed down it would turn off and vanish. But how many cops were there on the local force? A dozen? How many had a reason for following him? He did not mention it to Sam, or to anyone. But he would look for his chance to have it out with the angry little man. He left his mother's car with his old friend Tony Pascarelli, and stepped over the low concrete barrier separating the automotive repair shop from the liquor store, eyes scanning the street along this alley of shops. Florist, coffee shop, post office, convenience store. Searching for the blue lights on top of an idling cruiser. Seeing nothing, he pushed open the glass door of The Cask & Flagon and went in.

The spectacles, forward-leaning posture, and especially the faded red Nantucket pants immediately identified Charlie Winthrop, standing at the counter.

"No, no, just a small dinner party with friends," Charlie was saying. "First chance we've had since Benji went back to school."

"Very nice," said Saul Markowitz, behind the register. The Cask and Flagon was Saul's store, and though he had people working for him, the silver-haired, acerbic fellow seemed always to be on duty. "How's he liking Harvard?"

"Oh God, not the *H* word!" exclaimed Charlie. "No, no, Benji's at Princeton, of course."

"Of course," Saul concurred, unfazed by his faux pas.

"My daughter now," Charlie went on. "Annie is, in fact, contemplating matriculation at that temple of arrogance down there in Cambridge."

"Is that right?"

"Sorry to say, yes. It's enough to make her poor papa weep. Ah, young William."

"Hello, Mr. Winthrop," Will replied, having failed to sneak past.

"'Mr. Winthrop,'" the man laughed, pumping Will's hand furiously. "Charlie! Everyone calls me Charlie. Look at you, you're all… Now how is your mother?"

"Good. She's been home two days, getting back to normal."

"That's great news. Just fantastic news."

Despite being a shameless snob, Charlie was friendly with Abby and had always been nice to Will. He even forgave the younger man for not going to Princeton. *Amherst is a fine school*, Charlie had assured him. *Whatever anyone says*.

"Tell her I'll stop by soon."

Charlie grabbed his six-pack and bottle, waved a parting salute and was out the door in a hurry. He was always in a hurry, but Will figured it was probably just his metabolism.

"Young William," Saul deadpanned.

"Saul," Will replied. "Everyone in town knows his son goes to Princeton."

The thinnest of smiles appeared on the wine merchant's face.

"Kendall-Jackson," Saul said. "And a six-pack of Corona. Big spender."

"I thought you liked Charlie."

"I like him fine," Saul said. "But these cheap WASPs are going to put me out of business. Glad your mother's doing better."

"Yeah, she's walking around the house without stumbling. We'll get her outside anytime now."

"Haven't seen her in here for a while."

"You kidding? She can't afford you—she shops at Kappy's."

"Not the *K* word," Saul moaned.

"I need a good spaghetti-with-red-sauce wine."

Saul squinted his eyes, but paused barely a moment.

"Palazzo Della Torre. Second aisle, middle of the Italians. Only nineteen bucks, you better get two."

Will did as he was told, then swung over to the whiskey aisle. A bent old crone was perched in front of the shelves, and he had to lean around her to get a bottle of Maker's Mark. He figured he should replace the one he and Sam had killed. The crone began to move aside, then froze.

He expected her to speak, or at least to look at him. But she only stared at a pricey bottle of The Macallan. Slack, liver-spotted face showing nothing. He felt a sudden chill. Sensing she was the source, he stepped away, but the chill stayed with him.

He barely made it to the register without dropping the three bottles. Saul rang them up swiftly, not noticing his distress.

"Sox going to do it?" Saul asked.

The Red Sox had lost two in a row to Oakland and looked likely to be bounced from the postseason in a hurry.

"I guess three in a row is possible," Will ventured. "No?"

"A curse is a curse," Saul replied.

"So it's hopeless?"

"Here it is," Saul said, placing his hands flat on the counter and looking serious. "They need to take a wooden stake made from Babe Ruth's bat. Okay? Stick it in Bill Buckner's heart, and bury him under home plate in Yankee Stadium."

"That's, um, elaborate," Will replied. "I didn't know you were a pagan."

"I try to adopt the customs of the local population."

Saul glanced to the side, and so did Will. The crone stood ten feet away, staring at him. He realized now that he knew her, but the cold analysis in her watery blue eyes froze his memory. He could not think straight. Her gaze seemed to fall not on his face, but on the edges of his body, all the way around. As if she saw something revealing there. There was a thin but elaborate silver chain around her neck. When she clutched it to bring forth whatever hung from the end, Will thought Saul was going to dive below the counter. But all that emerged was her reading glasses.

"Who wrote these tags, Saul," the old woman rumbled in

a wet-lunged voice, ignoring Will now. She put the glasses on her face. "I can't read anything."

While Markowitz went to assist her, Will picked up his bag and fled the store.

Outside, he took in big breaths of cool air, listening to the soft clinking of the bottles in his arms. Trying to remember Muriel's words. He was projecting fear and mistrust on every encounter. And yet Saul had felt something, as well.

When he got back to the garage, the Pascarelli brothers had the hood open and were bent over the engine.

"Like a thump, or a grind, or what?" Tony was asking.

"More like a *tap-tap-tap*," Ernie answered. "You don't hear it?"

"Okay," said Will, "since when does the taillight connect to the engine?"

"This car hasn't been serviced in more than a year," Tony replied, not looking up.

"It drives fine," Will said, knowing he was in a losing fight. "All I asked you to do is fix the taillight."

"Told you he'd say that," Ernie noted with disgust, pushing himself up and wandering off to find some other project.

"What's his problem?" Will asked.

"Nothing," Tony shrugged, looking at him now. "Just tired of cheap pricks who don't take care of their cars."

"Tony—"

"I know, I know, it's your mother's. But the oil was so low I'm surprised the engine didn't seize. And now Ernie's hearing a knocking sound."

"Tapping, I think he said."

"That's right," Tony agreed. *"Tap, tap."*

"Do you know what it is?"

"I don't even hear it. But Ernie has sharper ears than me."

Ernie Pascarelli was the best mechanic around, and handled a wide range of makes and models. But somehow a two-hundred-dollar job always ended costing five, or eight. Abigail never got her cars serviced. Sometimes Muriel did a quick fix, or else Will brought them to the Pascarelli's shop, and he preferred dealing with Tony.

"What do you need to do?" he asked.

"Maybe nothing," Tony decided, wiping his hands on a filthy rag. "If it's not giving you problems. But keep your ears open. What the hell are you looking at?"

Will realized he had been scanning the street again. He turned his eyes to Tony, who gazed back with puzzled amusement. They were the same age, had been all through school together, from elementary to high school. Along with Sam, Christine, Brendan Duffy, Danny Larcom. So many old friends, so long ago now.

"Just making sure Jimmy Duffy isn't lurking somewhere," he said finally.

"Jimmy?" Tony laughed. "Why, you banging his wife?"

"Ex-wife. And no, I'm not," said Will, realizing he should have reversed that. "So he's done this to other guys?"

"I only heard of one. Some, like, housepainter from Gloucester. Pretentious shit."

"A pretentious housepainter?"

"He was an artist or something. Anyway, that was a year ago. I didn't know he was still doing that. I would have said something to him when he came by."

"What, he came by here?" Will asked.

"Comes by a lot. Well, he used to. Him, Brendan, me and Ernie used to play poker Fridays. Not big money. A few bucks, a few beers, with the game on."

"How's Brendan doing?"

"You didn't know?" Tony looked surprised, then shook his head. "In Walpole. Beat a guy pretty badly. Some bar in Southie. Put him in the hospital."

"Damn," Will said quietly. Brendan always had a temper, and he was a big man.

"Yeah," Tony agreed, gazing at his blackened fingernails. "Wasn't the first time either. Those Duffys. You know their mom died years ago. Old man's got cancer too. Kevin keeps reenlisting, now he's in Iraq. Brendan in prison. The sister, Marie, married some guy in New Hampshire, won't speak to her brothers. Thinks they're bad influences on her children."

"Oh man, Tony," groaned Will. "This is a sad tale."

"All I'm saying is Jimmy's in a bad way. Don't make too much of what he says."

"Did he ask about me?"

"Yeah," Tony answered. "Matter of fact, he did."

"Really? What did he ask?"

Tony glanced up at him with a sly grin.

"Asked if you'd gotten your mother's taillight fixed yet."

CHAPTER

TEN

Night was coming down. Darkness after sunset took hold more swiftly in these weeks following the autumnal equinox. It was not safe to take his eyes from the twisty road, yet Will was certain he had spotted his stalker. A hundred yards back and closing. Will accelerated, but the police cruiser kept on until it was right behind. No siren, but the blue lights flashed once. Will waited for a straightaway, then pulled onto the shoulder.

Jimmy looked more agitated than angry as he came up to the window.

"What did I do this time?" Will asked, keeping his voice even.

"Nothing," Jimmy replied. "We have to talk."

"Look, she's been my friend since before—"

"It's not about Sam," the cop said impatiently.

"No? What's it about?"

"Stuff that's been going on," said Jimmy evasively.

"If this is your idea of talking…"

"Not here. Out in the middle of the road."

"Where then?" Will asked. "The station? If you wanted to talk, why didn't you come by the house?"

"I did," Jimmy claimed. "A couple of times. You weren't there."

"I'm there every night. You're telling me you can find me on these godforsaken roads but not in my mother's house? What the hell kind of cop are you?"

"You're pushing it, Conner."

"No, *you're* pushing it. This is harassment, and I'm not taking it." He put his hand on the key in the ignition. Then dropped it. "I'm sorry about Brendan. I didn't know."

"Didn't know," Jimmy echoed. "He was your friend, right?"

"We were friendly. Didn't keep in touch. I'm sorry about the stuff with your sister too. I guess it's a bad time for you."

Jimmy's mouth was working with no words issuing forth. The way it had that night a week ago.

"Fuck you," Jimmy rasped. "This ain't about me."

"Okay," Will replied. "So if we're clear that there was no cause for the stop…"

Jimmy slammed his hands on the car door and leaned in. Instinctively falling back on intimidation. Will could smell his sour breath.

"Every time you come here, bad shit happens," Jimmy declared. "You think nobody has noticed? Well, I have. And I'm not the only one."

Will gave him a long look, but Jimmy didn't budge. Like he was some TV cop, awaiting an admission of guilt. Will started the engine. Then he hit the button that rolled the window up. Jimmy only pulled his fingers out at the last moment. Fury on his face. Looking like he would shatter the glass with his forehead. Will gave him several moments to try, then put the car in gear and pulled away.

The thing to do now was turn off somewhere quickly, or get home as fast as he could. Will did neither. He drove slowly, waiting for the cruiser to appear in his rearview mirror once more. When it did, he felt his facial muscles pull. It took a few moments to identify the action as a smile. There was no mirth in him. It was someone else's smile. It disturbed him, yet his mind was elsewhere. Working on the next step.

Right turn onto Orchard Road. The cruiser followed. Will bent toward the freshly cleaned windshield, peering through the gathering gloom. Old Forest Lane was un-marked, so he had to be alert. There, that break in the tightly packed trees. He turned hard onto the narrow road, small branches brushing the car. Jimmy missed the turn and Will slowed to see if he would back up and pursue. It was a bad road, no longer in use. Both vehicles would take a beating, but the patrol car did not belong to Jimmy.

Nevertheless, here came the cruiser again, swinging onto Old Forest Lane, headlights casting a ghostly glow over the interior of Will's car. Will's hands on the wheel looked strange to him. Too large. He sped up. Broken tarmac gave way to rutted dirt, and the car began to rattle and buck. An invisible pothole bounced him off the seat, banging his head on the roof. The impact made him vaguely dizzy, but also felt good somehow. The clarity of pain. It was not that late, but the woods were very dark. After shaping a turn, Will stopped abruptly and killed the engine. The police car was not visible yet, and he opened the door and got out. The ground smelled damp and mulchy. A familiar and pleasant scent. Will had spent a lot of time here when he was young. Fifty yards farther was the clearing where high school kids used to make bonfires and have parties. Maybe they still did. Across the road was swamp. Difficult to negotiate by day, impossible by night. Behind him, through some narrow trees, a rocky shelf rose almost straight up. There were paths, or you could just haul yourself, hand-over-hand. Will had done it many times, but not for years.

He heard the cruiser's engine, saw the lights shaping the turn. Jimmy would not be able to get around his car. And driving in reverse all the way to Orchard Road would be a challenge. Will felt that nasty smile on his face again, felt an anxious flutter of mischief in his stomach. In his whole body. He stepped off the road into the trees.

Headlights lit up his mother's car, the driver's door hanging open. He could hear Jimmy's curses through the police car's windows. The cruiser stopped, engine idling, lights still on. Jimmy sprang out and went to the other vehicle. Searching around inside. As if Will might be hiding behind the seats? Or maybe looking for evidence. Drugs, paraphernalia, something to justify a bust. Had he left the keys in the ignition? No, here they were in his pocket.

"Conner," Jimmy called, facing the trees where Will stood. Thirty feet away. "Where are you?"

Will turned and reached for the stony slope, scraping at dead leaves and moss before he got a solid grip. The incline was shallow enough to push himself up without much difficulty. But he made a lot of noise, and could hear Jimmy ducking through the trees.

"What are you doing?" Jimmy said, as Will rose away from him. "Get down here. You're being an idiot."

Anger was giving way to something else in Jimmy's voice. Caution, uncertainty. Just the same, a moment later Will could hear the cop scrambling up the stony slope behind him. Two men playing at boys. Or maybe it was the other way around. When he got to a broad ledge about thirty feet up, Will felt the adrenaline surge abandoning him. He sat down suddenly on the spongy soil. Drew his legs up and put his forehead against his knees. There was a pressure in his head. A flickering spasm in his eyelid and a picture forming there. Bright light and dry heat. A desert landscape and another rock face. Climbing, struggling to reach the top, where a dusky-faced man smiled down at him. *That's right, brother, just a few more feet. Then we rest, and speak to the sky.*

"Will," Jimmy said, near at hand. Will looked up to see the compact shadow of the cop rising over the rim of the ledge. Jimmy was silhouetted against twilight sky. Seated in shadows, Will must have been invisible.

"I'm here."

Jimmy took a few wary steps in his direction and crouched. Still not able to see him clearly.

"What the hell are you up to? Driving out here."

"Someone was chasing me," Will replied.

"Come on, man."

"Just reliving my youth. The old Boy Scout camp is up this hill. Another hundred feet, maybe."

"Yeah," Jimmy agreed. "I was never a Scout."

"Me neither. You ever come out here?"

"In high school. To drink."

"Never walked in the woods? There are lots of trails."

"Brendan did that," Jimmy said irritably. "With you."

"I thought you were with us once or twice."

"Kevin, maybe. Look, what are we doing here?"

"I didn't ask you to follow me."

"You kind of did," Jimmy countered. "Acting like that. And now you got me boxed in."

"What bad shit happens when I'm around?" Will demanded.

"You want to talk about this here?" Jimmy dug at the moss with his finger, looking like a little boy. A little boy with a pistol hanging off his belt. "I'm not accusing you of anything. I'm just saying…"

"Say it."

"People have been dying."

"Every day. Is it against the law now?"

"A bunch of things have gone down in the last six, seven years. Starting with Doc Chester getting shot by Eddie Price."

"Hunting accident," Will replied automatically. In fact, there had been some suspicion about the shooting, despite the long friendship between the men. Rumors that the charming Doc and Sally Price had gotten a little too friendly.

"Maybe," Jimmy said. "Then Nancy Chester gets hit by a car walking home from the diner. Concussion, broken hip. Nobody saw anything. No one came forward. Louise Brown keels over in her garden. Heart attack. Fifty-three and fit as a horse."

"It happens."

"Sure it does. Then Marty Branford dies of a gas leak. It happens, right?"

"It did," Will said, annoyance creeping into his voice.

"And every time it happened, every one of those events, you were here."

"How do you even know that?" It was the wrong thing to say. Defensive. For all Will knew, he *had* been around for all those events. The point was that it meant nothing.

"There were twelve people in your mother's prayer group."

"Spirit circle," Will corrected. Prayer group! But was that so far off? "There was no fixed number. People came and went."

"There were twelve the night Johnny Payson died," Jimmy persisted.

"You have witnesses, I guess."

"My mother was there," the cop said. "She told me."

Here it was. Will thought of the Duffys as new blood. Working class Boston Irish, nothing to do with old family nonsense. He forgot Jenny Duffy had been Jenny Branford. He was surprised to learn she was there that night; she seemed only a casual member of the circle. But it explained Jimmy's obsession.

"Twelve people," Jimmy said again. "Most of them young. Seven have died since, some violently. A couple others had bad accidents."

There had been talk of a curse. Back then. Those first ten years or so after the incident, when three people died and others suffered tragedies. Like Molly Jordan, whose only daughter Christine was killed in an accident. Driving her mother's car to pick up her boyfriend, Will Conner. The talk went away after a while. If it had been stirred up again the last seven years, Will had not heard about it.

"What does this have to do with me?" he asked.

"I don't know," Jimmy confessed after a pause. "It's just, like, these coincidences."

"Your mother died of lung cancer, right?"

"She was getting better," Jimmy mumbled. "Everyone said she was getting better, and then something went wrong."

Relapse. It happens, Will wanted to say again, but thought better of it.

"Jimmy. I was fourteen when she died. I was nine when Doug Payson threw himself out that window."

"I know."

"Just what is it you think I have to do with this stuff?"

"I don't know," Jimmy snarled, standing quickly and running a hand through his hair. "I'm not saying you did anything."

"And you're not saying I didn't."

"Maybe it's something connected to you. Some person or some, some…thing. I mean every one of these times, the last seven years."

A thought formed suddenly: had he gotten this idea from Sam? Will hated thinking it, but it made sense. It didn't sound like something Jimmy would dream up on his own. More like something he would seize upon to justify his antipathy for Will.

"And here we are again," Jimmy said.

Here we are again. Will's tired mind tried to dodge the meaning of that phrase, but the words caught and held him. In a moment he was on his feet, rage surging in his muscles. He rushed at the other man.

"What are you saying?"

Jimmy gave ground and put his open hands out, stop signs.

"Hang on now."

"You miserable shit, what are you saying?" He growled more than spoke, in a voice that did not sound like his. "Do you think I pushed my own mother down the stairs?"

Will swung at his face, just catching the nose as Jimmy ducked away. The next moment the cop's open hand struck him on the side of the head, unbalancing him. His ear rang, his whole head rang and Will squeezed his eyes shut. Breathed deeply. It did not calm him, but worked like a bellows, adding oxygen to his rage. He was sweating anger out of his pores. When he opened his eyes, the cop appeared diminished somehow.

"Just calm down," Jimmy said, his voice shaking.

Will went at him again, seizing him by the shoulders, squeezing his fingers into muscle and sinew. Jimmy grabbed his forearms and tried to break free, but Will's grip was iron. Their faces were less than a foot apart, the cop's screwed up tightly. His eyes found Will's, and sprang open wide. His mouth let out a little moaning sound, and then his whole body became frantic with the effort of escape.

Startled, Will released him. Jimmy stumbled back quickly and was gone. Will saw one arm flailing and then no more. A moment later there was a thud on the rock face below, then a softer one in the dead leaves at the base of the ridge. Will stepped forward cautiously and looked down. He could hear movement down there, but could see nothing.

"Jimmy?"

He turned himself around and started down. His mind was blank, which was useful. An empty mind aided concentration. It was dangerous work trying this in the dark, especially with all his muscles quivering. He slipped several times, once banging his ribs hard against the rocky face. He heard a groan, and then a slow thrashing around in the leaves as he reached the bottom of the incline.

"Jimmy," he said more forcefully to the shadows.

A hunched figure went crashing through the saplings, bouncing off small trees until it reached the road. Will could see Jimmy clearly then in the patrol car's headlights. Turned sideways to him, bent over, with one arm hanging uselessly and the other pointed back at Will.

"You stay away from me."

Will couldn't think how to answer. He barely remembered what had happened, did not know who caused it. Jimmy was hurt and needed help, but moving toward him was not going to help things. After fighting with the handle a moment, Jimmy got the door open and jumped into the cruiser, slamming the door behind him. Will wandered into the road, alongside his mother's car and in the full glare of the lights.

The cop leaned forward, squinting. As if trying to make out who or what this being was. Then he jammed the cruiser into Reverse and began to back down the narrow road. Will was certain he would careen into the marsh, but Jimmy shaped the turn expertly and disappeared. His headlights and the rumble of the engine slowly faded. The darkness that followed was profound. A large bird of prey swept out of a nearby tree and vanished in shadow. It only then occurred to Will that Jimmy had never reached for his gun.

He could not remember later how he left the woods. Not driving in Reverse to Orchard Road, he was sure of that. So he must have gone forward instead, all the way out to

Seaview. God knew what that muddy track had done to the car's suspension. He drove aimlessly for a while. At one point he pulled up in front of the police station. Looking for what? The whirl of activity that would accompany the manhunt to find him? Will Conner: Cape Ann's Most Wanted. It was quiet. They knew where to find him. He drove home.

Quiet there too. His mother had made a vegetable stew with Moroccan spices. He ate some straight from the pot, standing in front of the stove. It was good, but he had little appetite. He opened a beer and went into the living room, where the Boston-Oakland game flickered on the muted television. His mother was asleep on the sofa. He checked her breathing before settling down to watch the game. Will was dead asleep long before the Red Sox pulled out a victory in the bottom of the eleventh inning.

CHAPTER

ELEVEN

Old families?" Margaret Price wore her usual self-satisfied expression, and poured tea from a chipped Blue Willow pot into matching cups. Will was pleased to note it was ordinary tea. "No. Winthrop, Larcom, Endicott. Those are the old families around here."

"I guess I mean the seven families," Will corrected himself.

"I guess you do," she replied. He wanted to wipe that smug look off her face. Reading his tension, Samantha squeezed his shoulder gently. Margaret did not fail to note the intimate gesture.

Coming here had not been his idea. It had not really been Sam's either. It was the elder Mrs. Price, Evelyn, whom she had telephoned. Hoping for some guidance on Will's "condition." Will had been against the whole thing and was surprised to learn the old woman—who must be in her nineties—was still living. Evelyn Price didn't have an answering machine, so Sam could not leave a message. Nevertheless, daughter Margaret called Sam the next day, insisting she and Will come for tea.

"The seven families haven't been here more than six or seven generations," Margaret continued. "Which isn't old at all for this part of the country."

"They were up in Maine before," Sam prompted.

"The Camden-Warren area. Ship captains, lawyers. Many of the Prices were soldiers."

"Halls too," replied Sam. "And back to England before that?"

"Yes. West Midlands."

"Price is a Welsh name, isn't it?"

Margaret paused, studying Samantha's face.

"I've heard it said that Price comes from the Welsh *ap Rhys*. The sons of Rhys. I don't really know about that."

"And the Chesters take their name from that town, on the Welsh border?"

"So they say. Your Halls are from the area around Coventry. Branfords also."

"Wales to England," said Sam, retracing the steps forward in time. "England to Maine, Maine to here."

"That's right."

"Never staying anywhere more than six or seven generations."

Margaret nodded deliberately.

"You want to know about the curse."

"Curse?" Will sat up as if prodded. His ribs still hurt

from slamming the rock face on his rapid descent. And there was a bruise on his left cheek that Margaret had stared at but not asked about.

"Careful of the tea, dear," she warned, handing him a napkin. "Am I wrong?"

"No, you're not wrong," Samantha replied. "That's just what we want to know."

In fact, she had not been at all clear why they had come. Sam did not have the same faith in Margaret Price that she did in Margaret's mother, but she was sure the invitation was no coincidence. Will pointed out that Evelyn could not even know they had called, but Sam was unmoved. You did not ignore signs. Now she was tossing out random details to see what stuck. If Margaret thought they had come to learn of a curse, well then, that's why they had come.

"The curse is legend," Margaret said casually. "Not really history."

"Of course," Sam agreed.

"And there are many people better versed in the telling than me."

"But they haven't invited us to tea," Sam answered. "And you have."

Margaret set her cup down on the cherrywood coffee table and leaned back against worn sofa cushions. Late-day sun through sheer curtains gave her hair a silver sheen.

"Back in England, or Wales perhaps, in medieval times, a demon was ravaging the countryside. Killing cattle, stealing children. Beguiling young women and poisoning crops. Doing what demons do."

"Where did the demon come from?" Will asked. Both women looked at him in surprise. You did not interrupt the telling of a tale. He should know better.

"That isn't part of the story," Margaret said, regathering herself. "Several brave men went to confront the demon. To slay it or drive it off, but each one came to grief. The people of the region called on their most trusted leaders to save them. Seven of them. Sages, holy men, warriors. One from each of the prestigious families gathered to hunt down the enemy. The fiend feared their strength and fled, but eventually they caught and bound it. Of course, you cannot kill a demon. But working together, they conjured a spell by which to banish it from the world once more. Back to the abyss."

She paused for a sip of milky tea. Despite her false modesty, Will noted the stylized language and dramatic pauses of a seasoned storyteller. She might find the tale nonsense, but she had clearly told it more than a few times before, and on some level was enjoying this.

"Demons are ancient beings," she continued, "and clever. No man alone is a match for one. But now I'm telling the professor his own subject."

"That's okay," said Will, hesitantly. He neither wanted to intrude nor fall into some trap. "Every tradition has its own rules. This isn't my story."

"Of course it is," she countered, gazing steadily at him once more. "I mean, all of us. We're all the heirs to this tradition, as you call it."

"Go on. Please."

"The demon tried to bargain. It would give them riches, long life, knowledge. Whatever they wanted. I don't know if demons have the power to give those things, but I suppose we'll all say anything to save ourselves. Yes? Some of the men were tempted, but in the end they stayed the course. They performed the rituals and enacted the spell that banished the fiend. However, before its parting from this world, it hurled a curse on the seven men. A curse on them and their children, and grandchildren, and all their ancestors down the generations."

She looked at them expectantly, as if awaiting their verdict.

"What was the curse?" Will finally asked.

"Ah, yes." Margaret bent forward for more tea. He wondered if he could drown her in that little cup. "Versions vary with the telling," she finally said. "What do you imagine it was?"

Plague? Insanity? Bad skin?

"Restlessness," said Sam.

"I had a feeling you'd heard the tale before," Margaret answered, settling back against the tired blue cushions.

"Long ago," Sam replied. "And not told like that."

"Wait," said Will in dismay. "That's the curse? Restlessness?"

"*Restlessness* is too gentle a word," answered the older woman. "More like a profound unease. A constant sense of struggle, of searching. With no hope of fulfillment."

"Sounds like the human condition," Will said. She smiled at him. Whether in agreement or in pity at his ignorance, he could not say. "So what happened after that?"

"After, yes. The community dissolved. Mistrust and strife took hold in that place." Her tone had grown darker; her eyes gazed at the floor now. "The old learned to live with the sense of loss. The young moved on to new lands. The same people who had turned to the seven to save them, now turned *on* them. Blamed them for their unhappiness. Drove them out."

It seemed to Will she was taking this awfully hard for a mere legend.

"And the same thing kept happening," Sam said. They both looked at her. "I mean the unease. It kept happening wherever they went. That's why they kept moving from place to place, isn't it?"

Margaret sighed. Looking sorry that she had started talking of this.

"One generation would find a new home. A land that held some echo of the richness and mystery of their old home. The next few generations would build up their place there. It was in their natures to prosper. To become leaders. And then another generation would ruin all they had achieved. And the young people would scatter again."

"How would they ruin it?" Sam asked.

Later, Will would understand that this was the most important question of all, though Margaret appeared to have no answer. At the moment, in that following silence, he only sought to shake off the unsettling enchantment of the tale.

"You're trying to say that these seven families traveled as a pack? Between continents, over centuries?"

"Now we move from legend to history," Margaret replied, unconcerned with his doubt. "And history is not so tidy. Every generation, children grow and move on. It's like that for all families. We can't even be sure of the number. We say seven, but maybe it's six, or eight. Probably some died out, and others come into the story later."

"Yeah?" mused Will. "Which?"

"Well, for instance, the Browns. They *claim* Brown derives from Bronwyn, which is an old name in Wales. But some say they didn't become one of the families until

Maine. Always been working people, you know. The Paysons are another question mark, if you ask me."

"You're telling me there isn't even agreement on who the seven families are?"

"Oh dear," laughed Margaret. "There's very little agreement about anything."

Then why the hell should we take any of this seriously, he wanted to say. Except that she had not asked him to. She had all but dismissed it as a fairy tale, even if her tone said differently. He had nothing for which to chastise her. He had walked into this room with that gnawing unease already inside him.

"Are we at the time in the cycle when the young people scatter?" asked Sam.

"I think we're past that point," said Margaret, a bit sadly. "I mean, yes, many have gone. William here, for one. My own children. You're still around, aren't you, dear? But you are the last of the true Halls. Doc and Sally Chester had no children. There are hardly any Branfords or Staffords left."

"Still a few Browns," Will couldn't help but say.

"Yes," the older woman conceded, "but they do themselves in at such an alarming rate, don't you think? And, well, not to be too hard about it. But they don't really embody the essence of what the seven families once were."

Will knew that Muriel would be proud of that judgment, so he felt no need to dispute it.

"No," said Margaret Price softly. "It's all going away. The history, the sense of community. The families themselves."

"What about the curse?" asked Will.

She held him in her gaze several long moments before

speaking. Will thought her expression looked kind. Maybe a bit tired, but not at all haughty.

"The first thing we need to do is find you stronger guardians," she answered.

He felt like he had missed a part of the conversation.

"The Duffys are troublemakers," Margaret went on. "The whole clan, everyone knows it. You can put one in a police uniform but it doesn't change anything. I'm sure the boy had coming whatever you gave him, but we can't wait until it happens again. To someone else. You don't want to end up hurting Samantha, for instance."

"What the hell are you talking about?" Will asked, baffled and alarmed.

"I worry about you, William," said Margaret. "My mother does too. And generally speaking, she doesn't give a damn about anyone."

"That's good of you, but there's no—"

"It's not about goodness," she said sharply. "Some of us still remember our obligations, that's all. We take responsibility for our own, whatever their behavior or affliction."

"Is that what I am? Afflicted?"

"What would you call it?"

"I don't call it anything," he shot back. "Except maybe superstition. Paranoia? Bad luck? Life is hard, stuff happens to people. We get worked up. Why does it need a name?"

"Why are you here?"

"Because my mother fell down the stairs."

"Why are you here in my house?"

"To tell you the truth, Mrs. Price, I have no idea. Why did you invite us?"

She took a deep breath, her eyes hard. This was it, Will thought, now it would come out. Whatever she believed was amiss, whatever role she had assigned herself in fixing it. But then something changed. She released her breath slowly, without speaking. Her eyes became gentle again.

"Do I need an excuse to invite old friends for tea?" she said finally, and he knew at once that the moment had passed. There would be no point in pressing her now. "You should really try those sugar cookies. Old family recipe."

"So was that useful?" Will asked, with only part of his attention. Most of it was focused on the small package in his lap. Margaret had handed it to him just before they left the house. *From my mother*, she said, tucking it into his arms.

"A little," said Sam. She was driving. It had not taken much effort to convince Will that bad things happened when he drove. "Might have been more useful if you weren't so rude."

"I wasn't rude."

"You kind of were."

"What, *you're* going to play Miss Manners now?"

"I'm not rude to people," she said, her voice uncertain. "Wait, am I?"

"The woman has been rude to you your whole life."

"That's no reason."

"Look," he said, squeezing the package's blocky contents with his fingers. "I'm sorry if I embarrassed you. My social skills have abandoned me since I came back here."

"It's not about that."

"She's a blunt old battle-ax," Will maintained. "If she can dish it out, she ought to be able to take it. I thought I might crack her cool. Make her say something she didn't want to."

"Well," Samantha considered, turning on the windshield wipers. "It almost worked."

"No, she's too smart."

"Actually, I think she was told not to say too much."

"Told by whom?"

"What is that?" she asked, meaning the package.

"A book."

"Just what you needed." Her attempts at humor cheered him. "What book?"

Will undid the clasp and slid out the dense object. Gilded edges and no words or markings on the black leather cover. He turned the thin pages, unable to understand much at first. Except that the book was old. Two hundred years or more.

"It's in Latin," he said.

"Can you read that?"

"Only in theory."

"There's a dictionary at my house."

Tom Hall had many books in Latin, Greek, French, German, and dictionaries in all those tongues. Will would have to rely on such help, because his mind was bouncing off the pages now, unable to absorb the words. Thinking of other things.

"She knew about Jimmy," he said.

"Yeah," Sam agreed.

"I didn't think he told anyone what happened."

Sam had heard about the incident in the woods before Will could tell her. The only thing she revealed to him was that Jimmy's arm was hurt, but he was otherwise all right. And that he had not reported the encounter to anyone.

"He had to get the arm looked at," she said now. "Somebody had to know something."

"Did you speak to him?"

"No. His father."

Kevin Senior. Who, when drunk, used to beat Brendan, though Will's pal insisted he deserved it. Now the old man had cancer. His wife was gone. His youngest was fighting in Iraq, his oldest was in prison. And Will had just made his life a little harder.

"What did he say?" Will asked.

"That Jimmy hurt his arm struggling with someone. That he was taking a short leave of absence to recover."

"Didn't mention my name?"

"When are you going to accept that people here know things," she said, exasperated. The rain intensified, and Sam leaned closer to the windshield. She drove slowly and cautiously, unlike him. "Those old women knew when I got my first period. They knew which boys I liked. Your face tells them things. Just sitting in front of them, they can read your whole life."

"I hope you're exaggerating," he said after a moment.

"Not a lot."

"I need to get out of this town."

"That won't help," she said quickly. Urgently, it seemed.

"How do you know?"

"Weren't you seeing that shadow before you came here? Back in New York?"

Had he told her that? He must have—he had told her so much.

"I think you just like having me around," he said with a smile. She did not smile back.

"I do," said Sam quietly. "I never thought you would leave."

"When? Like, go to college?"

127

"I mean, I knew you would. On some level I had to know that's where your life was headed. College, job in the big city. Anybody could see that was for you. But on another level, it wasn't real. That you would leave here. Leave me."

"Sam. We weren't even close anymore by the time I went."

"Is that how it felt to you?"

Yes was the only honest answer. But he had forgotten or misremembered so much else about his life, why not this also?

"Maybe you're the one who needs to get out," he said.

"Hah," she laughed. Like it was a ridiculous idea.

"Why not? What's keeping you?"

"I can't leave," Samantha said in dismay, glancing over at him.

"Of course you can. Unload that mausoleum and hit the road. Lucy Larcom is making generous offers, I hear."

"Your mother isn't selling, is she?" There was panic in her tone.

"She hasn't even mentioned it." Muriel had assured Will that no deal was imminent, and suggested it was better not getting Abby riled up by asking. "Has Lucy been after you too?"

"She cannot sell that house," Sam insisted. "Not yet."

"For God's sake, why not?"

"Because everything started there. This…thing, with you. You have to be living in the house until we figure it out. It's critical."

"Oh man," he sighed. "Should I also sleep in a pine box full of native soil?"

"I'm serious, Will."

"That's the thing, I know you are. I swear, you need to get out of here more than I do. I might have to kidnap you."

"I cannot leave this town," she said flatly. "There's some of us who are meant to stay. Everything I am is tied to this place, these people. You must know that."

He did not know any such thing, but the certainty in her voice stopped him from saying more. That, plus the fact that he had reached the first woodblock illustration in the book. It was primitive work, but compelling, and his eyes could not look away.

"Her mother wanted me to have this," he said. "What does that mean?"

"If it's from Evelyn, there's a message in it."

"What message?"

"I don't know," Sam replied, "it depends on the book. You figure out what it is yet?"

"Yeah," Will confirmed. Gazing at the shadowy, cross-hatched figure hunching in the billowing flames. "It's a demonology."

CHAPTER

TWELVE

The wine was good, Saul had not steered him wrong. Abigail wasn't up to more than a glass, and Sam hardly had a sip. Which left Will and Muriel to kill most of two bottles, but somehow they managed. Will made a variation on his mother's Bolognese sauce. More onion, less meat, a healthy splash of wine. They all seemed to enjoy it. Even Muriel, who never liked anyone's cooking but her own.

"Of course she liked it," Sam whispered, as the two of them carried empty plates to the kitchen. "Her little boy made it."

The tone might have annoyed him another time, but Will was in too good a mood to be thrown. Muriel and Sam did not like each other, and there was nothing to do about it.

Except not invite them to the same dinner, but tonight he wanted things his way. Wanted his favorite people around him. He only poked Samantha's arm, then kissed the top of her head. It was an odd thing to do, but he was buzzed and there it stood at chin level, her hair warm and summery. She did not move away. He squeezed her arm and she tipped her forehead against his collarbone. They stood that way for several moments.

Abby's raucous laugh startled them, and Sam stepped back. Will could not see the dining room from where they stood, but he could hear Muriel's voice. Talking low and fast, the way she did when telling a comical tale. Abby laughed again. He had not heard that sound in a couple of years, and it filled his chest with good feeling. The tension between the old friends seemed to have vanished, which was the main thing Will had hoped to accomplish this night. He was pleased. Something had gone right.

"Sorry," said Sam. It wasn't clear what for. Her comment? Being startled? Letting him touch her?

"Sounds like we're missing a funny story," Will said.

"Probably about me." It surprised him how much Muriel got under her skin.

"I'll do the dishes later. Let's go back in."

"Do I have to?"

"No," he said, disappointed. "I'll walk you home, if you like."

"Come with me," she said eagerly.

"I've got to play host."

"Come over later, then." She stepped closer, lowering her voice as her words became more urgent. "We have to look at that book."

He had left Evelyn Price's demonology with Sam. Know-

131

ing he would need the Latin dictionary, but also because he did not want it in his mother's house. He had not forgotten the book for a moment, but resented having to think about it just now.

"I'm curious too, but—"

"It's not about curiosity," she pressed him. "It's important."

"So is spending time with my mother. Which I haven't done nearly enough of."

"Yeah, well." Sam tipped her head toward the other room, the laughing voices. "Good luck with *her* here."

"She'll clear out soon," Will said. For all Sam's talk of knowing him, there was an awkwardness between them. It was Muriel who knew what he needed at any given moment, without his having to say. Did Sam see that? Was it the reason she resented the woman?

He took her by the hand and walked back into the dining room.

"Shhh," said Abby, noticing them. She leaned into Muriel's shoulder, both of them giggling. Maybe they were talking about Sam. Or him. Or telling dirty jokes the children shouldn't hear. The flickering candlelight made them look conspiratorial. He watched both women's eyes focus on the space between Sam and himself. Saw a cool appraisal on Muriel's face, and a warm smile from his mother. He looked down and saw that he was still holding Samantha's hand. At that moment, Sam tightened her grip, as if he might try to shake her loose. Her fingers dug into his knuckles, and she glared defiantly at Muriel.

"I need a cigarette," Muriel said.

"Me too," Sam replied.

"Yeah?" Muriel looked both suspicious and amused. "Well, come on, then."

"Outside," Abigail commanded.

"Yeah, yeah, we know."

Sam's hand was suddenly gone. Then the front door shut behind the two women, and just like that he was alone with his mother. He sat down next to her, the chair still warm from Muriel's fidgeting ass.

"You look happy," Will said.

"Why shouldn't I be?" Abby put her hand over his, so recently abandoned. "You were sweet to do this—it was fun."

"It's been a while since you had friends over. I mean, when I've been around."

"It's been forever," she said wistfully. The buzz cut had grown out a little, beginning to hide the scar. She was still too thin, but her skin was pink and glowing. And the lack of hair and flesh brought out her cheekbones and dark eyes. Candlelight danced in those eyes; her smile was playful. She looked good, if not quite like herself.

"You used to have people here all the time."

"I know that's how you remember it," said Abby. "But after Johnny died, there wasn't much of that."

"No?"

"My friends still stopped by. The real friends, the ones who stuck with me. The rest of them moved on to the next thing. It was about having a good time in those days, and this house was bummersville."

"Maybe they were scared," Will suggested. Her eyes met his for a moment, darted away.

"Maybe," she said. "Death does scare people."

"I didn't realize. That they abandoned you."

"That's a heavy word. *Abandoned.* I'm sure they didn't see it like that."

"Is that how it felt?"

"I guess," she admitted. "But you know, I wasn't keen on seeing them either. Made me have to think about that night. We lived through quite an ugly thing there, you and me. We needed that time together. That was our special time."

Will nodded, betraying nothing. He wasn't even angry, which had to count as progress. It was just strange how two people could remember the same thing so differently. She had filed it away as special time. He remembered her as a ghost. Huddled in a blanket on the sofa. Crying every time she saw him, until he hid from her gaze. Or simply comatose on sedatives, her friends coming over to cook for them. Who was right? The heavily medicated adult or the traumatized five-year-old? Both. Neither.

"Muriel was one of the true friends."

"Muriel," she said, almost scornfully. "The queen of your youth."

"She was good to us."

"God knows," Abby conceded. "There were times I never would have made it without Mure." *Murr.* "But that happened later."

"She wasn't part of the spirit circle?"

"No, she was what? Eighteen, nineteen? A kid. I guess she sat in once or twice. Even then, even that young, you could sense how contemptuous she was of it."

That fit the woman he knew, but Will was still taken aback. Muriel was always around, as far back as he could remember. He had assumed she was part of the gang.

"Also," Abigail said, reclaiming her hand to rub her tired eyes. It seemed like she might not complete the thought, though the words finally came. "She had a thing for Johnny."

"Muriel did?"

"Yeah. Needless to say, she wasn't coming by right after that went down."

"A thing for him, or..."

"More than that. They were a couple, I suppose. Although Mure was so young."

She shook her head at some memory. Will's fingers drummed the table until he made himself stop. He up-ended the dregs of a wine bottle into someone's glass. His own or Muriel's, though he did not drink the murky stuff. So many revelations, so many things he had not cared about until now. So hard to fit each piece into its place.

"When did you two become pals?" he asked.

"It happened slowly. We bonded when we were taking those art classes together. She was always looking over my shoulder, trying to copy my style."

"I was ten or eleven by then."

"That's right."

"I remember her being around before. Taking me shopping. Going to the Topsfield Fair. Showing up at my Little League games."

Abby eyed him watchfully.

"She might have done all that. I wasn't the most attentive mother. Grew up with an idea that the whole community raised the children. It was that way then. You were in and out of people's houses, I didn't know where you were half the time. Sleeping over at the Halls. Kids would sleep over here, kids I hardly knew. Everybody took care of everybody else's—it was just like that."

"And the thing with Johnny didn't come between you?" he couldn't help but ask.

"He and I were done before they started. Then later, I don't know, maybe it was part of what drew us closer. Not that we talked about it much."

"Johnny stayed in the spirit circle, after you and he split."

She rubbed her eyes with both hands, then looked at him hard.

"Is this what you want to talk about?" Abby asked calmly. "On this lovely evening?"

"It was you who wanted to talk. In the hospital, a week ago."

"Right," she sighed. "I was having those dreams."

"About what?"

"You. The night Johnny died. Awful stuff. You should have let me tell you then. I don't remember it so well anymore."

He picked up the wineglass and swirled the purple dregs. She was right. She had gotten healthy enough to reconstruct her defenses. To take all those memories from the fields where they had been grazing and lock them up behind the castle gates once again.

"The spirit circle was your thing," he said. Groping blindly for a way in. "Right? Kind of like your invention?"

"No, no. Groups like that have been around for generations. I used to sit in on Jane Hall's circle when I was a kid."

"Tom's wife?"

"Yeah. Sweet woman. Very calm and wise. Knew everything about everything."

Sam's grandma. Who was still giving herbology lessons from beyond the grave.

136

"Was it like yours?" he asked, smirking despite himself. "Swilling wine and holding hands and chanting?"

"There was some of that," Abby answered, taking no offense. "Minus the wine. And it was mostly Jane doing the chanting. In Welsh. Everyone else kind of closed their eyes and listened to her."

"Welsh?"

"Gaelic? Some language I didn't understand. But there was a power to it."

"You could feel it?" he asked quietly. Watching her dark eyes turn inward, her mind drift back to that time and place.

"I was outside the circle. In the corner, keeping quiet. Not touching them. That was an order, don't touch. But sometimes I could see the energy go through those women, like an electric current. Straightening their backs, shaking their arms."

"No kidding?"

"That was only some evenings. Other times, they would just knit and gossip. Talk about any old thing. Oh, and the healings. I nearly forgot those."

"Tell me." He kept his voice low and even.

"Jane would place her hands on people, wherever they were hurting. That's old medicine, laying on hands. I guess some still do it. Mostly, like rheumatism or arthritis. Common ailments. But she laid hands on Edgar Branford's stomach, when he had that terrible cancer. And damned if the man didn't live another fifteen years. Then later, much later I guess, when Jane was sick herself and her circle was breaking up, Lucy Larcom had that bad pregnancy. I was pregnant with you at the time. Jane got herself up and went over to Lucy's. Put her hands on that big belly and murmured some words. Three months later, out popped Danny, healthy as a horse."

"Huh." The laying on of hands, like so much else he was learning, seemed familiar. Certainly the idea that Jane Hall was a kind of medicine woman was well-known.

"I don't think the women nowadays have that strength. But it was amazing to watch."

"So you were there?"

"With Lucy? Yeah, Jane needed help getting around."

"Tom couldn't help?" Will asked.

"He drove us. Gosh, he would have done anything for Jane—they were so close. But the healing, the whole business really, it was a woman's thing. I know that sounds silly, but I don't remember men in Jane's group. They came to get healed. The older men did, like it was nothing strange. Like going to the doctor. But they weren't in the circle."

"They were in yours."

"Yeah," Abby said. A little twitch around her mouth. "I let the boys in."

"Why?"

"It seemed like the thing to do. The girls liked having them around. They brought enthusiasm, new ideas. Doc and Nancy Chester had been all over the world. They told us about the Mayans and Aztecs. Even the druids, back in England, where we all come from. Johnny brought these Navajo… I think it was Navajo, but prayer beads. And the prayers too, which we tried. We tried everything. We were figuring it out for ourselves. Jane was going to have me in her circle when I was old enough, but she got sick. I learned stuff from her, but I never got the full idea of what it was about. I had to make it up."

"One of the other women couldn't have taught you?"

"I don't know how much they knew, or how much they just went along. Jane, she was the one. We lost a lot when we lost her."

"What about Evelyn Price?" he asked, surprising himself.

"Evelyn." Abigail looked surprised too. Less by the name than that her son would know to invoke it. Her reverie was broken, and she studied his face. "Yeah, I could have gone to Evelyn, but I don't know if she would have helped."

The front door thumped open, startling them. A moment later Muriel came into the room. Her face was flushed and her pupils dilated.

"That must have been more than one ciggie," Abigail said.

"Yeah, well, we had quite a talk."

"You and Sam? Really?"

"Where is she?" Will asked, suddenly spooked by her absence. Muriel gave him a quick glance, then put her arms around Abigail.

"She went home. Which is where I'm going now."

"So early?" said Abby, though she looked beat. "You don't want coffee or something?"

"No, I'm good." She marched over to Will and kissed him loudly on the ear, cigarette smoke enfolding him like perfume. "Thanks for a great dinner, Willie. This was fun. We should do it more often."

Then she was gone again, and the evening was over. He tried not to make anything of Sam's leaving without a word. She didn't stand on ceremony, and the dinner had been no pleasure for her. Just something she had put up with, for him.

"Go over and see her," Abby suggested. He looked at

her tired expression. Not so tired that she couldn't see clean through him, as easily as Sam did. It would be good to get back to New York, where there were no women reading his mind.

"I'm sure she's fine."

"Well, I'm done in," Abigail replied, which was no more than Will had already figured. He didn't know whether to feel badly for pushing her so hard, or frustrated that he had not pushed more. She had more to tell. A lot more, and he wanted it.

"Go crash. I'll clean up down here."

"You know, I'm doing a lot better."

"You are," he agreed, eyeing her warily. She had started to rise, but sat again.

"If everything goes okay with the checkup tomorrow, maybe you should think of getting out of here. You know, back to school."

"Hey," he laughed. "You trying to get rid of me?"

"I don't want you to go," she answered sadly. "I just…"

"They're not going to fire me," he assured her, though he was far from certain about that. "You've been saying for years that I don't see you enough. And you were right."

She locked her tired gaze on him again.

"I'm not sure that being here is good for you."

She knew. She knew about Jimmy, and everything else. Everybody knew everything. There were no secrets. He ground his teeth and looked away. No more outbursts, be a grown-up.

"I'm all right," he said. "And I'm not going anywhere until I'm certain you're well. Do you understand?"

"I think I do," Abby said evenly.

"Good. Now go to bed."

CHAPTER

THIRTEEN

He ran. Not swiftly or well, but it felt good. He wore a soft brace on his left knee and labored to breathe evenly. It was odd to think he had once been an athlete. Track and baseball. An average fielder and below-average hitter, but a pretty fair middle-distance runner. Through sophomore year at Amherst, when hc blew his knee out. He was supposed to use a treadmill or bicycle, but seldom bothered, and had gotten out of shape.

Muriel would say he was projecting his mood onto the weather. Gray and misting. The clouds seemed to sit right on the houses, swallowing the tops of trees. Millions of droplets danced sideways, gently soaking everything. His sweatpants and shirt hung heavily on him. At the three-mile mark he meant to turn back, but caught sight of the Congregational Church steeple. A narrowing white shaft, vanishing into the ghostly vapor. He slowed, but felt a nudge at his back. Will knew better than to look. He also knew better than to ignore the hint. He picked up his pace and followed the winding road into what passed for the center of town.

Had he missed an evacuation order? A few cars passed, but there was no one else on the streets. It was poor weather to be out in, though that never bothered the locals. He scampered across the road and under dripping oaks to the edge of the churchyard. Then entered through a remembered break in the stone wall, toward the rear. Near the graves.

There were older graveyards in town, but as Margaret Price noted, the seven families were late arrivals. The oldest stones here bore dates from the early nineteenth century, just when the Halls, Prices and the rest started showing up. He ambled over uneven ground toward the secluded and tree-shrouded back wall. The graves were smaller here. Pale and pitted, and covered in lichen and moss. An older woman in a light blue dress knelt in the corner where Will was headed. The first soul he had seen today. She was slim, with silver hair and graceful movements. No umbrella, but the rain had backed off, or perhaps the oaks were shielding them. She was plucking weeds from around one old slab and arranging some flowers. Will lingered where he was, turning to the stone nearest.

Nathaniel C. Branford
Born June 9, 1809
Died November 11, 1859

His wife, Dorothea, who outlasted her husband by fifteen years, was beside him. There were more Branfords scattered about, but Nathaniel and Dorothea appeared to be the oldest of them. The woman in the blue dress stood and turned her face to Will. Handsome, familiar. She smiled briefly, then wandered away. He watched her for a few moments. A proud and erect posture that he could almost place. Then he proceeded to where she had been kneeling. The final resting place of the Halls.

He was instinctively drawn to the stone she had been tending. It was the smallest here. Probably marble, and so badly worn now that he could hardly read it. But he knew this marker, the great-granddaddy of them all.

Samuel Isaac Hall
Died March 3, 1848

The first Hall to come down from Maine. Possibly the first among all the families to make the move. Why did he come? Why did the others follow, if that was indeed how it had worked? And what lesson might there be for Will in this knowledge? He was deep in thought when his pocket buzzed, making him jump.

The phone. He normally would not have taken it running, but he wanted Abby to be able to reach him wherever he was. He dug it from his wet pocket.

"Hello?"

"Hey, stranger." Beth. Such a sane, friendly voice. How long since he had heard it? "How goes it up there?"

"Um, okay," he tried. "I don't remember when I last checked in."

"Your mom had just come out of the coma."

"Right." At least he had reported that much. "That was, like, a week ago."

"Exactly," she laughed, or it sounded like a laugh. "How is she?"

"Doing much better." He stood up and turned a slow circle, as if looking for spies. "Still weak, but a lot better."

"She's home?"

"Oh yeah. I'm sorry I didn't call."

"You don't need to apologize to me," she said. Implying that he did need to apologize to someone. "I'm sure you have your hands full."

"How are classes going?" he asked, beginning to walk. Back toward the church. Gazing at gravestones as he passed them.

"Under control. I told you Bryce took over American Lit."

Thomas Samuel Hall, died 1917. Old Tom's grandfather, who built the house.

"I remember."

"He's shown up twice. Figured out pretty quickly I was doing all the work."

"Good," Will answered mechanically. "And the seminar?"

She laughed again. It was a sweet laugh, but seemed a bit nervous or self-conscious now.

"Asa Waite seized control from the first day you were out," said Beth. Succubus girl. That figured. "They're a pretty self-propelled group. I wouldn't worry about the seminar."

"What should I worry about?" he asked.

"Dean Wagner."

Anne, beloved wife of…rests with the angels…

"What about him?"

144

"Will," she said firmly. "There's a right way to do this, and you're ignoring it."

"I spoke to him before I left."

"That was fine. It was an emergency—everyone understood. But it's ten days now, and you've checked in exactly once."

Alice Elizabeth Hall.

Will stopped short.

Born April 30, 1912
Died August 11, 1919

"Hello?" said Beth. "Anyone there?"

"What do I need to do?" he asked, gazing at the grave of his childhood playmate. If he believed Samantha.

"Apply for an official leave of absence. Did you get the forms I emailed?"

Emails, right. The wide world.

"My mother's computer is crap. There's a dial-up connection, but it takes ten minutes. I haven't seen anything."

"You haven't read any emails?"

"And I'm still alive," Will replied. "It's a miracle."

"Sarcasm isn't necessary."

"I don't mean to… It's like you said… I have my hands full. There's more stuff going on here than I expected."

"Sorry to hear it," she answered, sounding tired of the conversation. He didn't blame her. "We'll survive down here, but you're pushing it with Wagner."

The dean of faculty was gruff, short-tempered and formidable looking, and everyone was afraid of him. Yet Will noticed that his decisions were never malicious or arbitrary. He sensed a basically decent soul who had grown a tough skin. Of course, he could be wrong, but Will had been unconsciously trusting his academic future to this instinct about the man, a fact that had only become clear to him now.

The next grave stopped him again. It was the newest in this section and at the top in large letters it simply said HALL. Below and to the left it was inscribed:

> *Jane Marian, wife of Thomas*
> *Born October 22, 1910*
> *Died November 1, 1970*

To the right was inscribed: Thomas Isaac, Born May 23, 1913 with space below to list the date of death. But it was Jane's name that drew his eye back. Healer, herbologist, glue of the family, who had died too young. An image sprang to mind, and a sickening unease rose up in him.

"Beth, I have to go."

"I'll snail mail the forms. Deal with them. And for God's sake call Wagner."

"Thanks for everything. Really."

"Yeah, right."

The connection was broken. He put the phone away and looked around for the older woman, but she had vanished. Without thinking, he began walking quickly toward the break in the wall by which he had entered. But someone was there. Standing right in the open space. Will turned away quickly. He did not want to know who or what it was. He made for the front of the church, past the newer graves. The ground had changed since he had last been here. New stones had gone in, trees and bushes had grown up, yet he suddenly realized where he was. He stopped, reversed a few yards and went over one row to stand before a polished granite slab. Looking as fresh as it had that day. The last day he had visited this church, sixteen years ago.

Christine Rebecca Jordan
February 20, 1970
September 30, 1987

They had only known each other a couple of years. Had only been going out for six months or so. He could not say who she was as a person, who she might have become. It was this tragic thing that had occurred in his past. He hardly mentioned Christine to anyone. Good friends of his didn't know he had a girlfriend who died in a car crash in high school. And yet hardly a day went by that he did not think of her. He might see her face in the face of one of his students, or a girl in a coffee shop. He might smell privet or honeysuckle, scents she had made him aware of that summer. He might simply dream about her. Alive again, happy, full of plans for both of them.

No one had blamed him. Her mother did not speak to him at the funeral, but she didn't speak to anyone. Her brothers had been kind, patting him on the back, saying words he did not remember. But her father had pulled him close and spoken kindly in his ear. *Nobody is putting this on you, Will. Understand? Don't you do it either. It's just one of those things that happen.*

Did he blame himself? Not consciously. He was not in the car with her. He had not even asked her to come over that afternoon. It was her idea. Yet the fact remained that she had flown off the road on the way to his house. To see him. Had she not been his girlfriend, she would be alive today. Judgments aside, that simple truth was inescapable. Haunting.

He turned away from the grave, turned a slow circle again. No older woman. He was alone. What had she been trying to tell him? Why had his steps directed him to this place? Only one idea occurred to Will.

She opened the door after his second ring. He hadn't seen Molly Jordan in ten years or more, and was startled by how much she had aged. Her face was thicker, her hair grayer, and she gazed blankly at him for a moment or two. Then smiled. It was a brittle smile, but did not seem false, nor did she appear surprised.

"Will. You're soaked."

He looked down at his wet clothes. Why had he come here like this? Why hadn't he gone home and changed? It was as if he traveled to her doorstep in a dream and was only waking now. Yet if he had thought too much, he would not have come.

"Sorry, I should have called. I was out running and saw the house…"

"Come in."

She stepped back and pulled the door open farther. The big wooden door, still painted forest green, with that useless little window near the top.

"I don't want to interrupt anything."

"Really, it's fine. Please come in."

She put a dish towel on a kitchen chair and made him sit. Then busied herself making tea. More tea. If he got out of this town alive, he would never drink tea again. The kitchen was as he remembered. The creamy beige walls, blue Dutch tiles around the counters and appliances. He could vaguely remember Christine moving about in this space, but only vaguely. She was slender, wasn't she? He was not certain anymore. He had looked at her picture in his high school yearbook the night before, and been surprised to find it not quite matching up with the one in his dreams. He was losing her, making her up.

Molly brought the cups to the table and started talking, about anything. She didn't mention the divorce, but Will had heard about it. Her older son, the banker, had moved from Boston to Charlotte. Which meant seeing less of her grandchildren. The younger son was doing something with an environmental group in Boulder. She didn't ask why he had come, though the question hung in the air between them.

"How is Abby?" she finally said.

"She's doing really well," Will assured her. "Almost back to her old self."

"I have to go over and see her," Molly said firmly, as if trying to convince them both. "It's been so long."

Molly had been a core member of the spirit circle, but her relationship with the Conner family had not survived her daughter's death. She had been friendly to Will the two or three times he had bumped into her since, but she avoided Abby's house.

"Will you leave now?" she asked, looking at him closely. The way all the women around here seemed to do. "Now that she's better?"

It was not such a strange question, but her leaping to it so swiftly felt odd. Lines were forming. The people who wanted him to stay and figure things out. Which was really only Sam and himself, although you might throw the Price women in there. And the people who wanted him gone. Which was pretty much everyone else.

"Not yet," Will answered, returning her gaze as steadily as he could manage. "She needs me a little while longer. And maybe I need to be here."

"Do you like coming back?"

"There are people I like to see. But not really, no."

"You were smart to get away," she said, breaking eye contact. Sipping her tea. "I don't know why I don't leave."

"Some people feel attached to the place. Like they couldn't live anywhere else."

"The old families, yes. But that's not us. My sons have gone. My husband too, as I'm sure you've heard. Just me now, and this house is too big for one."

"You don't want to leave Christine," he said, his mouth ahead of his brain. But her expression turned warm, and she put her hand on his knee.

"That's right. I think that's just what it is. It's nice that you understand."

"She's very…" Will fumbled for the right word. "She's very present to me when I'm here. Well, all the time, but especially here."

"You don't still…" A worried look came over Molly's face and she squeezed his knee, seemingly without knowing. "You've moved on, haven't you? You have a girlfriend or fiancée or something?"

"Sure," he replied awkwardly. It was weird having her ask him these questions. Weird, too, that he had not thought of Helen once since he'd been home.

"It was so long ago. Of course, you meant the world to her. Dear God, she was mad about you. Wanting to spend every moment with you that she could. Picking colleges just to be close to where you were. It made me a little nuts."

"She meant a lot to me too."

"Oh, I know that. I know that, Will. It's just that you were both so young. And it was useless for me to say that you don't spend the rest of your life with your high school sweetheart. Or anyway, it doesn't usually work that way."

None of it was ill meant. She was just spilling things out of her bag of grief. Probably grateful to talk about it, and sensing the same desire in him. Yet he felt bludgeoned. Incapable of speech. As sick in body and spirit as if the news of Christine's death had just reached him.

"I'm sorry, is this all too much?" Molly asked.

"No, it's…"

"Do you see her?"

There were darting spots in his vision, and he closed his eyes. Trying hard to disappear from this place, but the pressure of her hand on his leg kept him tethered. Something both comforting and unsettling about that pressure.

"I see her sometimes," Molly went on. "Or just feel her close by. Sometimes she's hurt and needs my help. But I can't help her."

"I know," he whispered. He tried to say more but all that emerged was a sob. And then she was holding him while he cried. Pulling him against her and making soothing noises while his whole body shook. He tried to stop several times but could not, until his ribs ached and he pulled desperately for air. At length he drew away from her. Shamed. Wanting to flee, but knowing that would not be right.

"What does it mean?" he asked at last.

"I'm not sure," Molly mused. Looking a bit lost, or bereft. "I think it means we haven't let her go. Maybe we're holding her here."

What a hideous thought. He did not want to believe it, but there was poor Alice. Wandering the woods. Who was keeping her?

"How do we release her?" Will asked.

"I don't know, but we have to try. It's not fair to any of us, going on like this. Poor Will, I think I've made you feel worse for coming here."

"No, it's all right."

"Is there something I can do for you?"

"Yes," he replied after a moment. Looking at her again. "You can tell me what you were all doing the night Johnny Payson died."

She nodded, unsurprised by the question. But the nodding motion mutated somehow into a shaking of the head.

"Of course you want to know. The only wonder is you waited this long. Or maybe you've been asking others?"

"Actually, you're the first," Will told her. "Believe it or not. I mean, besides my mother."

"Lucky me. Well, I'm honored, but I can't. I'm sorry. We agreed not to talk about it."

"I was there, Mrs. Jordan."

"Molly, please. I know you were there."

"I was too young to understand what was happening, but it's never left me. I have a right to know."

She closed her eyes, pained lines gathering in her forehead.

"You have a right, no question. But you misunderstand. It wasn't a casual agreement." She opened her eyes again but looked away from him, thumb and finger rubbing the bridge of her nose. "More like an oath."

"You swore an oath? Why?"

"It was his idea. We all went along. I can't say any more."

"Who is 'he'?"

"I can't say any more," Molly replied harshly. Her head was clearly hurting her badly, and she had gone pale. He should stop now, but the deflection was driving him mad. Why did everyone have a right to know what had happened to him, *except* him? Maybe if she did not have to tell, but only confirm?

"You called something. Johnny brought a spell and you summoned something."

"I didn't know what we were doing," she said. "Most of us didn't understand."

"But something came."

"He said it didn't," she moaned. Closing her eyes again and rocking back and forth in the chair. "He said we failed. But there was this…"

"Go ahead."

"After the lightning. Right after, while we were still in shock. Before we understood what happened. Something rose up in that room. We all felt it. Some powerful presence. It was—"

She bolted up from her chair and rushed to the sink, vomiting tea. Then sagged weakly against the counter. Will rushed to her before she reached the floor, and held her, unsure what to do. Within a few moments, he felt strength return to her limbs.

"Do you need to lie down?"

"No," she said hoarsely. "Just help me back to the table."

She hardly needed help and was fully under her own power by the time she sat again. But she was still pale, and very worn.

"I'm sorry, I shouldn't have pushed you like that," he said.

"I had it coming. We all do, for whatever we did to you. I thought Christine was my punishment. I thought that would be enough. But I guess it doesn't end."

"Please don't talk like that. Do you need help? Can I get you anything?"

"You need to go."

He waited another half a minute, then stood.

"I'm sorry I troubled you, Molly. It wasn't what I intended."

"No, Will, I mean go. Get away from here. You want to understand, I know. You're a seeker, just like…like some men are. But it's better to let some things be, if you can. Let us alone—we've suffered enough. You've suffered enough. Leave this town. Just leave."

CHAPTER

FOURTEEN

It's possible," Samantha said. Looking away from the demonology long enough to consider the question. "Depending on the kind of oath and how it was given. Trying to break it could definitely make you sick like that. More than sick."

"What?" asked Will, straightening the framed photographs on the wall. A twitchy habit of his. "Stroke? Heart attack? Spontaneous combustion?"

"You can laugh."

"Do I look like I'm laughing?"

She shrugged and turned her face to the window. It was a bright day, but little light penetrated the room. Had Tom Hall liked it that way? Would he be offended that they commandeered his study to discuss such fanciful matters? Will sat down across the desk from Sam, his attention drawn back to the names on a sheet of paper. He tapped each one with his pen, counting silently for the fourth or fifth time.

"You can keep doing that," she said. "The number isn't going to change."

"Abigail Conner," Will read. "John Payson, Doug Payson. Eliza Stafford. Jenny Duffy. Louise Brown. Doc and Nancy Chester. Molly Jordan. Marty Branford. That's ten. We're missing two."

"Because Jimmy said so?"

"Why would he make that up?" Will asked. "Besides, twelve is the traditional number for a coven."

"You would know," she sighed. "Eddie Price."

Big Eddie. Shambling and social until the day he "accidentally" shot his best friend, Henry "Doc" Chester. Since then he had become a bitter, angry lout.

"You know that or you're guessing?" asked Will.

"He was around, wasn't he? And you don't have a Price on there."

"So?"

"Look," she said, stabbing a finger at the list. "You've got all six of the other families."

He checked. If his mother stood in for the Halls, it was true.

"Does that matter?" he asked, "having all the families? Does that add strength to the circle or something?"

"If you need to ask that, you haven't been paying attention to anything you've heard."

"Then we add Eddie," he said finally. "Johnny gets killed by lightning that night. Four years later, his brother Doug throws himself out a window. Eliza Stafford drowns in Chebacco Lake, what, a couple of years after that?"

"Yeah, about then," Sam agreed sullenly. Rubbing the edge of the Latin dictionary with her thumb. His obsession with identifying the coven members and their fates made her uncomfortable, but she let him go on.

"Another couple of years and Jenny Duffy dies of lung cancer. Then a gap of a dozen years until Eddie shoots Doc Chester. Then Louise Brown has a heart attack in her garden. And last Christmas Marty Branford dies of a gas leak in his house. That's seven of them."

"Can't argue with your math."

"Seven counting Johnny," Will went on. "Over twenty-seven years. Some of them pretty odd or violent deaths. Plus Nancy Chester getting hit by an unknown driver."

He did not add Christine Jordan's death in her mother's car. Or Abby falling down the stairs. It was too painful to include those. Yet if he did include them, that left only Eddie Price unscathed. Unless you counted killing Doc as the bad thing that had happened to him.

"And we're still missing our twelfth," he mused aloud.

"And where is any of this getting us?"

"I'm trying to understand. Isn't that what all of this is about? Understanding what's happened so that we can…"

"So that we can what?" she challenged. Blue eyes boring into him. "The important thing is making you right. Getting rid of whatever is hounding you."

"You don't think information is useful?"

"It might be. Anything might be useful. But look, you're just guessing. The people who know are the people who were there."

"Right," he snapped. "Which is why I'm trying to figure out who they are."

"But think," she said, pleading now. "Molly said they all took the oath. Which means *none* of them is going to be able to tell you. Not even your mother. Why do you think she's ducked it all these times? Why does she just get tired and can't speak? About something so important to you?"

He slumped back in the hard wooden chair. She was saying no more than he had been thinking since leaving Molly's house. If it was true, it would be true for all of them. In a funny way, it would let his mother off the hook. But he was not willing to swallow it yet. Both because of how far-fetched the idea was—an oath that sealed their lips for thirty years!—and because he so desperately wanted the truth. Whatever Sam thought, Will was convinced that understanding what happened that long-ago night was the key to everything.

She slapped her hand down on the old tome. Releasing dust motes into the shaft of golden light reflecting off the yellow basswood outside the window.

"This book," she said.

"Be careful with that, it's fragile."

"Have you looked at it at all?"

"Yes. The fifteen minutes you were in the kitchen."

Cleaning up days' worth of dishes, she said, but he was sure he could hear her on the telephone. So what? She was allowed to talk to people. Yet he kept listening for the front door. As if afraid of being ambushed.

"And?" Samantha asked.

"What did Muriel say to you the other night?"

Now she slumped back in her grandfather's leather chair, hissing like a stuck balloon.

"Hell, William, what does it matter?"

"It's a secret then?" he said casually, toying with his pen. He could sense her ready to leap over the table and shake him in frustration.

"She told me to leave you alone. That I was filling your head with bad ideas. Upsetting you about stuff that was better left undisturbed."

"What did you say?"

"Nothing, I just listened. Wasn't much point in trying to argue. She was pretty, um, vehement?"

"That's a good word for Mure," he said, ready to let it go. Then his brain veered back. "She wasn't threatening you or anything?"

"I don't know what she thought she was doing. She likes to act tough."

"You don't think she is?"

Sam gave him a hard look. It always surprised him when her soft eyes got stony like that.

"I'm not threatened by her," she said.

Will returned her gaze, waiting for her to give up something more. Nothing more came. Turning, his eye caught one of the four black-and-white photographs he'd just been straightening. The only hangings in this room of bookcases. A man and woman on a porch, smiling. He felt a chill and looked away. She was watching him, so he tipped his head at the book.

"I didn't start translating," he said, "just tried to get an overall sense. It's an introduction to the subject of demons, then a list of types and names. I don't see anything that looks like a formula for calling them. Or for sending them away."

She bit her lip and started turning pages. Tense, annoyed.

"Evelyn gave it to us for a reason," Sam insisted. *Us*, Will noted. She had thrown in with him completely. As if the would-be curse were upon her also. "Do you recognize any of these?"

"Yes," he admitted.

She stopped at the fourth woodblock. A five–pointed star, bounded by a double circle, with lettering between the two rings. Overlaid with other lines and small circles.

"Astaroth," Will said. "Master of knowledge, especially the sciences. He'll answer any question put to him, but he'll seduce you all the while. Appealing to your pride."

She looked up quickly.

"You got all that while I was in the kitchen?"

"No, my Latin isn't that good," he said. "I recognize his mark. I run across a lot of demons in my reading. Of course, there are inconsistencies from source to source."

She started turning pages again. Faster and faster, as if some answer was going to leap out at her on the next yellowed page of impenetrable text.

"Can I make a suggestion?" he asked. She stopped and looked up at him again, a weary desperation on her face. "Why don't we ask her what she meant?"

"I've called her three times," Sam replied. "She won't answer."

"Do you know where she lives?"

"Yes."

"Then let's drive over and knock on her door."

She became very still. Looking at him, but her mind elsewhere. He would swear that she was frightened by the idea. And yet, after several long moments, she nodded her head.

"Okay," Samantha said. "Fine. We'll do it."

* * *

The town's contact with the sea was primarily via a large inlet, surrounded by streams, marshes and dunes. All low ground north to Plum Island, except for the dark green hump of Hog Island. Heading south there was higher ground. Rocky bluffs right on the water, and forested hills behind them. The roads were poor, so it was sparsely populated. Will was surprised to find that Evelyn Price lived in a brown-shingled shack in this part of town, but perhaps she coveted privacy. He was getting out of the car when Samantha grabbed his arm.

"Don't touch the doorknob," she said firmly.

"You're right. Those things are filthy."

"Listen to me. Don't touch anything you don't need to. Don't step into the house unless she invites you."

"Sam, the woman is ninety years old."

"She's a powerful witch."

"You don't use that word," he objected.

"I'm using it for your convenience."

"Ah, thanks. I thought she liked you."

"I haven't spoken to her in a while," Sam replied, gazing at the little house in trepidation. "Anyway, I'm not saying she's hostile. I'm just saying be careful."

The sun was waning, but the day remained bright. There was a salty breeze off the ocean and drying clothes snapped and shuddered on lines staked up in the yard. Sam rang the doorbell once, then again a minute later. They were crowded together on the small stoop, waiting.

"I guess she's not home."

"No, she's here," said Sam, turning in place with her face up. Like a dog on a scent.

She stepped down and headed straight for the laundry,

vanishing behind a billowing white sheet. Will wondered why she didn't go around. Maybe her homing device didn't work like that. He followed, fresh-smelling pillowcases and blouses slapping his face as he ducked and bobbed through waves of material. Sam appeared and disappeared ahead. Until he cleared the last flapping sock to stand on a green shelf of land, falling abruptly to the sea. It was windy, and white crests tipped the waves to the horizon. In a weather-beaten Adirondack chair sat the old woman from the Cask & Flagon, her back to the stirring view. She smoked a cigarette and drank what looked like a generous glass of whiskey. Watching her clothes dry.

"Hello dear," Evelyn Price croaked at Samantha. That damp voice. Spotted, deeply lined flesh and the palest of blue eyes. She gave Will the full up-and-down before speaking again. "I guess you were bound to show up sooner or later."

There was no kindness in her tone, but no malice either. She was past caring what anyone thought.

"I think your laundry is dry," he said.

"Yeah." She gazed at it. "Problem is, once I get into this damn chair, it's impossible to get out again."

"My grandma used to dry it on the line like that," Sam said. "I love that smell."

"Salt and mildew?" the old woman snorted. "It's only there because the dryer is broken. Haven't gotten around to fixing it."

"How long has it been broken?" Will asked.

She took a long squinting drag on the cigarette, considering.

"Six years?"

"I hope this isn't a bad time," Sam said.

"Hah," the woman laughed, or perhaps it was a cough. "Look at me. I'm ninety-two—all I have is bad times."

"We came to ask about the book," said Sam. Evelyn looked accusingly at Will.

"They don't teach you boys Latin in school anymore?"

"I can make it out," he replied, crouching down so that their faces were on the same level. "We just wonder why you wanted me to have it."

"You don't know?" Her gnarled face was incredulous. "Shit, it's worse than I thought."

"Your daughter," said Sam, "Margaret—"

"I know my daughter's name."

"She told us about the curse. The curse on the families."

Evelyn considered them both at length, her expression growing amused.

"I'm sure she told you something. You can sit if you like. Don't ask me to get chairs."

Samantha sat down in the long grass and began speaking. Of Wales. The demon. The seven heroes who caught and bound it. The promise of riches refused. The casting out and the curse. Will felt certain that she was repeating Margaret's version word for word. *Just ask me. I remember every damn thing I've ever heard.* To his surprise, Evelyn did not interrupt. Just sipped and smoked and listened while waves thudded and hissed on the rocks below, out of sight. They were all quiet for some time after Sam finished.

"Yup," said Evelyn at last, nodding to herself. "That's one way to tell it. What you might call the sanitized version."

"What's the true one?" Sam asked.

"No true one. It's a legend. You shouldn't go believing such things, no sir."

Shoont. Nossah. Will had not heard an Old Yankee accent so thick since his great-aunt died.

"Never mind true," said Will, settling himself in the grass near Sam, six feet from where the old witch's sandaled foot dangled. He was determined to learn what he could this time, without suspicion or quarrel. "Tell us a different version."

"Different," Evelyn rumbled, consulting her whiskey glass. If it was whiskey. "Okay, here's another way to tell it. Those seven fellas who went hunting that so-called demon weren't any heroes. They were doing what they had to do. What their women made them do. Cleaning up the mess they created."

"Because they had called the demon in the first place," said Will. Having suspected it since Margaret Price first told them the tale days ago. Evelyn nodded.

"Why?" asked Sam.

"Who knows?" the old woman replied. "They wanted knowledge, or a favor. Those are the usual reasons. But they misjudged its strength. Lost control of it. Had to go hunt it down once it cast its shadow over the countryside. Still, they weren't so swift to ignore its offerings. They wanted to get something out of the whole bad business. Some of them, anyway. They went ahead and made the deal. Knowledge for freedom. Once they had what they wanted, they went back on their promise and banished the old one."

"That's why it cursed them," Will said.

"Well, sure," she agreed, turning a mirthless smile on him. "Wouldn't you have?"

"What was the knowledge they gained?" he asked.

"Isn't it obvious?" She looked back and forth between the two of them. "You know, I always forget how young people resist answers that are right in front of them. Even the smart ones. Can't say I envy either of you. What they gained is everything that makes our families what they are. The lore. The sight. The healing."

"No," said Sam sharply. She shook her head quickly once, again. Will reached out and touched her knee but she flinched away. "I don't believe it. The healing isn't evil."

"You silly girl," said Evelyn Price. "Who said it was?"

Will recalled Sam's own words to him, which she seemed to have forgotten. There were things *not from here.* Things that crossed over. Whose true nature staggered our minds, defied comprehension. We gave them names. Angel. Demon. Old one. But they were just names. Such power was neither good nor evil; it simply was.

"And what about after?" he asked. "They were driven out by their community?"

"Maybe. Maybe they just felt they had to leave."

"But they were pursued by the curse. Of restlessness."

"More like the curse of stupidity," cackled Evelyn.

"What does that mean?" Sam snapped. Her bluntness restored by the old woman's incivility.

"It means we don't change," Evelyn replied, a weary remorse in her tone. "Going someplace different didn't make them different people. They got up to the same old mischief."

"You mean calling on…those powers again?" Will asked, dismayed. "That's why they kept getting thrown out of places? Christ, is it that easy to summon a demon?"

"No. Very hard. Even harder to get rid of one."

"Then how did they manage to keep doing it?" he pressed.

"Maybe they got lucky," Evelyn suggested airily. "All

it takes is one arrogant idiot every generation, thinking it's his birthright. Getting his hands on the right spell and giving it a whirl. Sooner or later someone hits the mark."

"Twelve idiots," Will corrected.

"Twelve bodies," she agreed. "Fewer, if necessity requires. But only one needs to know what he's up to. The others just have to do what they're told."

"Or maybe the first demon never went away," said Samantha. "Maybe they never really banished it. That's why they're…why we're able to keep recalling it again and again. Maybe that's the real curse."

Evelyn regarded the younger woman with a pleased expression. Then pointed the stub of her cigarette at Sam.

"I knew there was more to you than good looks." She turned her gaze on Will once more. "I'm sorry I didn't pay more attention to what they were up to in your mother's house. Never occurred to me there was any real danger. I was forgetting that they didn't have Jane watching them anymore."

"Jane was the knowledge-keeper," he said, again remembering Sam's words. "She died before she could pass on what she knew."

"Jane was a good soul," said Evelyn, shifting uncomfortably in the deep wooden chair. "An insufferable know-it-all, but a good soul. She died much too young."

"You should have stepped in," Sam scolded. "You should have shown them the right way. Instead of keeping it all for your own family."

"I didn't keep it for anyone," the old woman shot back. "I didn't even teach this stuff to Margaret. I wanted it to die with me."

"You *do* think it's evil," Samantha accused.

Evelyn waved a hand at her in annoyance.

"Stop blathering about things you don't understand. Honestly. It's the times, that's all. Modern medicine. Modern science. Nobody has any use for the old ways. And those who worship them become outsiders. Sad, stuck little creatures, unable to function in the real world. I didn't want that for anyone's child, never mind my own."

Will had heard the words not spoken. *Sad, stuck little creatures like you.* He was sure that Sam must have caught it, as well.

"But you were wrong," said the younger woman defiantly. "Because we don't have any choice about being this way. I don't. So it's only a question of using your skills well or using them badly. You should have helped and you didn't."

Evelyn fixed her with a cold gaze, but said nothing. Sam gazed back unblinking.

"In the wine shop," said Will, breaking up the standoff. "You felt something. Something in me."

Evelyn closed her eyes and took a deep breath, coughing wetly on the exhale. He didn't like to imagine the state of her respiratory system.

"Wasn't just me who felt it. Saul felt it too, did you notice?"

"I just thought he was afraid of you."

"Well, that's true, he is. But he was feeling what I was feeling. The Jews are very sensitive to spirits."

"Oh, Mrs. Price," groaned Sam.

"What, Saul's not a Jew?" she demanded, looking at him for some reason.

"I believe he's a druid," Will replied.

Her laughter terminated in a long fit of coughing that Will worried would finish her off. *Great*, he thought, as Sam rose to assist her. *Here's another one Jimmy will chalk up to me. Conner the destroyer.* But Evelyn waved Sam away and spat what looked like a generous section of lung into the grass. She slumped back in the chair, posture slack. Yet her reddened face showed something else. A sharp line to her mouth, and her eyes half-shut but hard as marbles. As if daring them to see her as vulnerable. She looked dangerous.

"I felt it," Evelyn wheezed. "Once before. When I was a girl. We spent summers in Maine then." She finished the whiskey and, to Will's horror, lit a fresh cigarette. "Our neighbor was a veteran of the Great War. Shrapnel in his head, some old books he brought from Paris. My parents said stay away, but I was friends with his daughter. Cindy. Summer friends. She got 'sick,' they said. Sure, sick. If sick means your eyes turning yellow and climbing around the roof at night. Hypnotizing her sister. Her cousin too. She smelled funny—all the dogs stayed away from her. They finally locked her in the basement, but she got out."

"She was possessed?" Sam asked.

"Only case I've ever seen," Evelyn replied. Looking at the laundry as she pulled deeply on the cigarette. The sun was dying and blue shadows crept across the yard. "Of course it's rare enough that most never see it. But at the tender age of thirteen I got to witness an exorcism and a banishment, all in one go. Performed by my own mother, no less. Man, that was some night."

"Jesus," whispered Will. "Did it work?"

"It did. But it was a struggle. And Cindy was never really the same afterward."

"So I'm possessed?" he asked, trying to laugh and failing.

"No," Evelyn said, looking hard at him again. "That's the funny thing. I get the same uncanny feel off you I did from poor little Cindy. But you're obviously under your own control. It's *with* you, but not *in* you. Damnedest thing."

He saw Sam put her face between her knees, but didn't know what to make of it.

"Is that better or worse?" he asked.

"Worse," she replied in a clinical tone, "in that it gives the demon freer range of action. It's not limited to your presence. But also better in that we don't need to perform an exorcism. Those are messy. The host can die. In your case, it's just a straight banishment."

"Could you do it?" he asked, surprising himself.

She closed her eyes again and exhaled, smoke shooting out her nose like an old dragon.

"That's what I figured you came here for. Took your time getting to it."

"What's the answer?" Sam asked. In a small voice, bled of all its former challenge.

"Do you have the summoning spell that was used?"

"No," Sam answered. "We've been looking for it."

"It would be better to have that spell," said Evelyn. "In case there's anything peculiar about the manner in which it was called. But either way, I should be able to do it. I know the ritual. I've seen it performed. That puts me way ahead of anyone else you're likely to find. There's a catch. Which, to go back to your first question, is why I gave you the book."

"What?" asked Will, already knowing the answer. Indeed, embarrassed at himself for not having figured it out before.

"In the banishment ceremony you have to say what you're banishing. You must speak the name of whatever's gotten ahold of you. So tell me, William. Do you know its name?"

CHAPTER

FIFTEEN

Sam was agitated the whole way home.

"Its *name*?" she said, squeezing the steering wheel until her knuckles stood up white. "They aren't like us, those…those things. Why would they have names like us?"

"She explained that," Will replied. Even if they could not know the true name and nature of a demon, a certain word—which we called a name—succeeded in bringing it forth. That sound clearly had significance to and power over the being.

"So why would some monk from hundreds of years ago know it?"

"The book is a compendium," he said. "It's just somewhere to start."

Will didn't know why he was playing devil's advocate. So to speak. The whole thing was as absurd to him as it was to her. Despite the strangeness of the last two weeks, he was not prepared to accept a centuries-old superstition as fact. He knew too much. He had studied how and why those superstitions developed, and what damage they had done. Persecution. Stoning. Burning. He had been trying to focus on concrete matters, like what happened on that long-ago night in his house. The harm that the coven members had since suffered. Jimmy's suspicions. Matters which, however bizarre, might have an earthly explanation. This business with demons was something else entirely.

"And did you hear her with that 'some of them'?" Sam barreled on. "'Some of them' were tempted by the demon. 'All it takes is one idiot a generation'?"

"So what?"

"The Halls. She's talking about the Halls."

"She never mentioned family names."

"Of course she didn't. You think I don't know who she meant? The Halls make a mess of things and the Prices clean it up. Poor, martyred Prices."

"For God's sake, Sam. I didn't get any of that. Everybody was in my mother's coven. Eddie Price was in it."

Or was he? It was Sam who put his name on the list. Did she believe it, or did she only want the Prices to be culpable in some way? He really did not need an ancient feud clouding up the already-murky facts.

"You won't find them acknowledging kinship with Eddie," she replied. "He's the black sheep of that family."

"You're taking this very personally," Will said. He would have expected her to embrace whatever solution Evelyn offered. Instead, she had become angry and resistant. "Something's gotten under your skin. What?"

She settled back in her seat and grew quiet. Possibly embarrassed.

"Nothing," she said finally.

"She said something that threw you. What was it?"

But she would speak no further the rest of the drive.

His mother was watering flowers in the blue dusk. She smiled when she saw him coming through the pines.

"Having fun with your girlfriend?"

"Yes," Will agreed, unwilling to be provoked. "You're energetic this evening."

"We haven't had enough rain. I meant to do this earlier, but I fell asleep. I never used to be able to nap and now I can't stop."

"You're still recovering. It'll be a while."

"Do you think this forsythia needs trimming?"

"Yeah, it's pretty leggy. I'll get the clippers out tomorrow."

"How's Evelyn?"

"Fine," he replied. Quick and easy, not asking how she knew. He was almost proud of himself. "She sends regards."

"Margaret stopped by with an apple pie."

"Only a pie?" he asked, taking the hose from her and bending over to get at the base of the blueberry bushes. "Not a turkey too, or a side of beef?"

"She said you'd been over to visit."

"She invited us. Me and Sam."

"You're getting quite chummy with the Prices," she said.

"Maybe because they're the only ones willing to speak to me," Will said bluntly. He looked at her face now, but the shadows flattened her expression. "We talked about demons. You know anything about them?"

"I know it's a word that frightened people use," Abby replied.

"Is that what Johnny told you? Is that how he sold you on the idea?"

"Stop. He didn't…" Her voice was weary, just that fast. "I can't talk about Johnny."

"Of course not," he said. "You can't talk about anything. None of you. You took an oath, after all. What else needs water?"

"Just the impatiens."

He sprayed the glowing white flowers for a minute or so while she stood where he left her. By the blueberry bushes, staring out into the street. Then he squeezed off the flow and went to the spigot against the house, turned off the water and coiled the hose painstakingly around the reel. He had to buy her one with a crank—she was always leaving the hose in the grass. Abby came up beside him as he worked.

"I didn't take any oath," she said.

"No?" he asked in surprise, turning to her. "I thought everyone did."

"I didn't even hear about it until later. Maybe I wasn't in the room. I certainly wasn't in my right mind. I couldn't have sworn to my own name."

"Then why won't you tell me anything?"

"Because I don't remember," she said. "I don't remember what happened. I can't make it all…"

The rest was inaudible. Will put an arm around her while she wept tears of frustration. He tried to recall if she had cried this much before the accident. His anger was subdued. He was finding it harder and harder to maintain, at least toward her. And he was starting to wonder whether she had not always been this scared and vulnerable. The careless, hard-drinking party girl an act from the start. A persona anyone could have seen through, except him. Her lonely, obtuse son.

"It's okay," he said, patting her back. "Let it go. I'm sorry I keep hounding you."

"I've tried," she gasped. "I've tried to pull it all together. All I get is bits and pieces."

"Don't get mad," he said as gently as he could. "But were you, like, drunk or high?"

"I'm sure I was drinking." She pulled away, rubbing her eyes. "We all were. I don't remember any drugs. We needed to be clearheaded that night. We were trying out a new way to contact the spirit."

"This was something Johnny had come up with?"

"Yes," she agreed.

"And he was leading the ceremony?"

"No." She shook her head and looked at the ground for a few moments, digging deep into her bruised neocortex. "He was supposed to, but he got scared."

"Scared? Johnny did?"

"Yes."

"And that didn't scare you?" he asked.

"It did. But he said I shouldn't worry. Somebody else would lead the ceremony."

"Who?"

"I don't know," she said firmly. Meaning that she knew it was a critical point, but his pressing was not going to help. "He didn't say. Whoever it was would be there that night and then we would all know. Everyone else wanted to go ahead with it, so we did."

"And then what happened," he asked, still mild in his tone. "I'll take bits and pieces, if that's all you have."

"My last clear memories are from before. Drinking and talking in the kitchen, with Jenny Duffy and Molly. Then there's a blank. And then we're in the middle of the ceremony, holding hands and chanting. But I'm completely out of my mind. I can't focus, I can't speak."

"Sounds like you overindulged in the kitchen."

"I know it does, but I didn't," she insisted. "I was being careful. Johnny told me I would need to be alert. He was very anxious about it."

"He told *you* that, or he told everyone?"

"He might have said it to other people, but I only remember him telling me. He took me aside beforehand. He was very nervous about the whole thing. I can't help feeling like he knew something bad was going to happen."

"Why didn't you call it off?"

"I couldn't."

"It was your house."

"I mean, obviously I should have," Abby said weakly. "But I had lost control of things. Lost control of the group. Lost control of my life. I couldn't seem to make decisions, I thought they were my friends."

"Never mind. What happened next? After the chanting?"

"There's no 'next.' It's a jumble. I'm putting this in the order I know it must go. From what I learned later."

"Just do the best you can."

"We were seated in the circle, but someone was standing. Wearing a robe."

"A robe?" he echoed.

"Yeah. Like a gray robe, with a hood. Speaking the old words."

"The ones Jane used? The Welsh, or whatever it was?"

"Yes. I thought it was an hallucination, the figure in the robe. Maybe it was."

"Did anyone ever wear robes?" he asked.

"They used to. Generations ago. Some of the families still own them. I remember seeing Doc Chester's robe once. But nobody wore them anymore, not by then."

"Go on."

"Someone left the room," Abby said, blinking. Forcing herself to remember. "Someone else went after the first one. The circle shrank. There was an argument, over by the stairs."

"Who?" Will asked eagerly.

"A man and a woman. I think the man was Johnny. I don't know what they were talking about it. But it wasn't long after that, you know, that it happened."

Johnny had headed upstairs for some reason. Why? And the woman had pursued him. They had argued. And then the bolt from the sky.

"I thought something exploded," Abby went on. "It was so loud. And deep, like it happened inside your body. No one said anything. I felt like I was screaming, but no sound came out. We were all in shock, I think."

"Did you feel anything just then?" Will asked. Remembering Molly's words, about the evil presence that arose at that moment.

"Panic," said Abby forcefully. "I felt panic, for you. Like the blast woke me up. I tried to get to the stairs, but they held me back. So I wouldn't see Johnny. They pushed me into the kitchen. I never saw you come down, but some of the girls were yelling your name. I started yelling too. Jenny said you weren't in your room, so I ran to the window and shouted. But they wouldn't let me go, they kept holding me back. Jenny, and Molly, and Nancy. All crying. Poor Doug screaming his brother's name. Eddie went flying out the door. I thought maybe he was going to look for you, but he was just running away."

"Did he come back?"

"No, I think he kept running all the way home. Doc went and found you."

He dimly remembered that. Doc Chester, the oldest person there, and the only one to keep his head, carried Will back to the house. There was a blanket wrapped around him, and Doc spoke calming words. Will couldn't remember what had happened to Sam. Did she come back to the house? Go home? He couldn't recall the others except as one grieving mob. He was sure he remembered Muriel holding him, comforting him. But why would she have been there? And Eddie Price running out the door like that! Which presumably meant he wasn't there when they settled down enough to take their oath of silence. In the middle of these ruminations he noticed that his mother was shivering. She wore only a short-sleeved T-shirt and the evening had gotten cold, but it likely had nothing to do with the temperature.

"Come on, let's get you inside," Will said, taking her cool arm in his hand. She resisted at first. Eyes fixed on nothing, on that night long ago. But then her feet were shuffling along behind him toward the broken concrete steps to the kitchen door. The door he imagined escaping through that night. But she had been in the kitchen. How did he get out of the house? Did he go out his window? He started doing that in high school, when he didn't want to wake her with his nocturnal comings and goings. He had been tall and strong enough by then to make the jump off the kitchen roof. He could not have done that at five. His mind veered away.

"Do you remember a name?" he asked her then, stopping short in the darkness. "Do you remember using a name to summon the spirit?"

"No," she said softly, after thinking a moment. "No, I don't remember any words that I actually understood. I'm sorry, Willie."

"It's okay."

"I'm sorry for the whole thing. I'm sorry I let it happen, I'm sorry it troubles you."

"I don't blame you," he said.

"Don't blame Johnny either. He wasn't the devil you make him out to be."

"What was he, then?"

A far streetlight caught her face as she turned to him. For just a moment he thought she might tell him. But the moment, like all the previous ones, passed.

"Don't blame anyone," Abby said. "Just try to let it all go. Can't you?"

He gave her a tight grimace, knowing she could not see his expression. Then he took her arm once more and guided her up the treacherous stairs. *No, Ma. No, I can't.*

CHAPTER

SIXTEEN

Every box he opened released a cloud of dust, until his sinuses ached from the onslaught. Sneezing didn't help much. There were four small windows and two naked bulbs, but the light was still bad in the cluttered attic. Yet there was enough to determine that the contents matched the black marker headings on each box. Old volumes of Lucretius, Petrarch, Goethe, Emerson in the one marked POETRY. Just like Tom Hall to prefer the philosophical poets. Will could picture his large hands holding *De Rerum Natura*. Gently turning brown pages, intelligent blue eyes scanning the familiar text. He opened the next box, BIOGRAPHY. Boswell on Johnson; Franklin on himself; Ellmann's fat volumes on Joyce, Yeats and Wilde. He did not remove every book, only enough to see the bottom of each box. Sam had said the grimoire was large. Of course she had been small when she last saw it. There was, alas, no box marked AR-CANE or BLACK MAGIC.

He slapped dust from his jeans pointlessly, hearing the phone ring far below. There were old dressers, desks, cabinets tucked into every corner or standing in the open. He had been through them, but not carefully. Each time he could sense Samantha there before him, seeing all he would be likely to see, and more. This was a fool's task, as she had told him two hours ago. Will turned off the lights and clomped down the narrow stairs.

He went to the kitchen to wash his face and hands, then to the study. Sam was hunched over the desk, in a circle of lamplight. Interrogating Evelyn's old tome, with the faithful dictionary at her elbow. She was going to teach herself Latin by way of reading that damned demonology.

"Satisfied?" she asked.

"No," he said, dropping into the chair across from her. "Just defeated."

"I told you, I've been through this place."

"It's a large house, with more closets, alcoves and secret cabinets than anyone—"

"I would *feel* it," she declared. Massaging her left shoulder with her right hand. "I would feel it here, and I don't. Anyway, I think I know where it is."

"Where?"

"The *name*, William." She looked hard at him. "The name. Without it, we're nowhere."

"I didn't think you believed that."

She continued staring for few moments, then put her head down on the book.

"I don't know what I believe," she mumbled into the pages.

"Sam," he said, rising and walking around behind her. "You don't have a bibliophilic bone in your body, do you?"

"What?" she asked, without moving.

"You're supposed to touch the corners of the pages," he said, lifting her head off the yellowed book. "Preferably with gloves. Not bury your face in it."

"Books are for using. That's what Grandpa always said."

"Well, yes." Her muscles from shoulder to shoulder were a knotted mass. He pressed down with the heels of his hands on either side of her neck. "Use and care are not mutually exclusive. Relax, I won't hurt you."

Her shoulders sank, her resistance giving way slowly. And then so completely that it seemed she would collapse if his hands released her.

"Too hard?" he asked, easing up a little.

"No, it's good. It feels good. Keep going."

She started turning pages idly. Will looked over her shoulder at the archaic script and ghastly illustrations. Seeing only the bolded names.

Halphas, Havras, Hermus.

"Who was on the phone?" he asked. She hesitated before replying.

"Eddie Price."

"Seriously? The same Eddie we've been talking about? What did he want?"

"What he always wants. This house. And every other one on the street."

Will's mind stumbled.

"Wait, what does Eddie Price have to do with houses?"

"He builds them."

"I knew that," Will said, only just remembering. "But what does he want with… Do you mean to tell me he's the one behind Lucy Larcom?"

"He owns Price Construction. He's in with a developer and some other people. They're putting up houses all over Cape Ann, as fast as they can build them."

She kept turning pages. *Labal, Lamia, Leraie.*

"Why is he calling you directly?"

"You can go harder on the right," she said. "Yeah, there. Because I've said no to Lucy twice. And Eddie doesn't like no. He was pretty, um, rude just now."

"What, like, hostile?"

"It doesn't matter."

"It does," he said, thoughts banging about anxiously. "It does matter. Because if he's harassing you, he may be doing the same to my mother. And if he is, I'll—"

"Will. You cannot let this distract you."

Malphas, Marchosios, Merihem, Murmux.

"What?" Samantha asked. She had felt the shock in his hands before he registered it. "What is it?"

"Turn back one page," Will said, his own voice sounding faraway. "There."

Murmux, also known as Murmus or Murmur. A cloaked figure riding a giant vulture. Where had he read of him before?

"Summon…" Sam's shoulders tensed again and she moved quickly from the page to the Latin dictionary and back. "Summon souls…"

"Can conjure the souls of the dead to answer the questions of the summoner," Will said. Partly reading and partly remembering. "He teaches philosophy, and his name is a whisper."

His bronchial passages constricted, and his vision spotted. His hands slipped from her shoulders, and Sam turned sideways in the chair to look up at him.

"That time you saw it," she said urgently. "In New York, when you looked on its face. It spoke a word."

"I heard a word in my head," he replied, his mind veering away again and again from the memory. Refusing to have dealings with it.

"Murder," she whispered.

"Yes," Will agreed. "It sounded like that."

"Could it have been Murmur instead?"

He had to sit. He went across the room and collapsed on the threadbare couch, ignoring the discomfort of the blown springs. Sam came over and sat next to him.

"You recognize the name? Like, from the Bible or something?"

"No. I mean, yes, it could be Christian mythology. But I think I read it in folklore. English, or American."

"Okay." She nodded quickly, as if expecting that answer. "So, if we can say…"

She paused. Asking silent permission to conjecture in his field of expertise.

"You can say whatever you want, Sam."

"If we say folklore comes from someplace. You know, however changed. Then somewhere in England, or New England, where our people come from, the locals knew this name. In their folk traditions, without hearing it in a Sunday sermon."

He could explain how freely source material flowed from one tradition to another, over great time and distance. But he knew what she was getting at.

"I suppose."

"We want a name like that," she continued. "A name our ancestors might recognize. Not the name of some Babylonian god or whatever."

"If Johnny was studying with your grandfather," Will said, the pain in chest subsiding. Trying to see the matter rationally. "I don't know if that's the right word. But if he was reading Tom's books, imbibing his ideas and interests, this seems like exactly the sort of demon he would have called."

"So maybe we've got something."

He hoped so, but then another thought suddenly hit him.

"Why the hell would it tell me its name?"

"Well." He could hear some of the enthusiasm drain from her voice in that one word. "It may not be that it was telling you, only that you heard it. Remember, it's not necessarily a name, like we understand names. It's a word. A word that means something."

Will closed his eyes and massaged his forehead. This was all too vague, not to mention completely ridiculous. They sat in silence for a minute or so.

"Sam," he finally said. "Where is the book? The grimoire?"

"I think it's at my grandfather's house," she answered in a small voice.

"This is your grandfather's house."

"No, where he lives now."

He opened his eyes and looked at her, still confused.

"I thought he was in a rest home?"

"I never said that."

"You told me he was, what?"

"Retired from the world," she answered. Exactly the phrase she used that night. "He lives in a cabin on Mount

Gray. This house was too big, and he didn't want to deal with other people. He almost never leaves there."

"Is he, like, functional?"

"More or less," Sam replied. "He can cook and take care of himself. He has a car. He can drive if he really needs to. I do most of his shopping."

"So you see him often," Will said, surprised.

"Once a week, at least. Sometimes more. Why?"

"I don't know, I just thought he was put away somewhere. I didn't realize he was up and around and you were seeing him. I mean, come on, Sam."

"Wait."

"He was there that night, after all the bad stuff went down. He taught Johnny. He knows about the book. Maybe he knows a lot more. My God, why wouldn't you tell me—"

"He's not right," she said. "He's not really himself. That's why."

"He's not right how?"

"He knows who I am, most of the time. But he doesn't always recognize other people."

"Is this Alzheimer's?"

"They haven't diagnosed it. There are days he's good. I mean, really sharp. He'll talk for an hour, nonstop. Like one of his old lectures. All the words he needs are right there, the history, the quotes from his philosophers. And then, the light just goes out, you know? He'll stop in the middle of a sentence and stare into space. Other days," she sighed, "he can barely tie his shoes."

"Is there a home health aide?"

"He doesn't need that."

"Because he has you."

"Don't make me into a martyr," Samantha complained.

"The man was the only parent I ever had. Why wouldn't I do this much for him?"

"Of course you would," he agreed. "It's only that you and I have spent so much time together. Talking about this stuff, the families and the history. And all this time you're going up there to see him and I don't even know?"

"I didn't want to talk about it." Her face showed that she knew it was a feeble answer. "He's fragile. Things upset him. Talking about my grandmother, talking about Johnny—it can mess with his mental balance."

"You've raised the subject with him?"

"No. He brings it up. But there's no way to have a good discussion, he just starts to shake and get confused."

An odd and disquieting thought occurred to Will. Had Tom Hall taken the oath as well?

"I'm sorry," he said at last. "I wish I knew sooner. I'd like to see him."

"I figured. Problem is, you're one of the subjects that upsets him."

"Because of what happened that night."

"Yes."

He said no more right away. The old guy had hung around them like a benevolent spirit during all the hours they had spent in this house. Will had known he wasn't dead, but imagined him in ghostly terms nonetheless. To learn he was living up there on Mount Gray, that she had been seeing him right along… Well, they all had their secrets, didn't they? What things had he not told her? Was it possible for two adults to trust each other completely? Ever? Never mind under these strange circumstances.

His eye caught the framed photograph once more. He

didn't look away this time. Tom and Jane Hall. Middle-aged, arm in arm, on a porch somewhere. Happy.

"Sweet, huh?" she said. "They were so close. In love since they were children. He's never gotten over her."

"I saw her," Will said calmly. "Jane. A few days ago in the graveyard behind the Congregational Church. Tending the Hall graves. Anyway, it sure looked like her." She was quiet long enough that he finally turned to look . He saw alarm in her expression. "What? You see her all the time."

"It's normal for me," Sam replied. "Seems like you're seeing things more and more. Like the line is getting thin."

"What does that mean?"

"The line between you and them. Between here and… I don't know what it means."

"Nothing good, judging by your expression."

She ran her hands through her hair vigorously.

"We've got to figure this out, William."

"You really think he has the book?"

"He must. Not anywhere obvious, or I would have seen it."

"So he hid it," Will said, letting them both chew on what that meant. "You're going to ask him for it?"

"No." She shook her head firmly. "I'm taking him to his doctors day after tomorrow. GP and heart. I drop him and pick him up later. He can be there two hours or more."

"And you plan to ransack his cabin in the meantime."

"You don't have to put it like that."

"No, I think it's a fine plan," Will clarified, making sure he had her attention for what he said next. "There's just one thing."

"Yeah, what's that?"

"I'm going with you."

CHAPTER

SEVENTEEN

The sidewalk was scattered with orange and brown maple leaves. Overhead, the oaks were touched with russet, but most clung stubbornly to their green. The promised documents from Beth had come the previous day. Will filled them out, dropped them into the out-of-town mail slot and had just left the post office when he caught sight of Eddie Price across the street.

Eddie had gotten paunchy, and his black hair was streaked gray. But he was still a large man who moved with dangerous self-assurance. Will watched him go into the Green Apple convenience store, then crossed the street after him. He had no plan, but his instinct said the opportunity should not be wasted. He stood by the store's entrance for a minute, then looked around. No police cruiser. He had almost stopped thinking about Jimmy. The street was lined with tightly parked vehicles, and he tried to figure which one was Eddie's. Probably the blue Ford pickup. Will peeked in the windows, as if to find evidence of foul play.

A moment later he heard boots scuffing and the creak of a leather jacket, and turned to see Eddie approaching, carrying a paper bag with a lime-green apple on it. The big man wore a pissed-off expression, his mouth opening to tell off whoever was peeking into his truck. When he recognized Will, he went back on his heels and his jaw snapped shut. Hardly missing a stride, Eddie stepped into the street and went around to the driver's side without speaking.

"Eddie."

Will went the other way, around the hood, and they met at the driver's door together. The older man was half a head taller. His close-set eyes looked Will up and down with something like contempt. He shoved the bag of groceries into Will's chest. Will caught the bag just before Eddie let go, then the big man opened the door and got in.

"How's your mom?" Eddie asked, in a voice wrecked by cigarettes. His knee seemed to bother him, and it took a little while to get settled in the driver's seat.

"Good," Will said. Sick to death of the question. "She's good. Unfortunately for you."

"What the fuck does that mean? I never wished her any ill."

"Yeah, but maybe I'd sell you the house cheap, with her out of the way."

"There was nothing cheap about that offer. It's more than anyone else will pay."

"Maybe she doesn't want your money," Will suggested. "Maybe she likes her house."

"That moldy, falling-down piece of crap?" Eddie gestured for the grocery bag, and Will handed it back to him. "If any house needed demolishing, it's that one. I'll drive the bulldozer myself."

"What about the Hall house?"

"What about it?"

"It's a beauty," said Will. "But you want to knock that one down too, right?"

Eddie pursed his lips, considering. Will could not imagine what.

"If that's what bothering you," Eddie said after a moment, "we can work that out."

"What do you mean?"

"I mean, if I left the Hall house alone, would you consider selling your mother's?"

What sense does that make? Will wanted to ask. *The Hall house has four times as much property. And I don't own either of them. How can I make a deal with you?* He heard Sam's voice, as if she were beside him. *You're getting distracted.*

"I need to talk to you," Will said. "Not about houses."

"Like the talk you had with Jimmy Duffy?" Eddie replied, sneering. "Is that the kind of talk you had in mind?"

His dark eyes bored into Will's for two or three seconds, then looked away. The muscles in his face quivered oddly. *He's afraid of me,* Will suddenly realized. *This lumbering, bullying psychopath is afraid of me.*

"Jimmy and I had a misunderstanding."

"Yeah, well, I'd just as soon not have one of those."

"These questions. I think you may be the only person who can answer them."

"I had nothing to do with it," Eddie barked, slapping a thick hand on the steering wheel. "I was just there. It was that silly bastard brought all this on."

"I know," Will agreed. "But he's not around for me to ask anymore."

"A lot of people aren't around anymore."

"Come on. I am not the angel of death."

"Tell those others that," Eddie shot back. "Heard you went to see Molly Jordan."

"Yes, and guess what?" said Will. "She's still breathing."

"For now."

"Listen to me."

"*You* listen," the big man insisted, leaning toward the door handle, which Will was blocking. He stepped aside and Eddie slammed the door hard. "I won't go down easy. Not like the others, all right? I can take care of myself. I've got a gun under the seat right now."

"Good for you," said Will.

"Got more at home. I don't care if you're a good guy, a bad guy, or if you mean to do it. I don't care if it's just something that *clings* to you. That doesn't matter, does it? Dead is dead. Don't come near me again. Don't come near my truck, my house. You do, and I swear I'll kill you. Understand? Next time I see you, I'll kill you."

Will nodded. Then stepped closer to the window, meaning to say something conciliatory.

"Not if I see you first," he said quietly. He had no idea why he said it.

Eddie looked at him closely. Like Jimmy had done that night. Then his eyes went big and he looked away fast.

"You sonofabitch," he whispered, turning the ignition and roaring the big machine to life. "Why did you mess with that stuff?"

The rear tire nearly ran over Will's feet as the truck pulled away. He was left standing in the middle of the road. Feeling that mean smile on his face, which he quickly removed. Feeling also like he had overheard a conversation between two other people.

Sit. Only that. No words, no thoughts. Just sit and be with yourself.

My knees.

The body complains, yes? The mind too. Ignore them. Sit with the pain. Sit with the thoughts. Do nothing. Say nothing. Breathe, if you must, nothing else. Shut up and sit.

But he has to rise. The room is dark and he goes to the moonlit window. The figure is there, by the bushes. First a shadow, then a girl, then a shadow once more. Back and forth it flickers. Darkness, golden hair, darkness again. What does it mean? It cannot be both things, can it? He leans closer to the window...

And came awake. Will stood in the middle of his room, wondering how he had gotten there. Something disturbed his sleep. A cry. Cats fighting in the bushes? He heard it again. Distant, human. Samantha? No, he was dreaming about her, that's all. He went to the window and gazed across the field. There was a single light on at the Hall place. First floor, maybe the study. At two o'clock in the morning? The light wobbled, and he heard the cry a third time.

He dragged on his jeans and, what seemed a moment later, was flying out the kitchen door, no memory of coming down the back stairs. Cold air prickled his bare skin, weeds and pebbles stabbed his feet. Yet he ran as fast as he could, because she was in trouble.

The pine branches raked him, scraping his ribs. A narrow branch caught him above the eye. He saw or sensed movement near her front door before he was even through the trees, but once he reached the porch he saw nothing. Will stopped halfway up the steps, nearly hyperventilating. Sounds caught his ear from every direction. A small creature scuttled through the shrubs below. The wooden stairs creaked underneath him. What might have been footfalls echoed around the side of the house and he took two steps in that direction. Then saw that the door stood several inches ajar. He pushed it open and slipped in.

There was, in fact, a dim light coming from the study. He went to the door to see the desk lamp on the carpet, the glare right in his face. A chair was knocked over, and a fat book—the Latin dictionary—lay facedown, pages mangled. It took him a moment to see Samantha. Sitting on the floor in the corner, her face in shadow. He moved toward her and saw her flinch. Saw her fold more tightly into herself. She had said nothing when he entered the room. Had not cried out to him for help. She remained as still as possible, as if hoping to be missed.

"Sam," he said, continuing toward her. Slowly, carefully.

He could see her clearly now. She wore only a white T-shirt and underwear. Her eyes were wide, and her hand clutched something. A letter opener. She held it out in front of her, like a dagger. Looking like she would strike him if he came closer. Will crouched down about four feet away.

"Hey, Sam, it's me. It's Will."

Her eyes softened. She dropped the weapon with a rattling clang and reached for him. He crawled over and took her in his arms. She grasped him fiercely, as if fearing being dragged away. Will fumbled for words, but his mind was distracted. Disturbed by her behavior, and listening for noises elsewhere in the house. His knee hurt and there was dampness on his brow.

"It was here," Sam finally rasped.

"Someone was here?"

"It was here, in the house."

"The shadow," he said. So that they would not have to use that other word.

"Yes," she answered, voice trembling. "I felt it, in my sleep. Then I woke up, but the feeling stayed. I thought it was looking for something. I came down here."

"Jesus, why? You should have…"

"I feel safer in this room. The energy is stronger."

He looked down at her bare legs, folded under, then saw marks on the floor. A circular shape scratched into the boards surrounding her. Using the letter opener, no doubt.

"You did a protection spell."

"It had been here already, scattering things. I could feel it moving through the house."

"Sam." His mind was not willing to face what was becoming plain to him. "When I came into the room, you were frightened of me."

"I thought it had come back. You came in and I…"

"But I don't look like a shadow," he said, a plea in his voice he had not intended.

"Sometimes," she whispered. "When you're angry, I feel the same energy in you. You feel the same way it feels."

He began, unconsciously, to release her, but she held on even tighter.

"Will, I have to tell you. I was afraid to before, I didn't want you to hate me."

"I couldn't hate you."

"This is my fault," she said, head still pressed against him, speaking into his chest. "When you call a demon, you have to command it. You have to tell it why you brought it, what you want it to do. If you don't, it overwhelms you. It does what *it* wants to do. It's free."

Why was she telling him this?

"When you came to me in the field," Sam went on, her words rattling around inside his rib cage. "When I saw the demon with you, I knew I had to do something. I didn't know the rules then, not exactly. But I could sense it waiting. Waiting for me to speak. I knew I had to give it an order or something bad would happen."

"What did you say? Sam, what did you ask it to do?"

"Protect you. I commanded it to protect you."

The words he remembered her uttering that night. Things made sense now. He had not been able to understand why the coven's act had become attached to him. Not to any of them, but to Will. Why would they have done that to him? But they had not. Samantha had.

"I'm sorry," she said. "I'm so sorry."

"You were very young," he replied calmly. "And scared. You were brave to do that. It was quick thinking. Who knows what would have happened if you didn't."

"It was a terrible thing to do to you. I didn't understand."

"So they were right," Will said with resignation. "All of them. It's been me all the time, doing this stuff."

"Not you."

"It's the same thing, though. The question is how it interprets the command. It must see the coven members as my enemies. It must think killing them protects me."

"Wait," Sam said, her voice growing stronger. "We don't know that. We don't know that it has anything to do with those deaths. You keep thinking of everyone else. You need to focus on you. All we know for sure is that you're haunted, and we need to free you."

The dampness on his brow dripped into his eye, and he blinked against the sting.

"You're bleeding," said Sam. Her head was tipped back, looking at his face. She put two fingers to his forehead, touching the wound. It should have hurt, but instead it felt soothing. "And here," she said, noticing the scrape on his chest. She put her lips to it, warm and soft, and the soothing was there too.

Stroking her back, his hand had gotten under her T-shirt. Caressing her skin, and the knobby path of her spine. He pressed more firmly, working from her tight shoulders down to the flesh around her tailbone. Her lips moved slowly across his chest. Spreading that soothing, and other sensations, as well. He pulled the T-shirt up and off as she unbuttoned his jeans, and they fell awkwardly on their sides. Kneeing and elbowing each other without complaint as they pressed relentlessly together.

CHAPTER
EIGHTEEN

He sat on the front steps, drinking coffee. Waiting for Sam to keep her promise.

Normally a late sleeper, Abigail had been up early that morning. Early enough to see Will stumble through the kitchen door in only his pants. If she had been worried about his absence, she did not let on. All she said was good morning, though he detected a smirk on her face as she filled the ancient kettle. Of all the local women, Abby was the only one undisturbed by his relationship with Sam. Given his mother's judgment about people, Will wasn't sure that was comforting. However, he had pretty much established that Samantha was not the dangerous one. He was.

Sam had patched his wounds last night. After they had

finished grinding each other into the study floor, but before they got started again in her bedroom. She was shy after the first time. Regretful, he assumed, yet she asked him to stay. He had no intention of leaving and lay down chastely on top of the blankets beside her. Within ten minutes, her hands came looking for him.

The hot shower stung both wounds, but the damage seemed superficial in daylight. Perhaps her witchy ministrations accelerated healing. He discarded the bandage and swept his hair over the cut. Then he got dressed and went down to make small talk with Abby, before taking his coffee out onto the steps. It was pushing eleven, and he was beginning to think Sam had changed her mind, when he saw her white Honda roll down the street. He hurried down the walk and slipped into the passenger seat. Sam pulled away fast, nearly spilling what was left in his mug. She did not look at him.

"I was starting to worry," said Will.

"I always sit with him in the waiting room," she answered tightly. "They took a while getting to him today."

"Will we have enough time to search?"

"I don't know," she grumbled. "Lost twenty minutes swinging back here for you."

"But there will be two of us looking now."

"Anyway, I'm the one picking him up, so I can delay. Not too long, he gets a little crazy waiting."

Three hours earlier she had been tender, defenseless. Stroking his hair and smiling, asking him not to go yet. He had to remind her of the plan, that she was going to be late taking Tom to his appointments. Now she was cool and distant. He should not have been surprised, this is how it often went with women. The delayed-action panic at having exposed their feelings. Somehow, he had expected Sam to be different.

"I'm sorry," he said, "if, um, if last night wasn't what you wanted. You were vulnerable and I shouldn't have—"

"Shut up," she said. "You think that was your decision?"

He felt slapped, but kept quiet. Her right hand slipped off the steering wheel and found his left, squeezing firmly.

"Don't be sorry," said Sam. "It was wonderful. I haven't done that in a long time."

"Me neither."

"I don't mean that's the reason it was wonderful," she added quickly. He squeezed back, not risking words. Knowing she would continue. "It's just, I don't know. I don't know if we were supposed to do that."

"There's no right or wrong about it," he replied. "It's something that happened. It doesn't have to happen again."

"That would be sad. I think what it is…"

"What it is," he said, pitching in after four or five seconds of silence, "is that you don't want to lose a friend over a fuck." She didn't reply, but he could see that he was near the mark. "But you're not going to, okay? Whatever happens, things will be all right between us."

"People say that, then later it gets ugly."

"I'm not Jimmy."

"Jimmy's not a bad guy," she said. "Sex complicates things."

"It's not sex that does that."

They were quiet then, but it was a companionable silence. She did not release his hand until they hit the steep road leading to Tom's place. Mount Gray was a large, pine-and-boulder-strewn hill, stuck between the highway and ocean. The top and inland side were public land, used for hiking and climbing. On the ocean side there were a hand-ful of houses, and Tom Hall's was the highest and most isolated of those. The Honda swayed and spun several times on the gravelly surface, Sam fighting with the wheel.

"You really come up here twice a week?" Will asked in dismay.

"Sometimes. Why do you think my car is kicked to crap?"

At length they pulled into the circular drive, which was big enough for many vehicles. The only one there now was an old forest-green Jeep, covered in pine needles.

"Now that's what you want for this road," said Will. "Why don't you switch with him?"

"I should," Sam agreed. "He almost never drives it." Her voice had gotten quiet. Like the house might be listening. Or the trees. She popped her door open. "Come on."

The "cabin"—which was easily as big as Will's mother's house—was hard up against the slope, even partway into it, and built on two levels, one slightly above and behind the other. With its low profile and russet shingles, the place was nearly invisible among the pines and pin oaks. A carpet of brown pine needles completely absorbed their footsteps, making Will uneasy. The cause was not hard to determine. The stealthy approach made him feel like a thief, which is what he was. Sure, he needed that book, more than Tom did at this moment. And it would only trouble the frail old man to confront him. Yet there was no escaping the fact that they were here to take something that was not theirs.

Sam stopped in front of the door. He heard her whis-per a few words. Then she touched the doorknob tenta-tively before inserting the key. In another moment, they were inside. The front of the house was one large room.

A kitchen and dining area on the right, a spacious living room on the left, with exposed crossbeams overhead. And above that, a slanted ceiling with two large skylights, letting in what sun the trees allowed. If it was an old house, it had been remodeled within the last ten or twenty years. Yet the furnishings were simple, even shabby. There were rips in the sofa and mildew on the walls in several places. At the back, there were three doors, and stairs going to the upper level. Bookcases and books, of course. Some looked old, but not old enough, and there were not nearly as many as Will expected.

"Cozy," he said.

"I guess," she conceded. "He seems to like it."

"Where do we start?"

"Not the bookshelves," Sam answered, seeing his eyes focused there. "I checked those already. Besides, he wouldn't put it someplace so obvious."

"Dark red cover, a foot square, no exterior markings," Will said, repeating her description while scanning the shelves anyway. Maybe she had overlooked it, or maybe there were other tomes of interest.

"That's what I remember. You look here, I'll check the bedrooms."

"We should stay together," he objected as she started for the stairs. "You might see something I miss, and vice versa. We need to be systematic."

"I have my own system," she tossed over her shoulder, continuing up.

Will wrote it off to her discomfort in being here, but it was still frustrating. They needed to work as a team. He went to the bookshelves, making sure his eyes touched every spine. If they were jacketed and approximately the right size, he took the jackets off for a better look. History, biography, essays, books on Renaissance and Baroque art. It was a hodgepodge, and the books were covered with dust. Will had the strong impression that Tom Hall didn't read much anymore. There was not enough room to hide such a large book behind the others, but he looked just the same. Nothing.

End tables, sofa cushions, oak buffet. Nothing. The kitchen was unlikely, but Will gave it a cursory going-over. Then he tried the doors. To his surprise, none led to a basement. One was a bathroom, one a closet, the third a small bedroom. Barely furnished. A single bed, a dresser and a shelf of brown paperbacks. Dorothy Sayers and Eric Ambler. For guests, no doubt. Though it didn't seem likely Tom had guests up here.

They had been searching nearly an hour by the time he emerged from the spare bedroom, to find Sam back in the living room. Arms out, eyes closed, turning a slow circle in the center of the worn Oriental carpet. Will said nothing to distract her, but she stopped at the point where she was facing him and opened her eyes.

"Come here."

He obeyed, stepping to within a few feet of her. She grabbed him by the shirt and pulled him closer.

"Stand right here. Good. Now close your eyes."

"Why?" he asked, but complied.

"What do you feel?"

"A headache coming on."

"Here," she said, slapping his gut. "What do you feel here? Or behind your eyes. At the base of your throat. If I can do this, so can you. What do you feel, standing right here?"

A presence. Palpable. Malevolent. His old friend was back. Not that Will thought it had really gone anywhere.

"The floorboards are uneven," he said, swallowing his unease.

She sighed in annoyance. But when he opened his eyes, he saw her testing the truth of his statement, shifting her weight back and forth.

"You're right," said Sam. "There's something under here. Come on, we need to move the carpet."

They went to the sofa, knowing they would have to drag it back in order to roll the carpet. Bent over, grabbing either end, they both saw the figure at the same moment. The gray hair had gone white, and the blue eyes behind their thick lenses were expressionless. Not alive with that remembered intelligence. Yet Will had no trouble recognizing Tom Hall after all these years. Sadly, the reverse did not appear to be true.

"Dougie?" the old man said, gazing hard at Will, something like fear in his voice.

Sam looked sick, and Will half expected her to run out of the room. She mastered herself and stepped up beside him.

"No, Grandpa, this is Will. Will Conner. You know, Abigail's son."

"Will." Tom's features softened immediately. "How are you?"

"I'm well. I'm very well, Mr. Hall." He felt sick himself now, ashamed of them both. Why hadn't they just played it straight and asked for what they wanted?

"What are you doing here?" Sam asked.

"Doctor Gardner's office didn't have the appointment written down," the old man answered, turning and heading for the kitchen. "So it was just Doc Miller today."

"How did you get home?"

"Jimmy was there, with his father. He gave me a ride."

Will had the impulse to rush to the window and see if Jimmy was lurking. He could see from Sam's face that she too was disturbed by the coincidence of her ex-husband delivering her grandfather here just at this inopportune moment. The only one not troubled was Tom, who had not even asked them what they were doing in his home.

"Does anyone want coffee?" he said, taking a bag of beans out of the freezer.

"I'm good," answered Will. "Had plenty this morning, thanks."

Tom looked disappointed and put the bag down.

"I suppose it's early for a drink," the old man said. "Willie, how are your classes going?"

"Will's a professor now," Sam replied, still looking unsure what to do. How to take back control of the situation.

"I know that," Tom rebutted. "He still has classes, doesn't he?"

"They're going fine," Will said. "I teach Survey of American Literature for freshman. And a seminar on myth and folklore." He could see that Tom was only half listening. Looking around the kitchen, puzzled. Their presence had thrown him after all, yet he seemed unclear on the cause of his confusion. "You know," said Will, "it's noon. I could go for a drink."

He felt lucky that Sam was so in control of her infernal powers. Otherwise, the look she gave him surely would have caused instant death. Tom, on the other hand, brightened again and went looking for a bottle. They sat in the living room. Sam commandeered the whiskey and poured two tiny glasses of the amber stuff for herself and Tom, and a spitefully large one for Will. Tom stared at his glass a few moments as if he wasn't sure what to do with it, then fired the contents down in one gulp. He closed his eyes a moment. When he opened them again, some hint of the wise old professor he had been returned to his face.

"Bibamus, moriendum est," Tom said, in that strong baritone Will remembered.

"Indeed," Will replied, though the choice of toast was unnerving. *Drink, for we must die.* He did not empty his own glass, but he took a deep gulp. The smoky fire burned his gums, and a calming heat filled his chest. Sam did not drink.

"Now," Tom went on, settling back in his creaking chair, voice friendly. "What are you two looking for?"

Will was about to speak when Samantha finally did.

"That old spell book," she said. "The one Johnny was obsessed with."

"Yes," Tom replied. "That. He wasn't the only one, was he?" he added, cutting his eyes at her.

"I only cared because you two spent so much time with it."

"I was indulgent with Johnny." Tom shook his head a bit ruefully. Will wanted him to go on, but Sam jumped in again.

"Do you still have the book?"

"Well. Haven't seen it in years. Let me think…"

"Mr. Hall," Will said tentatively, when it was clear that no amount of thinking was going to bring a swift answer.

"Please," the old man said. "Call me Tom."

"Tom." It felt odd, but why not? The professor's calm, scholarly presence had brought back some part of Will's own paralyzed rationality. "What is the book?"

"What is it? Oh, you know, old family stuff."

"Excuse me, but I think of old family stuff as, like, family trees and recipes."

"There are recipes in there," chuckled Tom. "As I remember. Some botany, herbology. Thoughts on our relationship to other people. To the world. The physical and the spiritual one. People put that kind of knowledge in books once. It's certainly not unique of its kind."

"There are spells," Will said. "Are there not?"

"There are rituals for various purposes. Prayer. Healing. Conjuring. You could call them spells, I suppose."

"And do you believe in their efficacy?" he asked, leaning forward. "Do you believe they possess actual power?"

"Words have power," the old man said, looking him in the eye now. "You know that."

"They have the power we give them," Will countered.

"True. To a degree. We are not unarmed. A strong will can decide to succumb or resist. But strong language will still shake a powerful mind, and overwhelm a weak one. Therefore it follows that the words themselves have power. Maybe a lot of power, over people or things unequipped to resist them."

Sam was right. The motor functions might be shaky, the short-term memory gone. But behind that superficial damage, the professor's mind was sharp as ever. Will's pleasure in finding it so was mixed with unease. If Tom was in a condition to answer for past oversights, Will had no good excuse not to confront his former mentor.

"Was Johnny's mind weak or strong," he asked. "Was it equal to those powerful words? To those spells?"

"Johnny was a dreamer," Tom said, with that regretful shake of the head again.

"And were you not aware of that at the time?" Will pressed. Sounding like a prosecutor. "How could you let him play with a book like that?"

"Will," Sam cautioned.

"No, it's all right," said the old man. "I wasn't careful enough with Johnny, that's true."

"You tried to help him," she said protectively. "I remember."

"I mistook his enthusiasm for strength," replied Tom. "But it wasn't in him. I should have guided him more wisely."

"Guided?" Will said. "You should have locked the book up. If you honestly believed in its power, you should have burned it."

"Really?" Tom asked, appearing genuinely curious. "Is that what you would have done? Burned a book? Knowledge isn't for hiding, William. It's there to be explored. Even expanded upon."

"All knowledge? The knowledge to summon demons?"

"Well, we all have our demons," said the old man quietly. Just a hint of a smile on his face. "I bet yours are more interesting than mine."

Will had to give his anger hard rein. However normal Tom seemed, his faculties were surely compromised. He likely had no memory or comprehension of what Abby and Will had suffered because of Johnny's reckless act.

"You have no idea what you're talking about," was all he said.

Tom put up a placating hand.

"I'm not making fun of you. I don't know what you've been dealing with. I don't keep up. Sam tells me things, but…" He shrugged.

"I'm not asking you to feel sorry for me," Will replied.

"Of course not."

"I'm asking for your help in getting rid of something dangerous."

"And that's what I'm getting at," said the professor, finger raised for emphasis. "You say 'dangerous.' Well, all right, you're the one to know. But I'm asking you to think about how much trouble we get ourselves into with our own ideas. Our preconceptions. Our fears."

I think I've heard this speech, thought Will.

"To the Greeks," Tom continued, "a daemon was an intercessor between men and gods. Perhaps a god itself. No evil connotation. Plato equated the term daemon with knowledge. Socrates had his own personal daemon who spoke wisdom to him and kept him from making errors. Didn't control him, mind you. Didn't tell him what to do. Just guided him."

"That's metaphor," Will said. "The unconscious speaking to the conscious."

"Well of course it is," Tom agreed, sitting back again in the creaking chair and smiling. "Unless it isn't."

"You believe there's more to it?"

"That's it." Tom shot a finger at him. "More to it, that's all I'm asking you to consider. Do I believe in Zeus up on a mountaintop, white beard and lightning bolt in his hand? Sending messengers down among us mortals? No more than you do. No more than I think Saint Peter is waiting for me at the Pearly Gates. It's the Christians that made daemons into demons. Devils. Something evil. You must have read this stuff if you teach it."

"Yes," Will said, trying to keep his cool. "But I read it, and teach it, as myth."

"Well and good," Tom fired back, heat coming into his face and words. "But now that *myth* has come and bitten you in the ass."

"Grandpa, stop," said Sam, badly distressed by the exchange.

"Now you're thinking there might be something more going on," the old man continued. "But where do you go for an explanation? Christian fantasy and propaganda. Instead of that older, purer understanding of the phenomenon. That's what Johnny was after. That's what every true seeker hopes to find. Contact with those messengers who used to bring us knowledge and comfort."

Will closed his eyes and breathed deeply.

"You don't understand. This isn't something I've chosen. It's imposed itself on me. And there is nothing comforting or enlightening about it. It's dark and ugly."

"It's a heavy load," Tom replied, pity in his voice. "I have no doubt. But what you're describing isn't the thing itself. It's your fear. It's your resistance."

"Resistance to what?"

"To whatever message the daemon is trying to deliver."

"It's trying to give me a message?"

"Could be," Tom said, less certainly. "Only you know that."

"I assure you I know no such thing."

"Then you had better figure it out, young man."

Another deep breath was required. Will could continue this sparring, but to what purpose? The Tom Hall who lived in his mind, the wry, wise surrogate grandfather who would have talked him down off the ledge of this madness, did not exist. Perhaps he never had. The man before him was what remained, and this man was as deeply owned by seven families' mysticism as any of them. The Price women. Samantha. Eddie, Jimmy, Molly, his mother. Even Will's own voice of reason rang hollow to him.

"If you two have finished," said Sam urgently, "can we please get back to the book?"

"The book." Tom turned to her as if she had just appeared, his eyes fluttering slightly. He went back and forth between the younger people, seeking for an explanation, his face beginning to go slack. They were losing him. "The book is no good to you."

"Why not?" Will asked.

"It's no good to you without a name. You need the name."

Sam knelt down next to Tom's chair, taking his hands in hers.

"We think we know the name."

His blue eyes fixed on her with a wild intensity, magnified by the thick lenses.

"You do?" he whispered.

"We need the book, Grandpa. It's very important. Please."

He nodded several times, a wobbly, jerky motion.

"You know," Tom mumbled, looking away from her now. Leaning away, even. "You know, I think I got rid of that old book after all. I think maybe I gave it to someone."

"No," she said softly, shaking her head. Willing it not to be true.

"I need to lie down," he went on, his speech becoming as slack as his face. "This is too much for one day. Can you help me up the stairs, dear? And then, you and your boy should go."

* * *

The drive over had been tense, but there had been hope mixed with it. Some anxious expectation that they were on the verge of a solution. Perhaps also on the verge of a new phase of their relationship. The silence between them now was only grim.

"He's lying," said Will finally.

"Don't put it like that."

"How should I put it? He would never give a book like that away. He would never just lose track of it."

"He's old and confused," she said, biting off each word. Eyes fixed on the road. "And you were agitating him."

"*I* was agitating *him*?"

"Yes," Sam insisted. "Every time we go see someone, you pick a fight."

"Every time we see someone I get treated to a bucketful of condescending bullshit by people who are not living with what—"

"You spent all of his energy arguing philosophy, instead of focusing on what you needed."

It was "you" now, he noted. Not "we."

"Damn it, Sam, it was…" He made himself stop and take another deep breath. They were not helping his anxiety, but they might just keep him from saying more stupid stuff. "I'm not trying to fight anyone. But what they know is as important as what they have. We still don't completely understand this."

"And you never will. No one completely understands this stuff. That's the nature of it. If we only had that book."

"What do we do?" he asked. Knowing it was foolish, but not knowing what else to say.

"I'll go back and look again," she answered, half-heartedly. "On my own."

Will felt a gap opening, much wider than the two feet that separated them. She was withdrawing from him. Backing away. Whatever her professions of friendship, he had crossed a line. He had violated the space between her and the old man, which was still the most precious bond she possessed. Understandably so. But her sudden coolness grieved him more than he could express.

"I'm sorry," he said.

"What for?"

What indeed? For being himself? Or for everything that had happened, and was about to happen.

CHAPTER

NINETEEN

He sat in the crowded room, drinking watery beer and watching the dream die. Again. Muriel and Saul, seated on either side of him, were as quiet as Will, but the tavern's other patrons were not taking the matter calmly.

"What the hell are they doing?"

"Jesus, Grady, get him out of there."

On the television over the long wood bar, Pedro Martinez looked tired. He had gone seven strong innings, spoiled only by two solo homers by Giambi, and the Red Sox entered the bottom of the eighth up five runs to two over the Yankees. Game seven of the American League Championship. World Series berth on the line. But Pedro had thrown more than a hundred pitches, and it was time to turn the game over to Boston's superb bull pen. The announcers knew it. Everyone in the bar knew it. Everyone in New England, not to mention retirees in Florida and transplanted Bostonians all over the country and world, glued to their television screens, knew it was time to pull Pedro. The only person who did not seem to know was Grady Little, the Red Sox manager.

A double by the hated Jeter. Howls of protest in the bar. A single by Bernie Williams. Little bounced out of the dugout and headed for the pitcher's mound.

"Thank God," said Tony Pascarelli.

Tony had been the only one to greet him when Will and Muriel entered Murphy's. Muriel said he needed to get out, and demanded he join her to see the Sox victory in some public place. Will reluctantly agreed, but regretted it the moment they entered the crowded tavern. Faces turned away from his gaze. Did they fear a hex? Will didn't even recognize most of them, but they knew him, apparently. Saul Markowitz joined them at their table against the wall, probably out of pity. The favorable progress of the game distracted everyone, until the ill-omened eighth inning. Grady left the mound with Pedro still on it, and the momentary relief of the bar patrons turned to dismay.

"What is he *doing*?"

"He's got to bring in Embree to face Matsui. Got to."

But he did not, and Pedro gave up a double to the dangerous Japanese batter, bringing Jeter and Williams home. Posada's single tied the game. Will looked over at Saul, who only shrugged.

"A curse is a curse," he muttered.

Couldn't have said it better, thought Will.

The faultless Mariano Rivera stifled the Sox batters and

the game went to extra innings. The atmosphere in the bar turned hostile. Will could smell anger on the men and women around him. The way Sam claimed to smell it on him. A hot, rancid scent.

"Let's go," said Muriel abruptly. Not waiting for a reply, she stood and headed for the door. Will hesitated. You didn't leave a tie game between the Sox and Yankees—it was disloyal. Yet he felt more allegiance to Mure than to the Red Sox. He dropped twenty bucks on the table, nodded to Saul and got up. A few hard looks followed him to the door. Traitor.

On the car radio, they listened to Aaron Boone hit the game-winning home run. Listened to the crowd at Yankee Stadium celebrate wildly. Another chapter in the book of Red Sox futility. Muriel jabbed the off button.

"Wasn't their year," she said. With the equanimity of someone inoculated against disappointment by a lifetime's exposure.

"It's never their year," said Will. "You thought they were going to turn on me, didn't you? The gang at Murphy's. That's why you got me out of there."

Early in the game, Will thought he saw Eddie Price enter the bar and leave again, but he couldn't be certain. The day before he thought he saw Jane and Alice Hall walking hand in hand down the street, so he did not trust what his eyes reported. *The line is getting thin. Between you and them. Between here and there.* Despite her warnings and her guilt, Sam had not been in touch for two days. He didn't know if she was trying to find the book or trying to forget he existed. He didn't know which was better. Muriel did not answer his question.

"So this thing with Samantha has run its course?" she said instead.

It was not reasonable to think that there was a conspiracy to provoke him. It had to be coming from him. And it was like Muriel to be blunt.

"We're friends," he replied. "I hope that's not something that runs its course."

Muriel shrugged, simultaneously lighting a cigarette and rolling down the window.

"Depends," she said casually. "Hard to be friends with a crazy woman." Then a mad cackle that was uncharacteristic. "I should know."

"You think she's nuts?"

"She's a strange girl. You don't need me to tell you."

"You're not friends with Sam," he said, zipping up his jacket against the chill invading the car. But it was better than choking on her cigarette. "I thought you might be talking about my mother."

"I was making a little joke about myself, actually. I never called Abby crazy."

"What happened that day," he asked suddenly.

"Can't let it go, can you?" she sighed. "Your mom is the only person who can help with that. I was out in the car. I wasn't even in the house when the lightning hit."

They were at cross-purposes, but maybe this was the way. By misunderstanding his questions, she was giving him more interesting answers. Could he perfect the technique and apply it to others?

"You meant the day Abby fell down the stairs, didn't you?" Muriel said, catching on.

"Yeah, but you can answer either one."

"What a lousy choice. She was just having a bad day. It

was like she never woke up from the dream. She was talking to me, but she was seeing whatever was in her head. And then she gave me this look. This, this terrible look, like…"

In the blue light of the dashboard gauges, he could see pain in Muriel's eyes.

"Like you were evil," said Will. Knowing it was so, but not understanding how he knew.

"Yeah," she answered. "Like that. Then she was out the door."

"Poor Mure," he said. "I can't tell you how many times I've been looked at like that since I've come back here."

"You must like it," she grumbled. "You won't leave."

"Why were you out in the car that night?"

"Oh man, you're going to squeeze it all out of me, aren't you?" She was trying to locate her usual sarcastic tone, but her voice jumped with anxiety and grief. "We were going to get you out," she said, so fast he almost didn't catch it.

"Get me out? Who was?"

"It wasn't safe for you in that house. They were going to involve you in the ceremony. They were going to *use* you. We had to get you away from here, but it didn't work."

"What the hell are you talking about?" The car was losing speed and her pale face had a frozen look. Will thought suddenly of Molly Jordan. "Pull over," he said quickly.

But she was already doing it. Before they had completely stopped, she had popped her door opened and leaned out to retch. The chill that spread through Will's body had nothing to do with the cold air rushing in. Logic should have told him that if she was there for the aftermath—as he remembered—she would have been under the oath. But this was Muriel. The woman who didn't believe in any of that nonsense. If she was subject to such control, against her will and even her belief, then what else might be true?

She sat up. The fear gone from her face, looking more embarrassed than anything.

"Shouldn't have eaten those nachos. Friggin' Saul, he knows I can't say no. Could you get me a tissue, hon? In the glove compartment."

He handed her the packet and she wiped her mouth. Then closed the door and put the car back in gear. She didn't speak again for another minute or so.

"You're trying too hard," said Muriel.

"Am I?"

"Yes," she confirmed. "Half this stuff you think you need to figure out, you don't. You know all you need to. You just can't see it. Because you're missing one piece of information."

"Okay," he exhaled. "And that is?"

"Ask Abby about your father."

"My father?" It was the last thing he expected. "What does he have to do with this?"

"It's connected, trust me. But I can't tell you. It has to come from your mother—it's only right. She should have told you a long time ago."

Even as he considered just how resolute her refusal was, if there might not be a way to move her, something bothered him. And then he had it. "Your father" she had said. Not "Joe," which was the only way she ever referred to the man.

"Get your answer and then get out of here," she continued. "I'll drive you to New York if I have to. If you won't do it because of the danger to yourself, do it for the pain you're causing everyone else."

They had swung around the bend and were passing

Sam's house when he saw the police cruiser parked along the roadside.

"Stop," Will commanded. "Right here, stop."

She complied, with a huff of annoyance. Will looked hard at the police car, but it was empty.

"What?" Muriel demanded.

"This idiot has been following me around since I got here."

"Who?"

"Jimmy Duffy. This must be his cruiser, the door is even dinged where he...never mind."

Her cell rang before they could say any more. Muriel listened a moment.

"Yeah, he's with me," she said into the phone. "No, we're right down the street, what's up? Yeah, sure. Call me back when you can." She slapped the phone closed and put the care in reverse. "Your mom."

"And?"

"There's something going on at the house. Jimmy is there and she doesn't want you anywhere near—Will!"

He opened the door and stepped out before she could hit the gas. He half expected her to get out and chase him, but he didn't look back. In a few seconds he was running. That sonofabitch, harassing his mother now. He would break his other arm.

It was late; most houses on the street were dark. The porch light was on at his mother's place, and several lights inside the house, as well. Will had almost reached the stairs when he saw a dark shape moving swiftly across the side yard. He hesitated. Was that a flash of blond hair? Then he was running again, around the house and across the little field. Trying not to stumble. For just a moment he heard voices, calling back and forth urgently, but could make nothing out. A jagged line of tall shadows marked the edge of the woods behind the house and it seemed like the voices had come from there. Anyway, he could see nowhere else they could have gone. He dodged around the rosebushes and headed for the trees.

The yard had been dark, but beneath the oaks and pines it was nearly pitch-black and he had to slow down. Holding one hand before his face to prevent getting scratched again, he took careful steps forward. His feet made too much noise among the twigs and roots, but even so he could hear others. Feet kicking through leaves. A male voice cursing. He wanted to yell to Sam, but restrained himself. Moonlight opened little gray pockets among the trees and he waited to see a figure pass through one of them.

"Will?" Samantha's voice, far off.

"Over here," he called.

"Shut up," Jimmy ordered from somewhere closer. "Get down on the ground."

There was a hard, flat bang to his left and a simultaneous thunking sound near at hand. It seemed a long gap of time, but was likely only a moment later that his brain processed this as a bullet striking a tree. A tree quite close by. A bullet aimed at him. All the blood seemed to flush from his head into his legs, and he dropped dizzily to his knees. This was the right move, he knew, even if accidental. Then another quick *bang-thunk* made his whole body jump.

"Motherfucker." A deep, angry voice. "I told you to stay away."

Will found himself flat on his stomach, clutching the cold earth. Pine needles were in his mouth and his heart beat hard enough to shake the ground. His brain felt sluggish. Too stunned and starved of oxygen to even accept what was happening, let alone make a plan. After long deliberation, he lifted his head slightly and looked back along his body to see if any of it was catching the moonlight. No. So it was his voice alone that had drawn the shots.

"Devil boy." The angry voice was closer now, only a few yards away. The speech was slurred. "Where are you?"

"Cool it, Eddie," Jimmy called. "This is stupid."

"Stay out of it, you Mick son-of-a-whore."

Will could see the muzzle-flash from the corner of his eye as the gun boomed again. Both men were quiet then. He was about to risk a look around when something struck him in the side. The force of the blow, coupled with his terror, made him flip all the way onto his back. A tall shadow loomed over him. All Will could see clearly was the big boot that had kicked him, and the flash of moonlight off the pistol's blue steel.

"Get up," said Eddie Price.

"Why?" Will rasped. Embarrassed by his strangled tone. "You can shoot me just as easily down here." It must have been that other voice inside him that spoke—he would never say anything that stupid. Yet it sounded like him. "I didn't go anywhere near you. You came into the bar."

"Nah." He saw the big, shaggy head shake. "Last night, night before. Standing there across the street. You going to tell me that wasn't you?"

"That's what I'm going to tell you, yeah. You going to believe it?"

"No," Eddie said, aiming the pistol at him.

"Why didn't you come out and face me then?" said Will quickly. Desperately. "If you thought it was me, why didn't you come out and shoot me then? Skulking around my mother's house, you coward."

His senses became suddenly, painfully sharper. As if someone turned up the moonlight, and he could make out individual trees around him, make out Eddie's face. Sounds came from far away. Animals scuttling through underbrush, alarmed by the human intrusion. He could see or somehow feel all four of them where they stood in this small, mystical forest of his childhood, and he thought how funny it was that he should die here. A woman's voice spoke from a long way off, but he could hear it right in his ear. Chanting incomprehensible words.

He came back into the moment to see the arm with the pistol shaking. Whether in anger or fear, Will could not say, and guessed he wasn't going to find out. He only wished that something would happen before he threw up or pissed himself.

"Eddie, you stop right now," said Jimmy, very close. "Put that gun on the ground."

Eddie exhaled deeply. Like a man done wrong. Then he spun around fast.

"I told you to stay out—"

Two sharp bursts came from five yards away. Eddie staggered backward, stepping on Will's hand. Will managed to extract his fingers from under the heavy boot as the big man straightened up. Swaying, fighting for balance. Then he crouched deeply, rocking there a moment. Then rolled over on his side.

Jimmy came on slowly through the trees. A tight black shadow, his arms forming a V in front of him, meeting where they clutched the pistol. There was a loud thrashing of branches farther off.

"Is he down?" Jimmy asked.

"Yes," Will said, too softly. Then again louder. "Yes."

"Is the gun still in his hand?"

"I don't know," Will replied, starting to crawl toward the fallen man.

"Never mind, stay away from him."

The thrashing sound got closer. Coming this way, fast and recklessly, snapping branches and tripping on roots.

"Will," she called.

"I'm here," he called back.

"Both of you stay where you are," Jimmy insisted, hopelessly.

But the figure came weaving and stumbling on. Through the last cluster of saplings separating them. Not slowing down, Samantha tripped over Eddie's outstretched leg and fell headlong on top of Will.

CHAPTER
TWENTY

Mike Conti had been chief of the local police force almost twenty years. His haggard face said it had been a few years too many. Not that there was much crime, but the mysterious deaths among the troublesome seven families must have been frustrating to the lawman.

"Let's go through it one more time," he said, massaging his cheekbones with the thumb and forefinger of one hand, tugging down the gray bags under his eyes.

Six of them sat at the dining room table. Or five, as Muriel kept jumping up to answer the phone or make coffee. Like any of them needed coffee. Abigail seemed the most put together. Sam looked as wide-eyed and shaken as Will felt, and held his hand under the table. Even Jimmy was subdued, but then he had just killed a man. His hands were pink from washing them a long time under scalding water, but there were still bloodstains on his sleeve. He had performed chest compressions until the EMTs arrived, even though all three of them knew Eddie was dead. Now his pistol was in an evidence bag on the table and he would be taking a few more days off. Standard procedure in a shooting.

What was not standard procedure, Will felt certain, was the group of them sitting around getting the story straight. They should be giving separate statements out of earshot of each other. Mike was a good cop, everyone said, and went mostly by the book. But Jimmy was one of his men. Family. As was Sam, by extension and despite the divorce. The troublemaking Conners were being cut some slack, and anyway the matter seemed a clear case of necessary force, even if the circumstances were cloudy.

"I saw Eddie out in the yard," Abby recited, for the third time. Mike sighed. "Sorry," she said, "I saw a *big guy* in the yard, a little before midnight. I waited for him to leave, but he didn't. He was standing behind the oak, messing with something." The thing he was messing with was a very full gasoline can, the purpose of which no one knew, but everyone could guess. "That's when I called the station."

Jimmy was conveniently "in the area" when the call came through from the dispatcher. Eddie, presumably, had been awaiting Will's return, either meaning to shoot him or burn the house down, or possibly both. He slipped into the woods while Jimmy checked on Abigail, but Jimmy saw him and pursued. Seeing the commotion and fearing Will might be in trouble, Sam ran into the woods after the men.

"And what were you going to do?" Mike asked incredulously.

"I don't know," Samantha mumbled, embarrassed. "Talk to him?"

"Talk to a big drunken man with a gun?"

"Sam can be very persuasive," Abby said. Not helpfully, Will thought.

Mike swiveled his gaze to Will, the only person in the room who seemed to bring a hint of anger to those sad eyes.

"Why was he looking for you?"

"He had it in his head that…" Will fought to steady his voice. "He thought I was dangerous."

"Do you know why he would think that?" Mike pressed.

He didn't know how to answer the question honestly without getting into weirdness.

"I could take some guesses."

"Let's leave off guessing for now. Did you threaten him?"

"No." Yet he could hear that voice in his head. *Not if I see you first.*

"But he threatened you."

"He said he would kill me the next time he saw me."

"You think he meant to?"

"A couple of those shots barely missed," Will answered steadily. "Yeah, I do."

"But in the end he hesitated." It was true, he had. Chief Conti let that sink in, then continued. "You saw him turn and aim the gun at Officer Duffy."

"Yes," said Will, without hesitation. In truth, he had not seen Eddie raise the gun, and he strongly doubted—despite the man's murderous intent toward Will—whether he would have shot Jimmy. Yet there was no way for Jimmy to know that, nor exactly where the gun was pointed.

"The phone call said to stay away from the house," Mike

went on, boring in on him. "But you rushed over there anyway."

The implication was obvious, and Will had not needed the police chief's words to contemplate it already. If he had stayed in Muriel's car, Jimmy might have talked Eddie down. And the black sheep of the Price family might still be alive.

"I thought my mother was in danger," was all he said in reply. What he did not say is that he had expected Jimmy Duffy to be the source of the trouble, not the one to save him from his own headlong stupidity. He owed Jimmy his life.

The chief nodded. He could find no fault with a man running to his mother's defense. He stood, scratching at his curly gray hair. The rest of them rose instinctively as he did.

"Well, you should all get a little sleep now, if you can. I'll need all of you down at the station in the morning to make formal statements."

"You want me to stick around?" Jimmy asked Sam.

"Sorry," Mike intruded, looking pained about it. "I need you to come back to the station with me, Jimmy."

"Sam will stay here tonight," Abby announced. "We won't leave her alone."

Jimmy nodded, but it was unlikely that the idea gave him much comfort. Will reached over and touched his elbow.

"Hey. Thanks. You, ah…"

"Just doing my job," said Jimmy, turning to follow the chief out.

"Oh, and Will," said Mike casually. "I don't know what your plans are. I assume you're staying on to help out your mom for a bit."

"You're telling me not to leave town," Will said.

"More or less. Until we get this squared away."

"No problem," he replied. "Funny, though. That's just the opposite of what everyone else has been telling me."

"Yeah, well," said Mike, not unkindly. "Too late for that now."

Muriel shot Will a look equal parts anger and worry. She stroked his face before heading for the door, but it felt more like a slap. As Abby came into the room from seeing them all out, her cool finally melted. She smacked Will hard in the chest.

"I said not to come. I told Muriel, 'Don't let him come to the house.' Why don't you ever *listen* to me?" Then she put her arms around him. "We could have lost you."

He might have replied that the message was vague. Disturbingly so. More designed to bring him than keep him away, but it only would have made her feel worse.

"I'm sorry. But you didn't lose me, I'm right here."

"Where are you going?" Abby said abruptly, and Will realized that Sam had been sidling toward the back door.

"I'll be fine at my place," she said. Her face conveyed that she felt an intruder on this emotional scene. "Really, I prefer it over there."

"Not a chance," said Abigail forcefully. "You're staying with us."

Sam slumped her shoulders in resignation.

"I can sleep on the sofa."

"No," said Will, going to Sam and putting his arms around her, without any reserve or awkwardness. She squeezed him in return and he felt her full, warm shape against him. "You take my room, I'll take the sofa. You know I hate those damn stairs anyway."

* * *

No one slept on the sofa. Samantha rocked languorously atop him, forward and back. Breasts brushing his chest, hair gently swiping his face. Her breath falling heavily on his neck. She had climaxed a few moments before, though the only signs had been a sudden clenching of her muscles and her thumbs digging into his shoulders. The embrace of her wet heat was lovely, but he felt nowhere near release.

"You don't have to keep going," Will said.

"You don't like it?"

"I do. I just don't think I can get there tonight."

She kept rocking. Speeding up very slowly as she recovered. Kissing his neck, his ear, his lower lip. He closed his eyes.

"You did something in the woods," he said.

"Shhh."

"Some spell. I heard you from far off. You made him, you made…"

A ripple of pleasure went through him as she concentrated her efforts. Then another. Then waves of it, until all his fear, hurt and urgency went rushing to his center to be expelled. Leaving his mind empty for five or six blissful seconds. They were still for a while.

"Speaking of spells," Will finally said.

"Oldest one there is. You feel better?"

"Yes." She began to slide off, but he held her tight and she stopped. He was nearly asleep when she spoke again.

"The thing in the woods. I was too far away for it to work."

"No, he felt it. We both did. And he hesitated, just long enough. You saved my life. You and Jimmy both."

"I don't know about that," she said, as if there was choice involved. "But if *you* believe it, then that's a kind of gift." She sat up and looked at him. "Right?"

"Sure," he agreed. "Yes."

"What are you going to do with it?"

"I don't know what you mean."

"What do you want, William?"

"There's a question," he said, taken aback. "How do I answer that?"

"Any way you like."

"What do I want from my life?" It was the kind of thing she would ask, but what could he say? It seemed a foolish idea for anyone over twenty-five to contemplate. At a certain point your life just became about getting through it. "Right now, I want the people I love to be safe."

"Good. And after that?"

Christ, Sam, he wanted to shout, *I almost died tonight.* But she knew that. What better time to ask oneself such a question?

"Stability," he said, grasping for a response. And it felt true. "I never had it my whole life. Dad left when I was three. My mother was, well, you know. I couldn't count on anything. I want a stable life. Useful work to do and, and…"

"Wife and kids?" she said.

"I don't know about kids. I don't want to screw up some innocent little bastard."

"The way you were, you mean?"

"The way all parents screw up their kids. It's not malicious, just inevitable."

"It's not," she laughed. Lying down beside him, right up against him. For such a pale creature, she radiated heat.

He craved her heat, and he wondered if he would ever be warm again.

"So you see a future for yourself," she went on.

"You think I'm trying to get killed?" he asked. "Is that what this is about?"

"Not necessarily on purpose," Sam replied. "But you can pursue a goal so intensely, you know? So relentlessly that it doesn't leave room for a future."

"Like Eddie."

"Sure, like him. What would he have done if he shot you? Get shot himself. Go to jail. He wasn't looking past his fear."

"All I wanted was answers," said Will sadly. "I didn't want for anyone to get hurt."

She pushed herself up on an elbow and made him look at her. Her blue eyes were gray in the darkness, but still bright. Hypnotizing.

"Eddie murdered Doc Chester."

"We don't know that," he protested.

"You doubt it? I don't. He's been in plenty of trouble since. Threatening people about selling their homes. He was going to burn down your house! With you in it."

Will had been thinking about that. The gas can, and Eddie's words to him outside the Green Apple. Was it possible that the entire real estate scheme was an excuse to demolish this one house? As if somehow that would stop the demon, stop the deaths?

"This is how Eddie was going out," Sam continued. "You can't feel responsible."

"Of course I do."

"Well, you need to get over it. Eventually." She kissed

his forehead and looked at him again. "So you're not after revenge?"

"Is that what you thought?" he asked. "Is that why you've been keeping away?"

"I wondered. We all put a demon on you. Why wouldn't you want payback?"

"I don't want revenge," Will said. "I just want it gone."

"Good." His answers pleased her. Her old enthusiasm was coming back, in spite of this hellish night. She was resilient. Or was it something else? "I haven't been able to get my hands on the book. It's in the house, but in a place I can't get at with him there."

"Under the floorboards."

"Yes," she agreed. "I'll try again, but I need you to do something for me."

"Of course. Anything."

"Not anything," she said. "Nothing."

"You want me to do nothing?"

"That's right, and I know it won't be easy. But I'm asking. I'll beg, if that will help. I especially don't want you going anywhere near my grandfather's house. Do you understand?"

"This sounds like something more than just the book," he said warily.

"There are things I need to look into," she conceded. "By myself. I'm not going to tell you what, and I'm not taking you along. No offense, but your presence is more burden than help to me right now."

Her tone was gentle, but absolute. If he had more energy, Will might try to fight, but he felt done in. And he had made such a mess of things...

"Sam." He stroked her arm. "Don't do anything risky."

"No one is going to mess with me. I just need to do some poking around, and I need to get that book."

"So what do I do in the meantime?"

"Nothing," she enunciated clearly. "Keep your head down. Stay out of trouble for a few days. Can you do that?"

"A few days." The words reminded him that it was only that long until the anniversary of that terrible night. Anniversaries held power, didn't they?

"I know," she said, reading him. "But you haven't answered my question. Can you leave this to me for a couple of days? Can you trust me?"

How else could he possibly reply to that?

"Yes," said Will. "Yes, I'll leave it to you."

CHAPTER

TWENTY-ONE

He couldn't sleep until dawn. Then he couldn't wake, so it was late morning before the three of them reached the police station. And middle of the afternoon before they left. Jimmy gave Sam a ride home, and Will tried not to mind. He took the keys from his mother as they walked to her car.

"Any objection to a drive?" he asked, starting the engine.

"No," said Abby, "that's fine." She agreed like someone submitting to punishment. He decided on Crane Beach, though he was unsure why. Because they had been there as a family?

"How did that go?" she asked, after they pulled away from the station.

"All right, I guess. There was a homicide detective from Boston. I don't know if that's standard. They mostly wanted to know why Eddie felt threatened by me."

"What did you tell them?"

"That he thought I had something to do with deaths in the community." He waited for a reaction, but wasn't surprised not to get one. "There was no sense in not mentioning it. Jimmy practically accused me of the same thing, so Mike must know."

"Eddie was crazy," she said harshly.

You're all crazy, he thought. *And me along with you.*

"Jimmy doesn't believe you killed anyone," Abby went on. "Why would he?"

"Because a lot of your old pals have died. None of them older than midfifties, most of them much younger."

"Did you put the gun in Eddie's hand?" she demanded. "Did you pull the trigger? Did you skip out on a Little League game to push Doug Payson out the window?"

"Ma, come on."

"Can you cause heart attacks? Can you call lightning?"

"You don't have to convince me," he snapped.

"He's jealous of you and Sam."

"That's part of it," Will agreed. "Probably that's most of it. And no, by the way, I can't call lightning."

"I know," she said, turning her face to the window. "Not many people can these days."

"Wait. Don't tell me Jane Hall could."

"She said she couldn't," Abby replied. "More like she wouldn't. She wouldn't perform any act without a good reason. But her grandfather did."

"Seriously?"

"Jane used to watch. Of course, there have to be clouds—

you can't call it from the blue. So there's no way to know if it's coincidence. But she didn't doubt it. He'd speak the words, from deep down in his chest. And pull with his arm." She illustrated the motion she had never seen. A strong tugging action. "And it would come arcing down."

He was such a sucker. Even with everything he knew, the image seized his imagination. Some grizzled old Yankee scholar or gentleman farmer. Rolling up his sleeves after dinner and walking up the hill to pull fire from the sky, for the delight of his granddaughter. It was the kind of magic he sought in all the adventure stories and fairy tales he read as a kid. The kind he had ended up teaching. An escape from his ugly, ordinary life. But it turned out that there was no escaping the ugly part, even if the magic was real.

"Well, that fits the pattern," Will said. "Right? The women heal. Teach. While the men make trouble."

"No," Abby said, reaching over to pat his knee. "Don't you believe that. The men can be good and wise. And the women can be plenty dangerous."

Houses became more widely spaced. Rolling green pasture dominated the landscape. Old stone walls. An orchard, a barn. Gold and rust leaves on the distant trees.

"Muriel said I should ask you about my dad. 'Your father' is what she actually said. I don't think she meant Joe."

"No," Abigail agreed, "doesn't sound like it."

She let the admission sit there as they traveled in silence. Past Goodale Orchards, with the long row of red maples leading to the converted barn. Rows of cars parked on the grass, families shuffling off to get apples, cider, fresh doughnuts. Did understanding come then? Or was it in the hours since Muriel's words last night? *She should have told you a long time ago.* Or before that, when Tom Hall mistook him for Doug Payson? Was it possible that he had known for a very long time and had simply been avoiding it?

"I should have found someone sweet," Abby said sorrowfully. Down the back alleys of her own thoughts. "Someone gentle. I always went for big personalities. Fiery emotions. Like Joe, with his laugh, and his temper."

"And Johnny Payson. With his...what?"

"Charisma? Magnetism? Johnny was a big bright halo of hair. Like looking into the sun. Not a dollar to his name. On the run, and yet so calm, so confident. Like he had a secret no one else knew."

"So you couldn't resist. What happened?"

"Joe and I had an apartment right off the base in San Diego. They let Joe have it because we were married. He was just waiting to be sent over. Johnny came to stay for a few days. He was going place to place, crashing with friends. Joe didn't like him being there. Draft dodger. He never liked Johnny, though he put up with him for my sake. He was at the base that day, like every day. Johnny and me were sharing a joint, talking about home, people we knew. How terrible the war was. One thing led to another."

"I don't need the details."

"I was nineteen," Abby said defensively. "You have to remember that. I met your father when I was seventeen, married him a year later. Never slept with anyone else. Joe was different than I thought he would be."

"Violent?"

"Sadder. More scared. It came out as violence. And now he was leaving me, maybe to go get killed."

The road passed through an inlet of beige sea grass. Water was all around, and the flat blue line of ocean was just visible. They traversed a low hill, like an island in the grass. Gnarled apple trees climbed the slope on the left, and the hulking shadow of Hog Island was on the right. The Crane Estate was on a little turnoff ahead, the black gates shut today. Then the road swerved right toward the sea.

"Was it just that one time?" Will asked, hating himself for asking.

"That's all it took. After all the times Joe and I... Anyway, yes. I didn't tell Joe anything. I meant to, but I just couldn't. I had to call him in Hawaii a few weeks later to tell him I was pregnant."

"Did you know it was Johnny's?"

"I kept hoping it was Joe's, but I guess I must have known."

"When did Dad know?" Dad? Joe? Will didn't even know what word to use anymore.

"I don't know," Abby said sheepishly.

"You don't...wait, he *does* know, right?"

"Yes. I mean, we never discussed it, but it was clear to me that he knew."

"How could you have never discussed it?"

"Your father... You know, his violence was always directed at objects. He got in a bar fight, in the army, but he didn't hit me, or you." She glanced over quickly. "He didn't ever hit you, did he?"

Will could have said that the destruction of countertops and televisions had been easily as terrifying as being struck, but all he said was "No."

"The one time I tried to bring it up with him, about me and Johnny, he knocked me flat."

"Seriously?"

"Gave me a black eye," Abby confirmed, "but that was

nothing compared to the look on his face. I was absolutely sure that if I said one more word he would kill me."

Will parked very carefully in the empty lot, near the dunes, and shut off the engine. Sadness hummed in his chest.

"That's, um, rough. I never knew that, he shouldn't have—"

"Oh, for God sake, Willie, you don't have to apologize for him."

"When do you think he actually figured it out?" he made himself ask.

"Honestly?" She was quiet for a long time, as if she would not answer. Then she did. "As soon as he saw you the first time."

Don't start conversations you can't finish, Will told himself. He had never been close to his father, had despised the man for long stretches of time, yet he now felt unaccountably grieved by this knowledge, this decades-late sundering. "Is that why he left us?"

"No," said Abby quickly. "I mean, who knows about things like that? We got married too young, that's all. We didn't really know each other. I was afraid to talk to him. He met Patty working one of his jobs. They spent a lot of time together. And, you know…"

"Okay," Will said, nearly choking on the word. "When were you going to tell *me*?"

"I meant to," she whispered. "Many times. You really didn't know?"

"How would I have known?"

"I thought someone… Somehow, I thought you knew."

And somehow he had, although he could not say how.

They sat in silence for a while and he could feel her gently shaking beside him.

"So that guy who got zapped by lightning at the top of the stairs was my father."

"Biologically. Otherwise, Joe is your father. Your only real father."

"What was Johnny doing upstairs?" Will asked, ignoring the family sentiment. His mind circled the problem. Maybe it was an excuse not to think of the other stuff, but he didn't care. He wanted an answer. "Muriel thought I was in danger that night."

"Muriel," Abby sighed in exasperation.

"Yeah, Muriel. What was she doing outside in a car?"

"How should I know? Waiting for Johnny, I guess."

"She talked about getting me out of the house. She said 'we.' So someone inside was with her. She thought they were going to involve me in the ceremony."

"No," Abigail said, looking at him in dismay. Her eyes were red. "Of course not—nobody in that house was going to touch you."

"You don't know," he said sharply. "Because you were totally out of it."

"Oh, you are never going to let me forget that, are you?" she said savagely. "Are you?" Then she shouldered the door open and hopped out. Marching off toward the beach. He was about to follow when the ideas swirling in his troubled mind began to coalesce. He sat still, letting it happen, letting the picture form. By the time he had it, Abby had disappeared over the top of the dunes. Only then did Will get out of the car and follow.

The wind was off the ocean, and the milky sun threw little warmth. His mother had slowed down to a normal stride by the time he reached her. She did not look at him as Will came alongside of her.

"They drugged you," he said. "So you wouldn't interfere."

He watched her open her mouth several times in the next half minute. Wanting to object but failing each time.

"It did feel like being drugged," Abby said at last. Barely audible over the wind and surf. "That's exactly what it felt like. And I know I didn't take anything."

"Johnny was going upstairs to get me, for the ceremony. One of the women went after him, to stop him. Maybe Muriel's accomplice. That was the argument you heard."

She wrapped her arms about herself, squeezing tightly. Shaking her head over and over, though less in denial, it seemed, than resistance.

"They wouldn't have. They wouldn't."

"It doesn't need to have been all of them. There's no reason to think Molly or Jenny were involved, for instance."

"Those bastards," she said, the savagery back in her voice. He found the tone disturbing. "If they did that to me. If they were going to do something to you, they deserve every awful thing that's happened to them."

"Come on, now."

"I'm serious," she insisted. Then she turned to him. "But honey, I don't believe it was Johnny. Maybe someone there had bad ideas, but Johnny knew you were his son. He would not have hurt you."

"No?" What to say to that? "He may not have looked at it that way. But he was twenty feet from my bedroom door. While the ceremony was going on downstairs, he was upstairs. He was there for some reason."

"I could talk to Molly," she said after a few moments. "It's been years, but—"

"I talked to her," Will replied. "She told me what she could."

"There's Nancy Chester. I think that's it, I think we're the last three."

Will put his hands on her shoulders.

"She'll be bound by the oath. Like everyone else. Even Muriel, who was only there afterward. Eddie was our only chance, and he took care of that. I appreciate you trying to help, but the last thing I want is anybody else getting in the middle of this."

"What will you do?"

"I'm trying not to do anything," he said. "After all the trouble I've caused."

"They caused the trouble, not you. All of us did. I thought you had escaped it. I thought it was history now."

"Sam is looking into a couple of things." He didn't know how much to say about the spell book. Probably nothing. "She told me to sit tight."

"Do you trust her?" Abby asked.

"Why shouldn't I?" She made no reply and he did not press her. "It's cold out here. Let's head back."

Abby made no argument, and they turned and headed back up the sandy slope of dune. A huge black-backed gull took flight at their approach. It's shadow, more immense than the bird itself, hung over them for several long moments before it turned out to sea.

CHAPTER

TWENTY-TWO

Namaste, baby.

    Hey Johnny. How you guys doing?

  We're doing fine, ain't we, Murr? Hello, little man, come over here.

  No.

  What's the matter? Uncle Johnny's your friend.

  I don't like you.

  Hear that, Abby? The kid doesn't like me.

  He's just shy.

  Well hell, that's all right. I was a shy kid too. Just like you, Willie.

  My name is Will.

Muriel calls you Willie. Oh, but you like Muriel, right? I mean, who doesn't? I'm mad about her myself.

Give it a rest, John.

See how the women gang up on me? That's what they do, women. They gang up on the men. Overpower us with their righteous chi. You and me, we should be allies.

Don't go filling his head with junk like that.

I'm telling him how it is between the sexes. His dad ain't here, someone's got to do it.

My dad is a soldier.

Not anymore, he ain't. He's a general contractor.

He's not a general. He's a sergeant.

That's funny. No, what a general contractor does, he builds stuff for rich people. Because rich people always need more stuff.

Has he been drinking this morning?

Why are you asking her, I'm standing right here.

My dad is a soldier.

Have it your way. Is he off fighting another war? Is that why he ain't here, with his son?

He's in California.

A war zone if there ever was one. Class war against the Mexicans and Chinese. Which side do you figure your dad is on?

We should be going.

Fathers. They fuck you up, don't they, kiddo?

Stop it, Johnny.

This is what happens when you try to speak the truth. People want to shut you up.

Please, you wouldn't know the truth if it bit you in the butt.

Listen to her, huh? Nineteen and she already knows everything. You need to know something, you ask Muriel. The teenage sage. Understand?

Okay.

Come on, we're leaving.

What, we just got here?

I'll see you guys later.

Not if I see you first.

The adults turn their backs on him. A terrible change is taking place. He knows that when they look at him again it will be with hideous faces, and he must run. To the door? He cannot see one. The stairs? No, not the stairs. But out, somehow. He must go, now.

His hand striking the bedpost stung him to consciousness. The pillow was on the floor. The sheets were tangled around his legs. He had kicked himself awake. A thin line of light showed along the bottom of the window shade. And there was the lingering impression of half a dozen shadows, huddled around the bed. Who disappeared into the room's dark corners just as his eyes sought them.

"That's right, hide, you miserable…"

Will sat up, examining his reddened knuckles. He was collecting a fine set of bruises. Who knew that dealing with the otherworldly was so much like a street fight? He reached over and tugged the shade, sending it flapping upward. The blaze of light was dazzling. And yet even at midmorning, it had a yellowy autumn cast. The sun was already losing strength. The red and orange leaves would soon be brown, then gone. The tree limbs bare. The long season of darkness was coming. And today was the day.

* * *

Muriel slammed the Subaru's hatchback, where a load of gear was piled. She froze when she saw Will coming up the drive, as if he was one of the specters from his dreams.

"Do I look that bad?"

She smiled, shaking off the wariness.

"Would you believe I didn't recognize you for a second?"

"All too easily," he replied, leaning on the car, hands jammed in his pockets. Despite the sun, it was cold. "Off to your mom's again?"

She tipped her head sadly and walked over to him.

"This could be it. I'll need to be there as long as it takes."

"I'm sorry, Mure."

"She's done well for a Brown. Most of us don't make eighty. I sure don't plan to."

"Don't say that."

"I'm just sorry to leave you alone with these crazies," she said, brushing his hair lightly with the back of her weathered hand. "You know what today is, right?"

"The day Johnny died." He hesitated a moment. "Or do I say 'Daddy'?"

"She finally told you." Muriel seemed almost grieved by the news. "About time."

"You could have told me."

"Wasn't my place—it had to come from her." Which was true, of course. "Was it a bad scene?"

"No," he assured her. "It was all right. She seemed to think I already knew."

"Does it upset you?"

"It's strange, but so much is strange right now."

"It doesn't make Joe any less your father. But you know that. Poor Joe."

"That's funny coming from you," he replied.

"What? I got nothing against him. Except he's mean, and I can't forgive him for ditching you."

"Right, besides that."

"He hasn't had an easy time. How you doing? After the other night?"

"Well, I'm still here."

"Any more visits from Mike Conti?"

"Not so far."

"Soon as they give you the all clear," Muriel said, "get out of here and don't come back. This place is poison. These people. Every one of them can go to hell."

"Why don't *you* leave?"

He waited for the usual response. She had spent her whole life here. Some people were meant to go and some to stay. Instead, she surprised him again.

"I'm working myself up to it," Muriel said. She glanced at him mischievously. "Hey, maybe I'll crash with you in New York. What do you say?"

"My place is a dump," Will replied with a smile. "But you could have the couch for a couple of days."

"No, I'm kidding. I'm not fit to live with other people. Though maybe you and me could do it. I imagined that once, when you were little. Getting you away from all this."

"What, kidnapping me?"

"*Rescuing* is the word I had in mind. But thanks for making it sound creepy."

"Mure," he laughed, squeezing her shoulder. "You did rescue me. But that would have been illegal."

"Why did you come over here?" she asked.

"I don't know. Johnny said if I ever needed to know anything I should ask you."

"Johnny? When?"

"Last night," he replied, realizing his playful tone was not reaching her. "In a dream."

"Don't joke about that," she said, in almost-menacing voice.

"Who said I was joking?" But he could see that her menace was hiding hurt. "I'm sorry. It was just a bad dream."

"Johnny, huh? He told you to ask me something?"

Something new entered her voice. Curiosity, or even hope. This quick succession of disorderly emotions unsettled him. Clearly Johnny had been more than a casual fling for young Muriel, and he was sorry to have toyed with her.

"It was more like I was remembering stuff about him. Things he said."

"He was crazy about you, Willie. He never made a big show of it, but he loved you."

Will had to swallow back whatever surged up in him before he could speak.

"Is that why he was going to use me in his summoning? Because he loved me?"

"No, you've got that wrong."

"So correct me. Oh right, you can't."

"If you're talking about that silly oath," she said, biting off the words, "I don't give a shit about that." Did he believe her words, or her manner? Which was becoming more and more agitated. He did not want to hurt her, not Muriel.

"What is it you think you know?" she demanded.

"That Johnny was coming upstairs to get me when the lightning hit."

"You're right," Muriel said, leaning right into him. "To get you *out* of that house."

This was the problem with memory. It distorted everything. He could not reconcile the big, threatening Johnny of his dreams with the worried and loving man his mother

248

and Muriel were trying to sell him. If he could have, he would have figured this part out long before.

"Johnny was your accomplice."

"More like I was his. I was just your wannabe momma—he was your real dad. But neither of us trusted those nuts."

"Those nuts, like my mother?"

"Not her," Muriel scoffed. "She was just a mess."

Could this be right? Could it be the truth?

"Who was the leader, then? That night. If it wasn't Johnny, who led the prayer?"

She closed her eyes and stepped back.

"I wasn't in the house. Johnny didn't tell me everything."

"You have no idea?"

"I don't want you thinking about this."

"Too late," he shot back, advancing toward her. "If you weren't there, then you don't know if Johnny might have been doing it after all. Playing some kind of double game with all of you."

"No," she maintained. "He was pretending to go along with them, but he was only there to get you. We were going to take you somewhere, until things settled down."

"How would that have worked?"

"But they knew," Muriel said desperately, still backing away from him. Driving her fingers up into her hair and tugging back the skin on her face. "They knew what we were up to, and they killed him."

"No, it was the lightning."

"Yes, the lightning. And I was in shock. Sitting out there in the car, waiting for him. Waiting for you. Then seeing that white flash and hearing the screaming." She was going through it all again, hardly looking at him. "And when they told me, when *he* told me what had happened, and that I had to keep quiet, I just went along."

"Who?"

"Like a frightened child," she growled. "Like a coward."

"Who? Who told you to keep quiet?"

"That old man," she shouted. Then she turned on her heel, took three quick strides and collapsed. Will rushed to her side. She had fallen so heavily that he did not know what to expect. But when he got her sitting upright, her eyes were open, and her face was calm. He even detected a faint smile. As if she had come through the other side of something and was proud of herself. She tried to stand but he held her down.

"You're shaking," Muriel said. "It's okay, Willie, I'm fine. In fact, I've never been better."

"I shouldn't have made you speak about that."

"It's over," she said firmly, tipping her head back on his shoulder and looking up at him with a soft expression. Her eyes just inches from his. "That's all over now. Those words don't hold me anymore. It's broken."

Could it happen like that? One will overthrowing another? He wished he knew the rules. Sam would know. And where was Sam, damn it?

"Who was the man?" he asked cautiously, testing her truth. "The old man?"

She blinked a few times, studying him with those hazel eyes. As if whatever mental victory she had achieved had wiped away the last few minutes.

"Who led the ceremony?"

"I don't really know, honey. But I think it was Doc Chester. I'm pretty sure."

"And he's the one who made you take the oath?"

"Corralling us like cattle," she mumbled in disgust. "Which is what we were, I guess. Explaining how nobody outside the circle would understand. We had to keep it to ourselves. I don't think we knew what we were promising. I sure didn't."

Doc Chester. It made sense. He was the elder of the group, knowledgeable about other cultures. It was he and Johnny who had brought new ideas to the circle, new rituals. And Abby had said that he owned a ceremonial robe.

"He's dead," said Will. Muriel nodded.

"There's nothing for you to do," she said. "There never was. Now help me up."

Will relented and tugged her to her feet. After a moment or two of getting her balance she seemed fine. Better than fine. Flushed and energetic, and ready to fight the world.

"You should lie down for a bit," Will said.

"No can do. I got to hit the road. Couldn't forgive myself if she died without me there. I'm the last child left."

"You need me to come with you?"

"You sweet kid," she answered, reaching out and holding him by the shirt collar. "That would get you out of here, anyway. But no, you need to be with your mom. You need *not* to go out tonight. You understand what I'm saying?"

"Yeah, yeah," he said. "Tonight's the anniversary. But they're all dead."

"Not quite all of them. Look what Eddie almost did. And there are children. How about Jimmy? You've made a lot of enemies."

"I know."

"Stay home tonight. Stay safe. Promise me."

"I already promised Abby," he said.

She released her grip and smiled at him.

"Good boy."

CHAPTER

TWENTY-THREE

Clouds rolled in. Despite the sunny morning, Will had been expecting them. A gray sky felt right for this evening, though no rain was forecast.

"Go over and check on her," said Abigail. "You'll feel better."

She sat on the green sofa with her feet pulled up and a sketch pad in her lap. The wreckage of an early dinner was still on the table. Neither of them had much appetite, and Will had been too lazy to clean up. He rolled a half-empty beer bottle between his hands.

"She's not there," he replied. "I haven't seen her for a couple of days."

"The lights are on."

That didn't necessarily mean anything, but it caught his wandering attention. His mind was unsettled. Thoughts circled the pile of inert facts like crows around carrion. Diving in now and then for an indigestible bite. He had learned some things, but how did they help him? How did they tell him who or what to trust?

"She was supposed to come here when she had more to say."

"Maybe she wants you to chase her," said Abby. Making it a romantic thing. Missing the point. Good old Ma. He was glad to see her sketching again, glad that the two of them had made their peace. They could never get back what they had lost, but they could still be friends. No small thing. Yet she was little help to him in this crisis. Sam and Muriel had abandoned him, both for their own good reasons. But on this particular night, he felt terribly alone. His body had not stopped vibrating since Eddie Price pointed that gun at him. Meaning to kill him. He tried to hide it from Abby, but could not manage to any longer. His skin went hot and cold, like a fever he needed to burn off, but how? Surely not by staying locked inside all night.

"Did Muriel say any more about Johnny?" his mother asked.

Johnny. His father. Another thing he had learned, but to what end? He hadn't really known the man. It did not change his relationship with Joe, except to make it more distant. It did make Johnny's death that much more terrible. But no less mysterious.

"What you said," Will replied. "That he wouldn't have hurt me. That he was coming upstairs to, um, protect me." Better to put it like that, he figured, than to say that her best friend and ex-lover meant to steal her child.

"That seems right," she said, sitting up and leaning toward him. "That sounds more like the truth. Do you believe it?"

But his ravenous thoughts veered off after a new target.

"What did you think of Doc Chester?"

"Doc?" She smiled a little. "He was a good guy. Smart as hell. Liked the girls too much, but then, they liked him."

"You included?"

"Nah, I was too close to Nancy. But plenty of the others. Louise Brown was mad for him. Not back then, I mean later. Right before he took up with Sally Price."

"Should have stuck with Louise," Will observed. "Might have lived longer. What about other women in the circle?"

"Louise, Liza Stafford, Jenny Branford." Abby ticked them off finger by finger. "Maybe Molly. She said no, but I was never sure."

"All of the women but you," he said.

"I guess." She looked a little perplexed, like she hadn't thought of that before. "It was a different time—there was a lot of sleeping around."

"Everybody looked up to him," Will stated, rather than asked.

"Sure. He had this calming, grown-up manner. And a doctorate in, like, anthropology. Or maybe archeology, I don't remember. He taught us all a lot."

"So he had a certain degree of control over the group?"

"Wait, you're thinking… No, honey, Doc was a good man."

"You think *everybody* was good," he said impatiently. "But somebody was up to no good that night."

"He went and got you from the field," she answered weakly.

He had. Did that exonerate or implicate him? Had Will fallen under the spell of this theory too quickly? It fit in many ways, but also left questions. What it mostly left him was nowhere to go. The man was dead. He could extract no revenge, or even explanation. Unless Nancy Chester knew something. He lifted the beer bottle to his mouth, then put it down again.

"How old was Doc?"

"When he died? Early sixties, I guess. Too old to still be fooling around."

"So he was what, forty back then?"

"Yeah," she agreed. "Not even. He always seemed older."

That old man. Would a nineteen-year-old girl think of a man that age as old? And wasn't a dead man exactly the direction Muriel would point him? Freeing him from both doubt and danger. Doc was a seeker, like Johnny, and clearly full of himself. But he was mature, calm. Whereas the summoning that night had a recklessness about it. Will stood up.

"I'm going to check on Sam."

"Good," Abby replied. "Bring her back here. She shouldn't be in that big house alone."

"Let's see if she's even there."

Through the cold glass of the back door he could see his mother standing in the kitchen archway. Exactly where the ruined specter of Christine Jordan had stood, moaning his name. What shadows would he see this night? What might be waiting for him in that dark field beyond the terrace?

"Come right back," said Abigail pensively.

"I will," he lied.

Clouds moved swift and low across the night sky. Black pines swayed. Dead leaves scuttled away from his marching feet. He crossed the broad yard unchallenged, and stepped carefully through the trees. The porch light was on. The

Honda was sitting in the driveway, yet Will was certain that Sam was not in the house. He could not feel her presence.

The front door was unlocked. Possibly an invitation. More likely acknowledgment of how useless locks were in a town full of witches. The front hall was dim and quiet. The parlor, dining room and kitchen were empty. He stood in the stairwell, thinking to call her name, but why? If she was there, she would have sensed his arrival. If she wanted to hide, he would not find her. Will went into the study.

The desk lamp was on. The leather chair protested as he sat down. Their books and notes were still on the desk. He picked up the demonology and flipped through it. Then noticed that the scrap of paper marking the Murmux/Murmur entry was gone. He looked again at the illustration of the hooded rider on the huge, ugly bird and felt an involuntary shiver. He slapped the volume closed and went to their notebooks. In the one Sam had been using, the passage translating the Murmur entry had been torn out. In his own, the page on which he had written the eleven suspected coven members was likewise missing. Someone might have come in and taken just those pages, but why? And why remove the bookmark? More likely Sam had removed all of these to keep them from prying eyes.

Will gazed about the room. One of the framed photographs was crooked again. He stood and went to it. A gray, grainy shot, one of the oldest in the room. A large white clapboard house filled the background. In front of it were four figures. The tallest was a middle-aged man in a white shirt and suspenders, with a haunted expression. His hands were on the shoulders of two little blonde girls, smiling shyly at the camera. To their right was a pale-haired boy, possibly a brother or other relation, tipping his head to one side. Will began to straighten it, then on impulse lifted it from the wall and carried it to the desk.

He studied the image a few more minutes, especially the faces. Then flipped the picture over and searched the brown paper backing. The elegant handwriting in one corner had faded almost to invisibility, and he had to look very closely: Gerald, Ethel, and Cindy Hall, with Tom. Warren, Maine, 1924. *I was friends with the daughter*, Evelyn Price's voice spoke in his head. *Cindy. Summer friends. My parents said stay away. Climbing around the roof at night and hypnotizing her sister. The only case of possession I've ever seen.*

She's talking about us, Sam had complained in the car afterward. *Halls make the messes and Prices have to clean them up.* Will closed his eyes and took a deep breath. He did not know everything, but he knew enough. He did not rehang the photograph. He simply turned and left the study, left the house.

The Honda was also unlocked. It had been too much to hope that he'd find the keys in the ignition. They were not in the glove compartment either, nor any of the receptacles around the seat or the door. He was about to go back in and search the house when he reached up and flipped down the sun visor. A chunky set of keys fell heavily in his lap. Willing his hands to stop shaking, he picked them up and squeezed hard, the cold metal biting into his fingers. Then he slipped the largest key into the ignition and the little car clattered to life.

Passing his house, he thought he saw Abby at the window, watching him drive away. He prayed that she would not try to follow him.

There were no streetlights on Mount Gray. Only headlights to guide him, and the occasional lit window, tucked back in the trees. The driveways did not have numbers, but that did not matter. Will remembered that Tom Hall's was the last. As soon as it came into view, he slowed rapidly, driving as far off the margin of road as the brush allowed. Small branches and saplings scraped against the car as he stopped. Well, she needed a new paint job anyway. He would even pay for it, if her friends and relations didn't murder him tonight.

As the headlights died, he saw how dark it was. The clouds had a weird luminosity, but allowed no moon or starlight to penetrate, and the wooded hill was utterly black. He opened the door and got out. The air was cooler here, and once again he wished he had grabbed a jacket. The long, sloping drive was just discernible between the trees. He walked swiftly upward, his feverish blood warming him. There was a roll of distant thunder.

Within moments, he sensed a presence nearby. Sensed rather than saw, because seeing would have been impossible. Yet his mind placed a shadowy figure just at the edge of vision, walking in stride with him through the dense thicket on the right. The ghost of Eddie Price? Or another of the dead or never-living companions he had acquired since coming home? More likely the familiar tormentor who had stalked him since childhood. Who might even be killing his enemies to protect him. Strange that though the presence instilled fear, it was a lesser fear to what lay ahead of him in the house. Or all fears had become one, and the need to know exactly what was happening had overcome them.

"I know you're there," Will whispered. "How about you leave things to me tonight?"

The specter made no reply, and Will continued.

Unlit, and backed tightly into the hill, the house was not visible until he was upon it. The shadows of at least five vehicles were in the gravel circle, and a faint orange glow came from somewhere. He walked the perimeter as far as the terrain allowed. The shades were drawn and that dim, flickering light came from around their edges. Candles. He listened a long time, first at the windows and then the door. Nothing. How could so many people be so silent? Were they upstairs? Or out in the woods somewhere? He had not considered the last possibility until then. Unless they were using some light source out there, he would never find them. But it seemed unlikely. No, they were in the house. He tried one of the windows in what he remembered as the kitchen, but it wouldn't budge. The sky rumbled once more.

A woman's voice. Inside, yet strangely muffled. Shouting a single word, then repeating it. *No*, it sounded like. *No, no.* Impossible to identify, and yet he was sure it was Sam. Panic jumped up in him. *Don't overthink things*, he heard his father say, and Will grabbed the doorknob.

His arm flying up in the air, nearly dislocating from his shoulder, preceded any sensation. Then the shock hit his whole body at once, punching the air from his lungs. He did not remember falling, but found himself on his back. Gasping for air, grasping for comprehension. *Thanks for the advice, Dad.*

In a moment or two, he could feel sensation in most of his body again, except the right arm, which was completely numb, like a club sewn to his torso. And the shoulder actually hurt. It had been some sort of electric shock. The door was wired. Idiot, he should have known better. Sam had warned him about touching things at Evelyn Price's house. Samantha, right. Where was she? What were they doing to her in there?

The front door opened, and a shadow stepped out and stood over him.

CHAPTER

TWENTY-FOUR

Will stayed calm until he tried to move. His left arm and right leg twitched, but there was no other response from his muscles. Fear set in then. He did not know if he could even fight this shadow, but being completely helpless before it terrified and enraged him. He spoke some incoherent words and tried to move again.

"Take it easy," said a familiar voice. The shadow separated into two forms. The second wore a sort of gown or robe that went to the ground. "Get his feet," said the first.

Jimmy Duffy, looking taller from ground level. Jimmy stepped from view and a moment later grabbed Will by the shoulders, lifting him. His head bobbed against Jimmy's chest while the robed figure tried with some difficulty to lift his legs. Will felt strength return and started kicking. The figure dropped his feet at once.

"What are you doing?" Jimmy snapped.

"He's kicking me," whined a young male voice, not at all what Will was expecting.

"Useless pussy," Jimmy grumbled. Then louder, in Will's ear. "Can you stand on your own?"

"I'm, I'm a…"

"I'll take that as yes."

The other two slipped under each of his shoulders and moved forward. Will found that his stumbling feet could keep pace with them. Through the open door they went, where it was brighter than Will expected. A glowing orange rectangle shone in the center of the living room floor. The sofa had been pulled away, the Oriental carpet rolled, just as Sam and Will intended days ago. And a three-by-six foot trapdoor sat upright on its hinges, revealing a narrow stair. The light wavered, and thin smoke drifted upward.

"There isn't room for us to go down like this," Jimmy said.

Will shoved the robed kid aside with his left arm, and Jimmy dropped his still-numb right one. And he was standing under his own power. Barely. Jimmy went first, a hand bracing Will's chest as he descended, one careful step at a time. The younger man came after, obviously afraid to touch Will again.

The chamber was small. Seven feet high and just wide enough for a long wooden table and low shelves crammed with books. Candles were on the table, flickering vigorously as Will came down. The scattered light caught parts of five seated bodies. At the head of the table sat a robed and hooded figure. A dark red book was on the table before it. The robe was gray and supple with age. Symbols were stitched along the sleeves and the belt.

The other four figures were women, and Will began to recognize them. Molly Jordan was on the robed figure's left, facing Will. A kind expression on her face. He was more surprised to see Margaret Price beside her. Her mouth was a hard line, and candlelight made orange flares of her glasses, obscuring her eyes. Beside her was an empty chair, and at the foot of the table was a very old woman he did not know. Also robed. Two more empty chairs sat on the near side, but between them a woman shifted painfully around in her seat, a cane beside her. Thickset, gray-haired, looking a decade older than she was, Nancy Chester peered curiously at him.

The young man who had come down behind Will took one of the empty seats. Splotch-faced and nervous, he could not have been more than a teenager, and his shiny black robe looked silly and cheap. Like something his mother had sewn for him just a few Halloweens ago. Will balanced himself against the empty chair to the hooded figure's right. Jimmy hovered next to him, as if fearing he would bolt back up the stairs. It took Will a few moments to notice the last occupant. Standing in the corner, her arms folded. Blond hair covering most of her downturned face. Will was about to say her name when the figure at the head of the table rose and folded back the hood.

"Welcome, William," said Tom Hall, a warm smile on his face.

"Took long enough," Margaret Price added.

"Are you all right?" Molly asked. "You don't look good."

"We knew he was coming," Margaret scolded Tom, seemingly annoyed with all of them. "You should have removed the protection."

"If he's fool enough not to knock," croaked the robed old woman at the foot of that table, "he got what he deserved."

Will didn't like the old hag's tone, but he was inclined to agree with her.

"What's going on here?" he asked, testing his own voice. Then, with more strength: "What are you all doing?"

"Making things right," said Nancy Chester.

"We're trying to undo the harm we did," Molly said earnestly, the candlelight playing wildly on her broad face.

Margaret Price sniffed. She had nothing to do with that earlier business, and clearly did not like being included in "we."

"Where's Evelyn?" Will asked her. "Shouldn't she be here?"

"My mother," said Margaret, adjusting her glasses, "does not wholly approve of this gathering."

"Then why are you here?"

"Why are you?" she shot back.

Because I didn't know what I was walking into, he thought. Though that was at least half a lie. Still, he did not like Evelyn's absence. She was mean, but he trusted her. He was not sure there was anyone in this room he trusted, however much it grieved him to think that.

"We're all here tonight to assist you in your struggle," Tom announced. "If you let us. I think you know most everyone. This," he said, pointing to the woman at the end of the table "is Ruth Brown, who came all the way from Maine. Eugene Stafford there," he pointed to the twitchy young man, "is her great-nephew, and not only consented to driving her, but to joining us in our ceremony."

They had gotten so thin on Browns and Staffords, they had to import them. Three in the room counted as Halls. There was a Price and a Chester. Jimmy represented the Branfords, and of course Will now knew he was a Payson. Which meant that old Tom did too, as there was no other Payson here. Did they all know? Had they known all along? Had Sam?

"Looks like you've got one of each," Will said dully.

"We're a contrary, bickering bunch," Tom replied. "But the families always pull together in times of need." His blue eyes behind the thick lenses were alive with intelligence. Clearly he had remained coherent enough at one stretch to organize all of this. Would he lose focus again in a few minutes? Or was the senile Tom merely a fabrication? Some kind of cover? If so, he was a very good actor, for Will had found his bewilderment convincing.

"Why didn't you tell us about this the last time we were here?" Will asked, fixing his eyes on the old man.

"There was nothing to tell," Tom answered. "It was only when I saw you that day that I knew what was wrong. What was necessary."

"And why are you the man to do this, when you screwed it up so badly before?"

"No," said Molly quickly. "That was a summoning. We didn't know what we were doing. This is a banishment."

"And I'm supposed to think you know what you're doing *now*?" Will challenged.

Tom shook his head slowly and raised his hands for silence.

"The ceremony was done properly. There was a break in the circle at a critical moment, and things went wrong."

"You never should have tried it," Will said.

"You're right," Tom answered sadly, his hands dropping heavily to his sides. He somehow managed to look regal in the ridiculous robe. "I've lived with it every day since then. But I can't change the past."

At least he had confirmation of that much. The men had argued, as Sam remembered. But it wasn't Tom telling Johnny not to tamper with evil spells. It was Tom *instructing* him in their use, and berating Johnny when he got scared. And finally, it was Tom coming over to lead the ceremony himself. The ceremony Johnny had ruined by breaking the circle, by trying to save his son. A transgression he had paid for with his life.

"Why did you do it?" asked Will.

"The same reason as every man before me," Tom replied. "To *do* it. To confer with a being outside of our normal experience. To gain knowledge unknown by men, and thereby add to the knowledge of our species. These aren't small things, Will. We don't know how much of human understanding, supposedly derived by science, was in reality brought to us by these messengers."

"I didn't think professors believed in shortcuts."

"Oh, there's nothing easy about it," said Tom.

"Clearly not. So what were you going to do to me that night?" The old man blinked several times but did not speak. "Tell me," Will demanded, slamming the table with his hand, toppling a candle.

"Mind your manners," Ruth Brown croaked. "You don't speak to an elder that way."

"I'll speak to this particular one as I please," said Will.

"Didn't your mother teach you better—"

"You don't even know what this is about," he snarled, energy returning to his body. "So just keep quiet."

"Oh yes," she murmured, nodding her ancient head. "Yes indeed. He's got a devil in him all right."

"You heard him," said Sam, springing from her sullen pose against the wall. "You shut up, old woman."

They were the first words she had spoken since he entered the chamber. And though he had come to depend upon her calm, her anger at this moment buoyed him. The others looked unnerved by Sam's words, and Will's.

"Can we get on with this?" Jimmy said.

"Answer me," Will persisted.

Tom sighed and hung his head. Less in contrition, Will sensed, than like a professor thinking how to make a complex idea simple. Thunder sounded overhead, rattling the house.

"There is always some risk in summoning a spirit. If done right, the being is caught and held in its own form. Or formless, yet present."

"What the heck does that mean?" asked Eugene Stafford.

"Hush," said Ruth.

"If the summoning fails, the worst thing likely to happen is the spirit departs. In some cases, very rare cases, the spirit gets free. Even then," Tom went on quickly, "there's little risk, because most are benevolent. And yet a few of them, without doubt, are mischievous, and may choose to stay."

"You're talking about possession," said Will.

"They may, for a time, take control of one of those present. Now, if the spirit is mischievous, and the body it possesses is strong, well, you can see what I'm saying, can't you?"

"Say it."

"There is almost no possibility that a being, a malevolent being, would occupy me, for instance. Yet were it to happen, with all that I know… It would be dangerous."

"What does that have to do with Will?" asked Sam.

"The spirit is likely to choose the easiest body to enter and control."

"A child," Will said.

"Dear God," whispered Molly.

"It's an old custom to have a child present for a summoning," Ruth Brown intoned. As if its being tradition justified it. "It soothes the spirit."

"Luckily," Tom went on, "that's also the body from which it can do the least harm. And from which it is most easily dislodged. Assuming it doesn't get bored and leave on its own."

"Tell cousin Cindy that," replied Will.

Irritation flashed in the old blue eyes.

"Cindy was a troubled girl long before that happened. Her father was a fool. No, that's not fair. But Gerald was damaged in the war, not in his right mind. He never should have attempted something like that."

"Sounds like you were there," said Will.

"I was around, yes. You can learn from bad lessons as well as good ones."

"So," Will said, standing up straight. "I was someplace to dump the malicious little fiend if things got out of hand."

"That's a hard way to put it," Tom replied.

"But true."

"It never would have come to that," the old man maintained.

"We don't know, do we?" But he felt the fight going out of him. They could debate the past all night. His mother and Muriel might want them all to suffer for their offenses, but all he wanted was to be whole again. He looked at Sam. "Do I do this?"

"I don't know," she answered, hardly able to look at him. "You have to decide."

It was what he expected. She had neither called him to this place, nor prevented his coming, which meant she was torn. Her grandfather at the head of the coven would have been enough to throw her all by itself.

"When you summoned the spirit," Will said, turning back to Tom. "What name did you call it by?"

"No name," Tom replied. "I know it's been done that way. But it seemed foolish to call a single being, who may or may not be real, or respond to that name. Better to open ourselves to whatever spirit might be within the range of our call."

"Then how the hell were you going to get rid of it afterward?"

"You continue to misunderstand," Tom said calmly. "Most of these messengers are friendly. I intended that it should come of its own volition, converse with us at whatever length it chose and leave when it wanted to."

"What if it didn't?" Will pressed.

"There are means for extracting a name," Tom said reluctantly. "If it came to that."

"And you have it in mind to use those means tonight?"

The old man looked confused.

"I thought you *knew* the name," he said. "That the being had spoken it to you."

Will glanced at Sam, who wore a guilty look on her averted face.

"It spoke a word," Will clarified. "Which might or might not have been a name. And which I might or might not have correctly understood."

"It's no good if it's the wrong name," Ruth tutted, shaking her head.

"Maybe this isn't such a good idea, Tom," Margaret said.

"Wait," said Nancy Chester. "What's the consequence if it's the wrong name? What would happen?"

Tom shrugged, obviously rattled by this unexpected turn.

"It won't work. I can't think of any consequence beyond that."

Will looked hard at Ruth Brown, saw her puckered old mouth drawn up in a pout, as if she might have more to say on the matter. But it was Tom's circle, not hers, and she kept quiet.

"Seems like Will ought to decide," said Jimmy. Reasonably enough.

"We don't have twelve people," Will said, stalling.

"Twelve is ideal," Tom replied. "But nine is sufficient."

All eyes turned to Sam, who stood apart. Each of her hands squeezed the opposite shoulder. At first Will thought she had not heard, but it wasn't that. She looked searchingly at his face. He had no idea what expression he might be showing, nor what she would see beneath it. Sam dropped her hands to her sides and stepped over to the table. Will began to sit down in the chair in front of him.

"Oh no," said Ruth Brown, coming toward him, "that's not your spot."

After a brief protest, he climbed onto the table and lay down on his back, forcing himself to relax. Ruth arranged his arms and legs so that each pointed to a corner. She took off his sneakers and socks with the careless ease of a mother. Then she placed the five candles. One between his knees, one by each hip and two bracketing his head. He could see the flames jittering, feel the warmth on his ears. Finally, she took a pouch from her robe and flicked a pinch of the contents into each flame, muttering unheard words under her breath. Will smelled something spicy, sage or rosemary. He wanted to ask what she was doing, but instead imitated the dead silence of the others.

When she was finished, Ruth returned to the end of the table and placed one hand on each of his bare feet. Eugene Stafford and Jimmy placed a hand atop each of hers. Margaret took Jimmy's right hand in her left, and Molly's in her right. With her free hand, Molly took Will's. Across the table, Eugene's free hand linked to Nancy Chester's, hers to Sam's, and Sam's to Will's. They were all joined, except Tom. Who now pulled the hood of the robe over his head and peered downward.

"Close your eyes," the old man said.

Will did so, and after a moment's pause felt Tom's hands clasp his temples and forehead. A current, low but strong, seemed to run through Will's arms and legs, to hum in his belly and quiet his mind. There was a particular warmth where Sam touched him, and his sore right arm and shoulder felt better. He had not guessed it could feel so good to be physically connected to other people. To be encircled by care and protection. He felt tears seeping from his eyes.

"That's all right," said Tom. "It's normal. Now, I need everyone's full attention. Center your energy on young William here. Clear your minds."

He began speaking in Latin. The older women recited with him, as if it was a familiar invocation, like the Lord's prayer. Will caught something about "the heart's circle" and "the powers of the earth," but his disused Latin and dulled brain could do no more than that. Indeed, he felt his consciousness shifting in and out, and he began to lose track of time. At some point, the words slid from Latin to another language, more obscure and difficult. Welsh, or an old form of Celtic. Now only Ruth's voice echoed Tom's, and even hers went silent for stretches. As if the old man were venturing into enchantments unfamiliar to all but him.

A long rumble sounded overhead. Again, Will felt himself slip out of and back into awareness. It took a few moments to realize the words had returned to English.

"...by the strength of our united and single will, and with the aid of those powers here present, we summon thee by the name of..." Will opened his eyes to see Tom's face, red with effort, staring down at him. "Speak the name," the old man instructed.

And a name came into Will's head then. An unexpected name. It was on his tongue, ready to come forth, when Molly spoke first.

"Wait," she said, and the energy of the circle wavered. "You mean banish, not summon. We're banishing it."

Tom huffed, and Will saw a frightening expression flicker over his lined face.

"We must summon it here first," Tom said, keeping his concentration locked on Will. "Then we can banish it."

"I'm not sure that's right," said Margaret uneasily. "Ruth, is that correct?"

Will could not see Ruth from his position, but the old lady made no reply. Tom's grip on his damp forehead had slackened, but now the strong hands reasserted themselves with great force. Will felt the current rip through the circle once more, felt his tailbone rise up off the table. The sensation was not pleasant this time.

"Speak the name," Tom said again.

Will tried to say something, anything. But the pressure on his head was making him take short, panicked breaths, and scrambling his thoughts.

"Speak it," Tom ordered.

"Don't" said Samantha urgently. "Don't say it, Will."

She seemed to be squeezing his hand, but then Will realized she was actually trying to release it. With the vise grip on his forehead, he barely managed to tip his eyes toward her. He saw her face grim with effort as she pulled her fingers away from his, one by one. Tom twisted Will's head back straight.

"Speak the name," he commanded again, in an ugly voice.

"What are you doing?" Will shouted through his fear. "What do you want?"

Tom's reddened face was inches away, his eyes bulging. Furious. Mad. And then his expression morphed swiftly from rage to surprise. Or even fear. As if the circle held him hostage, and not the other way around.

"I only want her back," he whispered.

Samantha's fingers came free from Will's, and the circle sprang apart. Will heard gasps and grunts all around the table, chairs scraping back. His own limbs quivered violently a moment or two and then were still.

He rolled onto his stomach, sweeping candles from the table, and rose to his knees. Tom Hall was collapsed on his chair. Arms at his side and glasses askew. The strong and fearful presence he had been just seconds before was utterly gone. He looked blasted, and Sam knelt by his side.

"Jane," said the old man weakly.

"She's not here," Sam answered, taking his hand.

"She wasn't supposed to leave." The voice had become that of a sulking boy. "Cindy said I could have her."

"Cindy?" Sam asked.

"No," said Will, guessing. "He means the thing inside of Cindy. The demon."

"They locked her in the cellar. She said if I let her out she would make Jane love me."

"Jane loved you all on her own," said Sam, her voice breaking. "But she's gone."

"I've *seen* her," the childish old man cried.

"I have too, but that's as much as we get. She won't ever be back the way she was."

"It promised me."

"That's why you called the coven that night," Will said. "To bring it back. To make it keep its promise." Tom made no answer. The long decades had vanished for him. He was a ten-year-old boy in love with the twelve-year-old Jane and willing to deal with the devil to have her. "I was going to be your host," Will went on. "Like Cindy was before. Except my father interfered, and you called down lightning on him. You struck him dead."

"Will," Molly said. She was bent over in her chair, looking hardly better than Tom. "I'm so sorry. You never should have seen that. We should have thought of you sooner. Someone should have gone upstairs. It was so awful. A boy should never see his father like that."

Her words were strange. His mind veered around them like negatively charged particulars. Refusing to adhere.

"I didn't see anything," he answered.

"Of course you did," Molly said, "you ran right by him."

"No. No, I went down the back...the back stairs."

Visions flickered in his mind. Nausea rose in his gut. He looked at Sam for help. She gazed back at him steadily.

"There are no back stairs in your house," she said.

There was a silver flash in the room above, and a loud boom. A ghost wind passed through the dank chamber and all the remaining candles were snuffed. Silence. And then one voice spoke.

"It's here," said Ruth.

CHAPTER

TWENTY-FIVE

The darkness seemed to deepen with the old woman's words. There were mutterings all around the table, and then someone screamed. Another voice picked it up. Jimmy shouted for calm but was drowned out. Chairs tumbled over and feet banged up the stairs. Will tried to jump off the table, but a strong hand seized his wrist.

Murmur, a deep and broken voice rumbled, right up against his ear. *Murmur* it said again fiercely.

Will tried to pull away. He knew that if a light were to shine that moment, he would see the burned, hideous face inches from his own. Those dead eyes. His flesh prickled at the thought; sickness rose up in him again.

"Let go of me," he yelled, but the words were lost in the din.

The beast obeyed, and he toppled off the table. His shoulder slammed against a chair and his forehead struck the floor. He was on his feet and stumbling up the wooden stairs before he was even quite coherent. Jimmy was still calling for calm, but there was no calm to be had in any of them. Will stood in the dark room above. With the curtains still drawn, the only light came from the rectangle of the open front door. He gazed at it for several seconds, wondering what to do.

"Get out of the house," a woman shouted, and Will ran. Barefoot and bleeding, into the night.

Within a handful of strides he was in the trees, his feet scraped and hurting. Through the branches above, he could see the clouds shredding and moving off. Moonlight filled the woods. A car engine started somewhere behind him, but moments later there was a heavy thud. As if, in his or her panic, the driver had hit a tree. Will should check on the driver, but his mind could not wrap around the thought. His feet would not move. Twenty yards away, a figure approached him through the trees. Large, lumbering, unnatural.

A bang, a flash, and he was out of bed. Voices screamed downstairs. A presence lurked. He had to get out. He ran across the muddy field.

"No," he said out loud, in the night woods, the figure much closer now. *Go back*, he said to himself, his head ringing with pain, his stomach surging. *Go back.*

A bang, a flash, and he was out of bed. The voices, the presence. He pushes the door open and enters the hall. A scorched smell burns his nostrils. A figure lies at the top of the stairs, smoke rising from it. He tries to tiptoe past. He tries not to look. But he has to look. And what he sees cannot be real. It's a Halloween mask; it's someone playing a trick on him. It is too horrible to be real. It is too terrible to be remembered.

In the woods again, the figure was there before him. Grabbing him by the ears, making him look on its destroyed visage. Will kept his eyes open for as long as he could.

Hello, little man.

He fell to his knees. Pounding the wet leaves with his hands as he retched up his poisoned childhood in hot, acid waves.

After some passage of time he was sitting up again. Pulling deeply for air, but calmer. The fever was burned out of him, and he shivered in the cold night air. The looming figure had vanished, and Will wondered if he would ever see it again. He would have to check on the others in a moment, but for now he just needed to pull himself together. A faint red glow began to touch the trees around him. Will thought at first that it was dawn breaking over the top of Mount Gray. Then he realized it was the wrong direction. He looked through the trees to his left and saw orange flames dancing. The house was on fire.

Sam.

He was up and running before the blood was even back in his cramped legs. The gravel drive was well illuminated as he came out of the trees. He saw the Stafford boy running down the long slope for the road, stumbling on his torn robe. The fire was inside the house, but had burst out of several windows. The green Jeep had been driven straight into the front door, blocking it. The door was open inward, and a figure was trying to crawl onto the vehicle's hood.

Will rushed over, his feet seeking some purchase on the front tire or fender, his hands reaching across to grab Molly's. Black smoke poured outward over her head. She clasped his outstretched hands, and Will leaned back with all his strength, dragging her across the hood to him. They fell in a heap on the gravel.

"Who's still in there?" Will asked, scrambling to his feet again.

"I'm not sure," Molly gasped. "I think Nancy was behind me."

With great difficulty, he pulled himself onto the hood and slipped the opposite way, through the dark door. The patch of carpet he landed on seemed to be the only thing not burning. The walls, the furniture, everything was wreathed in flame. The smoke hung thick about four feet off the ground. The heat made his skin begin to blister within seconds. He looked around quickly but could see no one. Then he turned and stepped onto the Jeep's bumper, climbing back out of the fiery maelstrom. He scrambled across the hood to Molly again.

"I don't see her," he shouted. "Where is everyone else?"

"I don't know. Most of them went up the stairs ahead of me."

The south end of the house was not yet engulfed, and he went that way. Around the corner, he saw a body sliding out of a window. Nancy Chester, coughing and wheezing, being lowered from inside by two strong arms. Will ran over and took hold of her before she fell, laying her gently on the grass. Then he stood and offered his hands and shoulders to Jimmy Duffy, who seemed a part of the gray smoke billowing around him. Jimmy leaned hard on him a moment and then leaped to the ground, falling on his side. His face was covered in soot and he breathed with difficulty.

"You all right?" Will asked. The other man only nodded. "Is anyone left in there?"

"Don't know," Jimmy coughed.

"Sam, what about Sam?"

"She ran out right after you. I thought she'd be with you."

Will stood and turned a slow circle. As if Sam would appear out of the night right there before him.

"Will," he heard a voice call. "William." Margaret Price, sounding not at all happy. She was in the woods up the slope, evidently seeking him. Will went the other way, back to the front of the house, looking about desperately in the glow provided by the flames. On impulse he ran back the way he had come, into the woods on the eastern slope.

"Sam" he called, moving quickly but more carefully now. His cut and battered feet were killing him. In fact, just about everything hurt. "Sam."

He thought he saw movement, parallel to him and a little below. He went around one tree, slapped aside some saplings and came into a small clearing. Her back was to him but there was no mistaking that blond head.

"Sam," he said again, and she whirled about. He could hardly see her face, but her body was tensed, as if ready for an attack. He had assumed she was looking for him, but she gave no answer, and he did not sense any welcome. Will took a step toward her and she took two steps back. A terrible idea occurred to him. The Jeep. If she was not using her Honda, then she was driving the Jeep, as he had suggested to her days ago. She had left the house right after him. She, or someone in the house, had yelled for him to leave.

"What did you do?" he said. The words—hard, accusatory—were out of his mouth before he thought them through. Before he realized that she had taken a small and cautious step toward him.

"What did I do?" she cried. Her voice high and grief-stricken. "What did *you* do?"

"No, Sam, listen."

He staggered toward her and she turned and fled. She was running away. Hurt, or worse, frightened of him. He was too surprised to move at first, but then he rushed after her. The slope fell off steeply just beyond the clearing, and he had to run to keep from plunging forward on his face. After a dozen yards he turned sideways to slow his descent, then took hold of a pine tree to stop himself. The scaly bark bit his palms and smeared pitch on his fingers. Sam was nowhere in sight. Will closed his eyes and listened. The slap of branches, somewhere to the left. He set out that way, slipping and stumbling as he went.

His mind, too, was stumbling. *What did you do?* Was she simply throwing the accusation back at him, or was there more? He thought he had come to understand himself, minutes before, in his revelation among the trees. That he had come to understand what it was that his mind had been avoiding all this time. But was there more to it than that? Could his body have been up to some mischief while his mind was elsewhere? No, that couldn't be right. He had not hurt anyone. He had not set the house on fire. How would he have even done it?

"Sam," he shouted again, but still she made no reply.

The slant of the hill blocked the house from sight, and flames no longer illuminated the woods. He could see very little but a silver strip of ground, twenty or thirty yards below. The road, bathed in moonlight. He could no longer hear any movement around him. He had not been far behind, but somehow he had lost her completely. Lacking a better idea, he made his way down the steep incline to the road.

As soon as he cleared the last trees, Will's eyes caught a black heap sitting in the center of the moonlit roadway. He went to the object at once and picked it up. Eugene Stafford's torn robe. He hoped the boy was wearing something underneath. He turned another slow circle, looking and listening with all the poor power of his ragged senses. Nothing. Where was the car? Farther up, near the entry to the driveway. Should he go get it and pursue her that way? But what if she had stayed in the woods?

As if in answer to his thoughts, he heard a car engine rumbling above. A moment later headlights descended the winding road from the hilltop. Will stepped to the edge of the narrow lane, but was caught in the beams before he could decide whether to jump back into the trees. He stood his ground as the familiar car pulled up alongside of him. The driver's window rolled down.

"Get in," said Muriel.

"What are you doing here?" he asked in surprise.

"Looking for you."

"I've got to find Sam."

"Good, we'll find her. Now get it the car, quick. That lunatic is right behind me."

On impulse, he went around the car and got in. Muriel pulled away before he had even closed the door. There was a determined look on her face. The interior smelled of cigarettes, and something more pungent.

"You didn't leave," said Will.

"No," she agreed. "You lying little shit, I knew you would come up here."

"It's not your job to look out for me."

"Yeah, whose is it? 'Cause they should be fired."

"Which lunatic?" he asked.

"Margaret Price. Man, the way she was cursing me, I should have grown a tail and horns." Muriel looked in the rearview mirror. "Speak of the devil."

Will twisted around in his seat to see headlights bearing down on them swiftly.

"I'm not afraid of her," he said. "Stop and let's see what she wants."

"I don't think that would be smart."

They reached the bottom of the hill and Muriel was forced to slow before the turn onto Seaview Road. The headlights raced up behind until their white glare filled the car. There was a bang and Will lurched forward, slamming against the dashboard.

"Crazy bitch," Muriel yelled, accelerating into the turn. The tires screeched and Will was knocked sideways against the door. "Put your seat belt on, for Christ sake."

He did so. The collision had not been that hard, but still he was shaken. He looked back and saw that the Volvo had turned with them, but it was rapidly falling behind.

"What was she cursing about?"

"You," Muriel replied, accelerating through the sharp curves of Seven Corners.

"What about me?"

"Hey, if you don't know, I sure don't."

"I didn't do anything," he insisted, praying it was true.

"No one said you did."

"I think it was an accident."

"What was?"

"Her hitting us. You stopped suddenly and she just—"

"Of course you think that," Muriel snapped. "In thirty years you haven't figured out how dangerous these people are. They killed your father. God knows what they tried to do tonight. Look at you. Where are your shoes?"

His sneakers, right. Melted, most likely.

"You look terrible," she said.

He gazed down at himself. Feet dirty and bleeding. Stains and rips on his jeans and shirt. He could only guess what his face looked like. How did he explain to her that most of it was self-inflicted? How did he begin to speak of the things he had come to understand this night? Before he could try, she turned the wheel hard to the left.

At first he thought she was driving straight into the trees. Then he realized it was a narrow, unlit road. The far end of Old Forest Lane, in fact. He had forgotten they were near it. When the car was twenty or thirty yards in, Muriel killed the engine. Darkness enveloped them. Will twisted in his seat again and looked back. About eight seconds later Margaret's Volvo went tearing by on Seaview. They had lost her.

"Clever move," said Will. He turned to see Muriel staring at him oddly. "What?"

"It's not enough that you have the same voice. Now you're using his words."

"Johnny?"

"You've said a bunch of things in the last couple of days that sound just like him."

"Clever move? That was a Johnnyism?"

"Yeah," she replied, smiling vaguely. "'Clever move, Brownie.'"

"Brownie?" he laughed.

"Oh yeah, he had a dozen nicknames for me. Brownie. Teen Queen. Mure-Mure."

There was a rushing sensation in his ears. As if he had stood up too quickly, though of course he had not moved.

"What?" he heard himself say.

"That was his favorite. 'Aren't you the clever one, Mure-Mure.'"

And why not? It was a perfectly obvious nickname. And perfectly logical that Johnny would pronounce it the same way that Abby did, or any of the old gang. Not Mure, but Murr. Murr-Murr.

Murmur.

CHAPTER

TWENTY-SIX

He did not speak for a full minute. The silence lasted long enough that he was certain she knew. Knew that something had changed between them in those few words. Perhaps she had only been waiting for him to grasp it. To notice that the pungent scent that the cigarettes could not quite hide was gasoline. Or to understand that it had been her voice shouting for him to get out of the house. Just before she blocked the door with the Jeep, then lit the place up.

A dozen clues must have preceded these. And he might have noticed them, had it not been her. Muriel. Queen of his youth, Abigail had called her. With a sneer in her voice. Did Abby know? She was the only one who might have understood, and still kept the secret. Will ran a finger over the fogging window glass. Why did it have to be Muriel?

"What's the real story with your mother?" he asked.

She took some time to answer.

"She doesn't have very long," Muriel said finally. "She's been mostly unconscious since the last time I was there."

"So she wasn't eagerly awaiting your visits."

"No. She hasn't known who I am for years."

"That day I arrived," Will said, the details coming back to him. "You were packed for a long trip. Because you didn't know when you would be back, or if you would. You didn't know if Abby would wake up or not, or what she would remember. Like you pushing her down the stairs."

"I didn't push her."

"No?"

"She stopped short and I ran into her. And then I couldn't grab her in time."

"But you were chasing her," Will pressed. "She looked at you like you were evil. You said so. She knew something. She was afraid of you and she ran, and you chased her."

"I wouldn't have hurt her, Willie."

"But you *did*. You did hurt her."

"It was an accident."

"And what about the others?" he demanded. "Were they accidents too?"

"Not accidents," Muriel conceded. She took a box of cigarettes and matches off the dashboard and lit up. Her hands were shaking, but her face was calm. "But not what you're thinking either. Every one of them deserved to die. But it was just, like, these opportunities. I didn't look for them."

"Were you in that hotel room with Doug Payson?"

"That's what I mean," she said. "No, I wasn't. He called

me. *He* called *me*. Drunk. Crying into the phone about how much he missed Johnny, how guilty he felt about the whole thing. How he just wanted to die. Wasn't the first time he called me like that. Like I was supposed to comfort him. Useless loser."

"What did you say?"

"The other times I just hung up. That time, though, I'd had enough. I said, you know what, Dougie? That's exactly what you should do. You should kill yourself. Because you're going to do it sooner or later, so you might as well get it over with and save everybody the pain of listening to you."

"And he took your advice."

"Yeah," she said, no remorse in her voice. "First smart thing he did in his life."

"And you didn't feel bad?"

"Why should I?" she snarled. "He asked my advice, and I gave it to him. Are you going to call that murder?"

"No," he answered, hesitantly. "But it's not exactly—"

"He was a grown man—he made his own decision. At worst I sped up something that would have happened anyway. Same thing with Liza."

Will would have sworn that he felt the temperature drop. Eliza Stafford. She had done that, as well. Half of him wanted to reach out and cover her mouth, to say "no more, tell me no more." The other half wanted to throw the door open and run away. Get far away from this creature he did not know anymore.

"She didn't drown skinny-dipping?"

"That's exactly what she did. That's probably what she would have done if I never existed. That, or drive off the road. She was a bigger lush than Dougie, and she loved

286

taking risks. Doing things she thought were crazy or cool. Instead of just stupid."

"But you encouraged her in some way," Will nudged.

"Bunch of us were at Murphy's. Or whatever it was called then. She was trying to get someone to go with her to Chebacco. One of the boys. Sometimes she'd take them out there to screw, then go swimming afterward. Mostly she went on her own, but for some reason she had to have a pal along that night."

"And you went."

"We took her car," said Muriel. "I drove—she was blotto. There was a pint of whiskey on the seat. Yes, I bought it. Did I make her drink it? Did I make her jump naked into that cold water? Did I ask her to swim after me into the deepest part of the lake?"

"I wasn't there."

"All her own choices," Muriel testified. "And it was mine not to help when she cramped up and panicked. I just swam back to shore. Put my clothes on and walked home in the dark. Took me over an hour."

"Jesus Christ, Mure," he groaned.

"What? Tell me what was lost? What was she going to do with her precious life besides spread herpes or kill some kid in a head-on collision? *That* deserves to live more than Johnny?"

How could he tell her? How could he explain how much more horrible these calculated nonactions were than a spontaneous act of violence would have been?

"What about Jenny Duffy?"

"What about her?"

"You didn't do anything?" Will asked.

"You think I can cause cancer? She died hard enough without any help from me."

"And the rest?" he said in a dull voice. Both sickly fascinated and wanting it to be over.

"How do you know there's more?" But she couldn't keep up the bluff, or she did not want to. "I told Louise about her beau. That old goat Doc Chester, banging Sally Price. That's all I did is tell her. Anyone else might have done it—other people knew."

"And?"

"She got mad. Did nothing for a while. Then she finally told Eddie, like I knew she would. And things took their course."

"How did Louise feel about that?"

"Freaked out," Muriel said, with a hint of pleasure. "She was the worst of them, Willie, the very worst."

"She was your cousin."

"That's how I know. The biggest braggart, and over what? What did she ever do? The biggest gossip, the meanest, most malicious woman. She was the one they sent upstairs to get you! Liza told me later. If Johnny hadn't stopped her..." She looked like she might reach out for him, but restrained herself. "Oh yeah, she was the worst of them, Louise. I should have *started* with her. She was my one exception."

"How do you mean?"

"I mean I didn't wait for fate. I did it myself. She suspected I had something to do with Liza. She also blamed me for Doc's death, instead of blaming her own big mouth. She was working herself up to accusing me. Or maybe that was just my excuse."

"What did you do?" he asked.

"She had a heart condition. I had this home remedy made up. I don't know what all was in it. Foxglove for sure, some other stuff. She was supposed to take just a little at a time."

"But you made sure she took a lot."

"In her tea," Muriel replied. "Sitting in her garden, with the mugs on our knees. Shooting the breeze. Like we were friends and did this all the time. I guess it didn't taste like much—she drank it down. Looking right at me, with this funny expression. Like she had indigestion or something. I watched the light fade in her eyes. Watched her check out right in front of me. She didn't even fall over, just kept sitting there. I sat a long time with her. Anyone could have seen us, but nobody did. I waited to feel bad, but the only thing I could think was that's it for you, bitch. You'll never hurt anyone again."

He glanced over and saw her wipe her eyes. Dampness glazed her face, in contradiction to her heartless words. She would not reach for the tissues, unwilling to register the hurt. Tough girl. It almost made him feel sorry for her.

"Abby," Will said after a moment. "That's who made the remedy for you."

"Yeah," she answered quietly.

"Did she know what you did?"

"Not then, but a few weeks back. You know, that day. She was going on about her dream, about imagining someone going upstairs to harm you. I flat out told her it was Louise. Told her what I thought of my dear cousin, in detail."

"She didn't know before?"

"Nobody did. They thought we were pals. Abby was so upset. 'But I know you cared about her, you had me make that heart medicine.' Then she just stopped. Like she finally got it. I guess I should have denied it, but I was tired."

"That's when she gave you the look," Will said, his muscles tensing. Like he was about to strike her. About to defend his mother, three weeks too late.

"It was the way she got up from the table," Muriel said, shaking her head. "Not just horror, but fear. Fear, of me. Like I was going to hurt her!"

"Was that so crazy a thought?" he said.

"Of course it was," she shouted. "She was as much a victim of those bastards as you. I hated her uselessness. I didn't like trusting your safety to her, but I wasn't going to hurt her. I got so angry. So angry, she could see it. She ran, and I ran after her."

And here we are, he thought. It all sounded so reasonable when she said it. Not right, but reasonable. The logic of revenge was a frightening thing. Had he been older, had he been a slightly different person, would it have been him? Would Jimmy have been right?

"Nancy Chester?" he asked. "Marty Branford?"

"Nothing to do with either," she said, with a wave of her hand. "Funny, huh? That's how it is with curses. People get hurt and die on their own, all the time. People looking for a pattern see one."

And yet there had been a pattern. In a weird kind of way, the very paranoia of people like Jimmy, and the need for reasonable people to reject that paranoia, had been Muriel's best protection. She had been careful in some ways, but totally reckless in others, and might easily have been caught at any point.

"Why did you come back?" Will asked. "After Abby woke up?"

"I never confessed anything to her. It sounded like her memory might be scrambled. I took a chance."

"You knew she wouldn't turn you in."

"I didn't know anything," she said. "Driving around the back roads of New Hampshire. Looking at maps of Canada, trying to figure out where to go." She shrugged. "I knew it wasn't in me. To run. This was home, and I would take whatever I had coming. I'm not ashamed of what I did. A lot of people would agree with me if they knew."

"Am I supposed to be one of them?"

She didn't answer, but put her hand back on the key and started the car.

"Louise wasn't your only exception," he said. "There was tonight."

"That's true."

"A lot of those people had nothing to do with the old coven."

"And a lot of them did. I couldn't believe it," she said furiously. "I couldn't believe they were starting that shit up again. Didn't they learn anything? They're either so damn stupid they don't deserve to live, or else they sold their soul to the devil. Either way, it was the fire for them. I made sure you got out first. And that idiot Stafford kid."

"And Sam."

"And Sam," she agreed, begrudgingly. Will wondered if Samantha had not, in fact, been intended for the flames. He had so many questions. His mind raced through the maze of the last twenty-eight years, down blind alleys, doubling back on itself. One thing in particular distracted him so badly that he barely noticed she was backing up toward the road.

"Where are we going?" he asked.

"Anywhere," she said, pulling the wheel to the right as they swung out onto Seaview, then hard left again. Back the way they had come. The opposite way from home. The way out of town. "You offered to come with me. Now you're coming. Until this blows over."

"This isn't blowing over," Will said harshly. Staring at her in amazement as she hit the accelerator. "Come on, Mure. We can't run from this."

"Just watch me."

He knew he should argue more strenuously, but his mind was still in the maze. Returning to a certain dark passage he had reared back from several times already. He bit down on his fear and plunged in.

"Why did you stop?" Will asked. "Those years between Eliza and Doc. What made you give it up?"

"I didn't stop or start," she said irritably. "I just took the chances that came."

They were sailing through Seven Corners, much too fast. Drifting over the centerline through the tight turns of wood-lined road. One car coming a little too quickly from the other direction would finish them.

"No opportunities came up in, what, fourteen years?" he pressed. That seemed unlikely. "You helped each other out, you girls. Cooking for each other, watching each other's kids."

"Don't include me in that."

"You were part of it. You were the mechanically inclined one." His throat was dry and his nerve was failing. "You fixed cars. My mom's, and some of the others'. Molly Jordan. I remember she used to bring you her car to fix. I just remembered that in the last few days."

He watched Muriel's head go back and forth in a slow

292

shake, but no words came out. Her expression was frozen. She had not lied to him yet and would not now, nor would she speak. They had come to the worst of it.

"You never liked Molly," he said. "What did you do?"

The car began to lose speed. They passed the Mount Gray road entrance, but he could see no sign of the burning house above.

"Muriel, what did you do?"

"You know," she said. Then paused a long time before going on. "That was Molly's car. No one else ever drove it. Ever."

Was that right? Christine had not been driving that long. Only a handful of times, usually in her dad's car. That might well have been the first day she had driven her mother's. So there it was. A monstrous coincidence. The miscalculation had scared Muriel out of her wicked practices for years. And then what had happened? Time and bitterness caught up? A chance to get in a dig at the hated Louise? Just a few loose words. Gossip. But it had been enough to start up the cycle of death all over again. Christine was the worst of it. But none of it was forgivable, and Muriel knew that.

"So that's it," she said. Her voice empty. "You're done with me now, right?"

Will was almost too sick with grief to speak, but he forced out two words.

"Pull over."

"Look, there's your girl."

They had hit a straightaway. At the far edge of the headlights a small figure could be seen, walking toward them along the border of the roadway. Even at this distance, the cap of blond hair glowed. Sam must have stayed in the woods to avoid being found, and come out way down here.

"Pull over," he said again, more urgently.

"Yeah?" she asked, her tone unreadable. "All right."

Will felt the car shake and slip as the tires hit gravel at the edge of the road. Muriel's hands tightened on the jerking steering wheel. She was pulling over, but too fast.

"Slow down," he insisted.

Her expression closed, her lips flattened and drew back. If anything, the car seemed to accelerate, and a startled-looking Samantha sped toward the windshield.

"Stop," Will shouted. "Muriel, stop."

There was nothing else to do. He knocked her near arm away with his left hand, then grabbed at the wheel with his right. Turning it as hard as he could. He saw Sam's stunned face pass by the side window, a few short yards away. The Subaru left the ground for a moment, banged hard off a little grass hillock, then shot into the air.

His head felt bloated, like it might explode. He smelled heat and plastic, heard a clicking sound. He was pretty sure that his eyes were open, but his vision was impaired. His arms hung uselessly above his head, yet below him. Things were turned around.

"Will?" said a voice nearby, but muffled.

A body was moving near him, forcing its way into the cramped compartment. He heard the crunch of broken glass.

"Hang on, now, I'm here."

Be careful, he tried to say, but it came out a grunting noise through sticky lips.

Hair brushed his forehead, and her breath was on his face. Hands reached up his chest, his stomach, finally found the seat belt release, which for some reason was above him.

She struggled with it for half a minute before it popped. Then he fell. No more than a foot, his head cushioned on her chest, his arms and legs collapsing in an awkward, painful heap around them. He let out an involuntary moan.

"I'm sorry," said Sam, gently in his ear. "Don't try to speak. Someone will be here soon. Can you hear me? Will, can you hear my voice? Squeeze my hand. Good. Now, you hang on, all right? I'm here with you. You'll be okay. Please, just hang on."

CHAPTER

TWENTY-SEVEN

Though the senior member of the old generation, Evelyn Price wore no robe. Only green corduroys with a black sweater, and a silver pendant. Will thought at first it was a pentagram, then realized it had seven sides. Well, of course it would.

He sat on the weathered old stump of the lightning-blasted pine, crutches beside him. Evelyn placed a hand on his shoulder. She could not take his hand on that side since it was in a sling. He was just glad that she did not squeeze his forehead. Samantha held his free hand, and Abby held hers. Then Molly Jordan, Nancy Chester, Jimmy Duffy, Ruth Brown, Eugene Stafford, Margaret Price and back to Evelyn. Some sitting quietly, some standing or shuffling nervously in place. Ten bodies, all seven families. Young Eugene—now dressed in blue jeans and a Metallica T-shirt—looked none too happy to be there, but Great-Aunt Ruth had bullied him into it. Will knew that several of those present had to be cajoled into coming after the last fiasco, but here they all were.

Evelyn began the Latin chant and some of the others picked it up. Will thought she looked regal. Her eyes were closed but her lined face was alive with strength. The wind lifted her white hair and the dark pines swayed powerfully behind her. A fire spit in the iron grate at the circle's center, and the ring of candles surrounding them fluttered but did not go out. Samantha thought they should hold the ceremony in Abby's living room, where the old one had been. But too many of them refused to be stuck indoors after that awful night two weeks before, and Evelyn decided that dusk on All Hallows Eve, on the lawn at the edge of the woods, was a proper setting for their circle.

"Close your eyes," Evelyn said, as Tom had that night. Will did so, and felt the strength of the group enter him. Felt peace. He also felt the worm of doubt that Tom's terrible desire had planted there, just as the old woman had warned he would. And as she had instructed, he did not fight or ignore it, but let it remain, small and ineffectual, in one corner of his mind. He took a deep breath and squeezed Sam's hand. She squeezed back. Ruth Brown's voice rose clear and strong above the rest.

No one knew how Ruth and Tom escaped the burning house. They had been the last two in the chamber, and Jimmy had not been able to fight his way back through the flames to them. Yet there they were minutes later, wandering out of the woods behind the house. Ruth still wore a bandage on her hand and much of her hair had been singed off. The smoke, or some other hurt, had felled Tom, and an ambulance had brought him to the hospital only minutes ahead of the one that brought Will. Sam went back and forth between their rooms all night, but old Tom's heart had given out before dawn. Will had been released five days later. Muriel, who made Will put on his seat belt, had not followed her own advice, and was still at that same hospital. In a coma, from which she was not expected to wake.

Evelyn was speaking in English again.

"To the unseen spirit present here among us, we say…"

While he was still in the hospital bed recovering, Will had told Sam what he thought had happened that long-ago night. They, in turn, had told Evelyn. The three of them in the study of the Hall house, with the old spell book—which Ruth had brought forth out of the flames—before them. Evelyn had given Will that long and searching look that Sam so often did. Then nodded her head and laughed her deep, wet laugh. As if the world was too perverse to be believed and you just had to enjoy it.

"Well, that's a different story altogether, ain't it?" she had said, turning pages in the red book. "And a different spell."

Now, on the dark lawn behind the house, with the faraway voices of the first trick-or-treaters just reaching them, Evelyn paused. It had been decided that Sam should pick it up from here, as it had been she who gave the spirit those long-ago instructions.

"We say," Sam echoed, "that you have faithfully fulfilled the duties assigned to you, and they are at an end. Your burden is lifted. By the single and united will of those here present, we release you by the name of…"

She looked to Will, as all of them now did.

"John Payson," he said, loudly enough for all of them to hear. Jimmy swore quietly, and Molly let out a gasp, but the rest were silent.

"Be at peace, Johnny," said Evelyn, "and follow those paths hidden from us but revealed to you. *Teithio yn ddiogel*." She finished with another Latin chant, and then slowly released Will's hand. The circle broke up.

Sam looked at him. Will shrugged. He felt good. Better than he had in a long time, in fact, but that could mean anything or nothing.

"I guess we'll see," was all he said.

Evelyn appeared pleased, so he figured the technical stuff had gone right. The others looked either confused or cautiously hopeful as they made their hurried goodbyes. Molly gave him a hug and looked like she wanted to say something, but kept it to herself. Jimmy just glared, like someone had pulled a trick on him. Sam took him aside, which had an immediately calming effect. Poor Jimmy. Even if they could get past their other differences, he and Will would never be friends. Not with Sam stuck between them.

Ruth Brown sidled up to him.

"Nice to see things done properly," she said. Which Will took to mean "done by women." He had no argument to make there.

"Thanks for saving the book," he replied, but Ruth waved that off.

"She didn't need the book. It's all inside her. Some of us haven't forgotten the old ways. The thing is…"

"Yes?"

"This was all well and good. Necessary, I mean. But there's still a demon out there."

Will only smiled at her.

"If that's even true, it's been true for eighty years," he said. "Or eight hundred, maybe. It's not for me to fix."

The expression on her sour face was so compassionate it unsettled him. She kneaded his good shoulder with her unbandaged hand, then moved on.

A Batman, a Spider-Man—the second of the evening— a scary zombie and an older sister who might be a hobo or a very dirty witch. Sam was too generous with the candy.

"We're going to run out," Will said. "What then?"

"They can fight each other for it," Sam replied.

"That's appropriate, I guess."

"What did your girlfriend say?"

He thought of explaining again that her name was Beth, and she was not his girlfriend, but suspected it was pointless.

"They'll have a hearing when I'm back," he said. Whenever that was. His injuries needed another week to heal before he could travel, but there were other complications. No one doubted that Muriel started the fire; there was plenty of evidence. What was less clear was whether Will had been victim or accomplice. What was he doing jumping in her car right after the event? Mike Conti seemed satisfied of his innocence, but they awaited the conclusion of the State's investigation. He had told no one but Sam about Muriel's other confessions. He didn't know when or if he ever would. "I imagine they'll let me go."

"Is that what you want?"

"No," he said immediately, surprising her. "I like teaching. I like my students. I understand this is all sort of embarrassing to the school, but I won't fall on my sword. I also won't fight to the bitter end. I can teach other places."

"Down there," she said.

"Somewhere," he replied. "I'm not coming back here, if that's what you're asking." She merely nodded. "But you could come to New York," he went on.

"Like, for a visit?"

"To start with," he said. She made no reply. "What is it?"

It was not as if he needed to ask. It was hard to contemplate the future right now. They had each lost someone they loved. Someone who had been a rock of stability in their chaotic lives. Yet those people had turned out to be strangers. Haunted, dangerous souls.

"Did you really think I started that fire?" she asked, hurt in her voice.

"Oh, Sam. I was a little out of my mind just then. You do remember that you threw it right back at me." *And ran from me, in fear*, he did not add.

"Yeah," she said quietly. An inexpressible sadness in that one word. "We didn't trust each other."

So that was it. Was she more disappointed with him or herself?

"That's right," he agreed. "For a few minutes we didn't trust each other. Only a few frightened minutes. Whatever else you may be, you're human."

"Thanks."

"You're allowed your doubts, your frailties. Like anyone else. I would not have gotten through this without you. I would not have survived the last month. You know that, right?"

After a long silence she nodded her head. Stroked the back of his hand with her finger.

"New York, huh?"

"It's an interesting place," he said. "Full of possibilities for mischief."

"Are you saying I'm a troublemaker?" she asked, grinning at him.

The doorbell again. Another Spider-Man. A cowgirl. A cell phone with two legs sticking out, which had to win best outfit of the night so far. Spider-Man had his mask pulled up to his sweaty forehead and eyed Will's leg cast and sling suspiciously.

"Is that your costume?"

"Yes," Will confirmed.

"What are you supposed to be?"

"A reckless driver. Let it be a lesson to you." He tipped his head at Sam. "She's a witch."

The boy eyed her skeptically.

"She doesn't look like a witch."

Will did not see what Sam's expression did just then, what her eyes conveyed. He probably would not have seen anything even if he was looking right at her. He wasn't a child anymore. But the boy's face registered sudden fascination. Then fear. He turned and raced down the steps howling. Cowgirl looked after him like he had lost his mind. Sam laughed and gave her extra candy.

"What did you do?" Will asked.

"Only what he wanted me to," she replied innocently. "Boys like to be scared."

* * * * *

ACKNOWLEDGMENTS

Thanks to Will Conroy for believing early on, to my father Neil for genealogical research (though his Halls are not these Halls) and for his fun, spooky stories, to all the Olsons for love and support, to Peter Joseph, Natalie Hallak, Roxanne Jones, and everyone at Hanover Square for encouragement and distraction in a dark time, and to Caroline for everything.